THE PROF CROFT SERIES

MORE COMING!

PURGE CITY

A Prof Croft Novel

by

Brad Magnarella

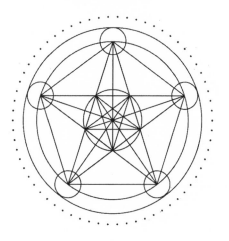

Purge City
A Prof Croft Novel

ISBN-13: 978-154419-021-1
ISBN-10: 1-544-19021-2

Cover art by Damon Freeman
www.damonza.com

First Edition

Printed in the U.S.A.

For my parents

1

"*Svelare.*" The word vibrated from my mouth, dispelling the magical veil over my floor-to-ceiling bookcase.

I paced the length of the shelves as encyclopedias and academic texts rippled and became magical tomes and grimoires. At a flaking, leather-bound tome, I stopped and pulled it from its slot. A book of Final Passage. I flipped it open to a marked page and set the book on a stand on my iron table. My gaze roamed across the ornate script to an old and sacred ritual that ensured swift passage for the deceased by calling forth a gatekeeper.

I took a resolute breath and nodded. I was going for it.

For the past week I'd studied the ritual, weighing the pros and cons of actually enacting it. But it wasn't like the Order had left me a choice. After several inquiries into my mother's death, the first sent four months ago, I hadn't received a single response. Not even a boilerplate: "*We appreciate your correspondence. Please be patient as we look into the matter.*"

So, yeah, the Order could bite me.

I consulted the book and some notes I'd jotted into the margins as I pulled spell items from my storage bins. Before long, the table top was arrayed with candles, an urn of graveyard dirt, a funeral veil soaked with a copal resin, a bloodstone, and a manhole-sized standing mirror. On the table's far end was the porcelain hair brush that had belonged to my mother when she was a girl, two strands of her light-brown hair caught in its bristles.

Two chances to get this right, I thought.

I walked in a circle, sprinkling the graveyard dirt into a symbol of the dead. I then placed five candles around the circle's perimeter and, chanting, lit them in a star-shaped sequence. As the flames rose and thinned, the room seemed to dim and cool by several degrees.

At the center of the circle, I propped the mirror on its stand and then placed the bloodstone and a strand of hair drawn from my mother's brush before it, covering both with the funeral veil.

"And now for my insurance..."

Focusing on the coin pendant that hung from a chain around my neck, I incanted softly, lips, tongue, and tone imbuing the family symbol with energy. The coin began to hum over my sternum. I switched chants, encasing the coin in a small shield. If I calculated correctly, the energy building up in the coin would overwhelm the shield spell in about five minutes.

A time bomb for if things went sideways.

"*Gatekeeper,*" I whispered in an ancient tongue as I stood

from the circle and drew my sword from my cane. *"You who grant passage to the dead and the dying, who safeguard the In Between. I beseech you to carry our beloved to the world beyond, to spirit her soul with all haste."* Wincing, I drew the sword's blade across my palm. I held the wounded hand forward, allowing the blood to drip over the artifacts in the center of the circle.

"Take her," I said.

The charcoal smell of the copal thickened, and the room dimmed further. A sound like distant thunder rumbled in. Black clouds filled the mirror, twisting slowly into a vortex.

"She is ready to pass, and time is short," I said, the spell elements amplifying the power of my mother's hair, wrapping it in a potent aura of fresh death. *"Take her!"* I repeated, fog issuing from my breath now.

The rumbling deepened and a powerful entity, more shadow than form, emerged into the circle and drifted over the blood-spattered objects. Aiming my staff at the circle, I cried, *"Cerrare!"*

The portal behind the mirror slammed shut. The gatekeeper jerked up and then circled several times, as though sensing its confined state. When the entity stopped, empty sockets, impossibly deep, stared back at me. A whispering voice spoke, raking me with chills.

"She is already claimed."

I went mute as I studied the being as ancient as humankind. Left to its work, a gatekeeper was harmless. When tricked and trapped, not so much. But I needed to know what had happened to my mother, and a gatekeeper could tell me.

"Yes, I know," I responded between grunts. Though I'd closed the portal, I could feel a force beyond, like a riptide, pulling back

3

toward the In Between. Even at my full strength, I wouldn't be able to withstand the pull for long. Beings from that plane didn't belong here.

"I need to know how she died," I said.

The room rattled around me. "Release me, mortal."

"I will once you tell me."

"Release me or I will claim *you*."

I planted my feet and leaned away from the riptide until I was nearly sitting, but the force only strengthened. My right foot stuttered through the graveyard dirt. The containment broken, a frigid hand emerged from the circle and seized my ankle. The cold bit into me like blades slicing into bone. I let out a ragged cry, but I was determined to get an answer.

"Tell me … what happened … to my mother!"

A second hand seized my knee and pulled me toward the portal. This wasn't going to work. I had to abort the summoning.

"Liberare!" I shouted.

The portal blew open like an emergency hatch on an airplane. The gatekeeper disappeared into the mirror, sucked back to its realm. But its ice-cold hands hadn't released me. I fell and twisted onto my stomach, dropping my sword and staff. They tumbled off behind me as though reality had rotated on a ninety-degree axis. My fingers scrabbled over the floor for purchase. When coldness enveloped my lower half, I realized I had entered the mirror.

I gripped the mirror's metal frame and struggled to kick my way back out. The numbness climbed like water to my chest, my chin. In the next moment, my head went under.

Stunned, I stared around a luminescent darkness of shifting shapes and roaring energies. I was in the realm between life and death. The In Between. Fingers slipping, I peeked between my legs. The gatekeeper's face stared back from the shadows like a grim reaper's.

I peered at the backside of the mirror, the image of my apartment beyond undulating into dimness. I could make out my hologram of the city, my lab table, my collection of esoteric books. A deep loneliness yawned inside me as I considered what I was holding onto: a life spent chasing nether creatures for an organization that barely tolerated, much less acknowledged, me—not even to tell me what had happened to my mother. Fallen to illness, as my grandmother had claimed? Or murdered, as insinuated by the vampire Arnaud?

At least in the afterlife I would know.

Yeah, but you'll be powerless to do anything with that knowledge, I countered, a defiant anger growing inside me.

I gathered my strength to shout a Word, but the strange ether that constituted the In Between gushed into my mouth like sea water, and no sound would emerge. The fingers of my right hand lost their grip on the mirror, and my arm fell into the cold. I could feel nothing below my chest now.

Just need to hold on for a few more...

The shield around my coin pendant fractured. For an instant, all the light drew inward, as though toward a collapsing star, before the coin's energy blew out in a detonating flash. The gatekeeper released my leg in a fading moan, and I vaulted up into my library/lab.

I landed back first into a bookcase. My head banged against the floor as tomes spilled around me. Dazed, I sat up and peered at the smoking ruins of the casting circle and fragments of shattered mirror.

"Nice timing," I mumbled, tucking the coin back into my shirt.

My mother's hair was gone, though, taken by the gatekeeper.

Meaning only one strand remained to cast from.

Maybe it was time to consult an expert.

2

Lady Bastet held the strand of hair on either end, her deep green eyes seeming to stare inside it. She hadn't moved for the last minute, the flatness of her dark face speaking to mild entrancement.

I gazed around the room in the back of her basement-level rug business. Beyond the tendrils of incense, a dozen or so cats stared back from shelves that held assortments of Egyptian charms and spell items. Lady Bastet had helped Detective Vega and me with a case in the spring in which her powers of divination had played a critical role. I was counting on her being able to duplicate that success.

"Yes," the mystic said suddenly. "The potential for magic once moved through these cells."

"What do you mean *potential?*"

"You did not tell me your mother's hair was from when she was a girl," she replied, setting it flat on the stone table in front of her. "She inherited magic from at least one of her parents, yes, but whether or not she ever developed that magic, I cannot tell you from a simple reading."

I noted her emphasis on the word *simple.* "You need to go deeper?"

She pushed up the band holding her thick hair from her kohl-lined eyes. "Yes, far deeper."

"Your price?"

"Your blood," she replied.

I had given her a vial's worth the last time, about which I'd been none too comfortable. Wizard's blood could be used in powerful magic, and if that magic turned black, well ... I would be in just as much trouble as the practitioner. "Can I ask what you did with the last sample?"

"I put it to good use," she replied enigmatically.

That the Order hadn't been in touch told me the blood had probably been used for benign purposes. Lady Bastet specialized in potion mixing, from anti-aging elixirs to male enhancement brews. *Better not to think about it,* I decided, rolling up my left shirt sleeve to my elbow. Even though I had undergone the procedure before, the sensation of her wooden needle sucking the blood from my bulging vessel was no less skin-crawling.

Lady Bastet returned the wooden needle to her hair, healed the puncture, and set the clay tube with my blood into her wooden box. When she returned to the table and drew away the veil that covered her scrying globe, I leaned forward, my stomach twisting into anxious knots.

She smiled apologetically. "I should have told you, Everson. For the kind of reading you're asking, I am going to need time."

"How much?"

"Until dusk," she said. "This hair belongs to a young girl. It represents her life to that point, beyond which lies a tangle of possible futures. I will need to comb them out, to align myself with the path she ultimately traveled—up to and including her death."

"Also, anything you can learn about my father..."

I knew even less about him than about my mother. According to Nana, my mother and father had met at a hippie commune upstate. Their relationship lasted just long enough for me to form a bump in my mother's belly before my father—whose name Nana couldn't remember—decided it was time to move on. Heartbroken, my mother returned home.

That had been the official story, anyway. But like with my mother's death, it now lacked a certain ring of truth.

Lady Bastet nodded. "I will tell you all I come to see."

I glanced down at the strand of hair, the final cellular link to my mother, the final link to the truth, maybe.

"I really need you to get this right," I said, raising my eyes to Lady Bastet's, but she gave no sign she'd heard. She leaned nearer, as though trying to read something beyond my face. I felt movement through my mind like fingers over a stringed instrument. Minor notes played fast, speeding my pulse. When Lady Bastet spoke, her voice was husky and distant.

"Trust in the one your heart trusts least."

"I'm sorry?" I said, the words catching in my short breaths.

She sat back, eyes returning to the here and now. She gazed at my mother's hair again. "With enough time, the reading will be the right one," she said in response to my earlier question, as though she hadn't just spaced out or spoken. "But are you certain this is what you want?"

My heart and breaths wound down again. *Why do you need to know?* she seemed to be asking. *Out of simple curiosity or from that age-old lust that has twisted many a man's heart into darkness: revenge?*

"Yes," I said. "It's what I want."

Lady Bastet nodded once. "Then it will be done."

I squinted into a liquid heat that rose from the West Village sidewalks and wobbled the buildings up and down the block. The mercury was forecast to climb over one hundred again today.

I checked my watch. The time, which had slowed way down in Lady Bastet's, seemed to have sped back up to the present and then some. If I didn't hurry, I was going to be late for my summer term class. Cane pinned under an arm, I hustled toward the nearest bus stop.

Within a block, sweat was streaming from my armpits and soaking through the back of my shirt. But I was more bothered by the knowledge someone was keeping pace with me. I peeked over a shoulder to find a young man in a tailored suit gliding around newsstands and oncoming pedestrians. His effortless speed, coupled with his bone-dry face, told me he was an undead.

One of Arnaud's, no doubt, I thought with a groan.

Up ahead, the city bus slowed toward the stop. I broke into a full run, arriving behind a small knot of people. When I looked back, I could no longer see the blood slave. I'd lucked out. He must've been on a different errand. When I straightened, the son of a bitch was in front of me.

"Go ahead," he was telling the driver of the crowded bus. "We'll catch the next one."

"Wait!" I cried, trying to cut past him. The blood slave moved deftly, blocking my attempts until the driver closed the door. With a loud chuff, the bus pulled from the stop and motored away.

"What the hell are you doing?" I said.

Like all of Arnaud's blood slaves, this one was young, his face smooth and handsome. Chilly blue eyes regarded me from beneath waxy eyebrows and a professional cut of brown hair.

"Arnaud Thorne would like you to see something," he answered.

"Well, tell him too fucking bad. I have a class to teach."

I hadn't heard from the vampire Arnaud since he'd held Detective Vega's son hostage in a game whose ultimate intent was to pit me against City Hall. He had cost me my friendship with Vega not to mention my contract with the NYPD. I couldn't imagine what he wanted me to see, or more likely get involved in, and I didn't care. I was done with Arnaud.

I spotted an on-duty taxi coming up Sixth Avenue and waved.

The blood slave gripped my arm and forced it down. "My CEO insists," he said.

The cab zoomed past.

Okay, that's it.

Stepping back, I yanked my cane into sword and staff. I angled the blade so sunlight glinted off a line of bright metal. "You see that? It's a little something called silver, a modification I made to better deal with your kind. Touch me again, and you're going to lose an arm."

The blood slave's lips broke upwards as his eyes sharpened. "Oh, come now, Mr. Croft," he said in a familiar, taunting voice. "Don't shoot the messenger. Or amputate him, as the case may be. I rather prefer him with all limbs intact." Arnaud had taken possession of his minion.

"What do you want?" I demanded.

"Like my associate said, for you to see something. We needn't go far. Why, that little establishment across the way should do."

I glanced over at the hole in the wall whose vertical sign read BAR. "Not interested."

"Oh, but I think you will be, Mr. Croft. I think you'll be *very* interested."

Something in the certainty with which Arnaud spoke made me hesitate. Or was that the vampire's power insinuating its way into my thoughts. I steeled my mind and cocked my sword arm.

"If you're not out of my face in the next second, I'll skip the amputation and go straight to execution."

"My associate is perfectly within his rights to occupy this public piece of sidewalk, Mr. Croft. And you should know that I will continue to badger you until you acquiesce to my request. Ten minutes of your time is all I ask. I will even pay your cab fare following. You'll arrive at the college before the bus you've just missed."

I squinted at him. "And you'll leave me alone?"

"You have my assurances, Mr. Croft."

Unlike agreements between mortals, a vampire's word held an innate binding power. Once made, especially by a vampire of

Arnaud's stature, they were hard to break. What in the hell was he up to?

"Leave me alone, as in never seek me out again?" I asked, to be certain we were on the same page.

"Indeed. *Should* we meet again, it will be because you have come to me."

I snorted. "Well, that's not gonna happen."

"All right." He clapped once. "It sounds like we have an agreement."

I sighed and sheathed my sword.

"Let's get this over with."

3

The blood slave held the door open for me, and we stepped into the dim bar. An assortment of fans blew around the stink of spilled beer, wet cigarettes, and what smelled like vomit from a back bathroom.

"Charming, isn't it?" Arnaud said through his slave, then glided toward the long bar. At one end, a trio of barflies sagged on stools, faces transfixed on the glow of a baseball game. The bartender, a hefty man in an undershirt with muddy sweat stains beneath the pits, stared at the game too.

"Ahoy, there!" Arnaud called with false cheer.

The bartender's head was eggplant shaped, broad at the jaw but smaller and shining around his crown. It rotated slightly as he shifted his smallish eyes toward us, his bulk remaining aligned with the mounted TV.

"My associate and I could use a cold drink on this hot day. A pair of scotch on the rocks, if you will." Arnaud scanned the top shelf of liquor bottles before stopping and pointing at a dusty bottle with a red label. "That one will do. And make them doubles, my good friend."

The bartender screwed up his eyes as though trying to decide whether Arnaud was toying with him. When the vampire set a pair of fifty-dollar bills on the scratched bar, the bartender must have decided he didn't care. Heaving himself from his languid lean, he plodded over to the bottle Arnaud had indicated and began pouring our drinks.

"Not the quickest study," Arnaud said to me as he climbed onto a stool, not bothering to lower his voice. "But beggars can't be choosers."

"You said ten minutes," I reminded him as I took the neighboring stool.

"Let's see..." Arnaud checked his slender wristwatch. "Yes, perfect timing."

As the bartender set our drinks in front of us, Arnaud pushed one of the fifties forward. "This will cover our beverages as well as a generous gratuity—despite that you only poured one shot apiece and then attempted to disguise the deception with common tap water."

The bartender's face clenched. "You calling me a cheat?"

"*This...*" Arnaud tapped the second fifty, ignoring the bartender's show of aggression. "...will be for additional services provided."

The bartender's gaze fell to the bill. "What services?" he asked suspiciously.

Arnaud broke into sudden laughter. "Oh, no, no. Nothing like that, my strapping friend. No, we would just like to procure your television for a short while."

The bartender's head twisted to look up at the TV. On the screen, an outfielder fielded a fly ball. When the bartender turned back to us, his brow was a bed of confusion lines. He scratched his stubbly chin.

"He'd like to change the channel," I said, acting as translator.

"The Mets are playing," the bartender said, as if that settled the question.

"And playing delightedly, I have little doubt." Arnaud checked his watch again. "However, we are interested in something for which time is of the utmost essence. And what we're offering in exchange is more than sufficient compensation. Wouldn't you agree?"

"Can't do it," he said. "Those guys at the end of the bar? The only reason they come here is for the games. They'd kill me."

The smile on Arnaud's face stiffened, and before I could anticipate his next words, he seized the bartender's throat. "I assume you're speaking figuratively in regards to your friends," he said in a fierce whisper. "I, however, am not, so I advise you to listen carefully."

The bartender gargled, his bald head already turning red.

"You are going to accept our payment," Arnaud said, "and you are going to change the channel, or I will crush your windpipe and end your pathetic life right here. Do you understand?"

"Hey, c'mon," I whispered, unlocking the sword inside my cane, ready to step to the man's defense.

The bartender pawed toward Arnaud's face, but a crunch of cartilage made him reconsider. He nodded desperately, his bulging eyes beginning to weep. In Arnaud's eyes, I saw a hunger to kill. But in the next moment, his hand popped open, dropping the bartender on the bar.

"Jesus," I breathed, notching my sword again. I peeked at the patrons. Their gazes hadn't moved from the television.

"There, there, my friend," Arnaud said, patting the bartender's heaving back. "Take a moment to collect yourself—a glass of water, if you need it—then kindly change the channel to four. Oh, and the shotgun you're reaching for is no longer beneath the bar. I removed it earlier in the event negotiations failed. I'm pleased we were able to arrive at a mutual understanding."

Arnaud slid the other fifty forward. The bartender stopped groping under the bar. He pulled a dish towel from his sagging pants to wipe his face, eyeing the fifty as though it might bite him.

"Go on," Arnaud said, "you've earned it."

The bartender took the bill and shoved it into a pocket. Protests rose from the barflies as he reached up and changed the channel. The ballgame flipped to a young woman making an impassioned plea to a grim-faced man over the custody of their child.

"A soap opera?" I said.

Arnaud held up a finger. "A moment."

Seconds later, the soap opera switched to a feed of Mayor Budge Lowder standing in front of a podium stacked with microphones.

"We interrupt this program for a special news conference," an off-camera news anchor said. *"The mayor is set to announce what he is calling a 'brave, new initiative' that could mean sweeping changes for the city of New York. We go live now to City Hall."*

As Budge wiped a cowlick of hair from his pudgy face and adjusted his round glasses, my thoughts cast back to the showdown at his mansion. Vega and I battling the mayor's wife and her werewolf brethren; Budge shooting me; me shooting his wife; Vega negotiating our release by blackmailing Budge and Penny with information we discovered during our investigation.

As it turned out, we hadn't had to worry about Penny. The shot that had ruptured her aorta had sent her into a coma, where she still remained. All summer long, Budge had been keeping the public abreast of her condition. It seemed to have had an effect, stalling his falling poll numbers despite the multitude of problems besieging his crumbling metropolis.

I guessed sympathy still held sway.

"How's everyone doing?" Budge asked from the podium. *"Good, good. As always, I'll start with an update on my beloved wife, after whom so many of you have been asking and offering your well wishes. At last count, we've been sent enough plants and flowers to turn Central Park into a profitable nursery."* He chuckled with the crowd of reporters, then paused as though to gather himself. *"Penny remains in a coma, but her doctors say she's stable. In fact, they're telling me I should talk to her because she can probably hear what I'm saying. So I've been telling her a few things. First, that what happened to her is my fault."* He raised his hands to the murmured protests. *"No, listen, listen. All you've been told was that she fell into a coma, but you don't know how she ended up there. I think it's time you heard."*

"Here it comes," Arnaud said above his glass.

"What?" I asked nervously.

"The Big Reveal."

"My wife was attacked," Budge announced.

The blood fell from my face. *He's going to out me,* I thought. *He's going to implicate me in his wife's attempted murder. Probably Vega, too. And with all of the sympathy pouring toward Budge and his wife, the city will eat us alive.* My eyes shot toward the door.

Arnaud's cold fingers rested on my forearm. "A moment."

On the television, Budge patted the air, assuring the press he would answer their burst of questions after he finished his announcement. *"Yes, she was attacked,"* he continued. *"But here's the thing. The entire City of New York is under attack. I'd heard the rumors and reports. But I ignored them. It took what happened to my dear wife to finally see the light. I'm talking about supernaturals. Beings that shouldn't exist. But I'm telling you, they do exist, and they're here. They're in our city. And they threaten each and every one of us."*

Instead of quieting the reporters, Budge used their swelling voices to bolster his own voice, like a preacher at a tent revival. *"Many of you have seen them. Some of you have been pursued by them. A few of you have lost loved ones to them. But not any more. Not in my city."*

In recent months, I'd observed an increasing number of ghouls scavenging the East Village garbage piles, a story even serious papers were starting to pick up. The monsters had graduated from the tabloids.

"Hey," one of the barflies said, "you remember that thing that chased us down Avenue C a couple months ago?"

"Yeah, yeah," his buddy replied. "Big and ugly with long arms. Think it was one of them supernaturals?"

The bartender shushed them.

"That's the second thing I'm telling Penny while she's fighting for her life," Budge continued. *"That the monster who attacked her isn't going to get away. We're going to hunt him down, along with every other supernatural that has infested our city, and we're going to eradicate them."*

"Damned straight," the third barfly said.

"So I stand before my city today to announce the creation of a one-hundred person force within the NYPD." He turned and opened an arm toward a late middle-aged black man with a somber face and thick mustache. *"Headed by Captain Lance Cole, the Hundred will lead the effort to root out and destroy the supernatural scourge on our city. The monsters are the true root of evil. Not taxes or the lack of city services or any of the peripheral issues my opponent would have you believe. Once the monsters are eradicated, once the streets and parks are safe, I promise you, the people and businesses that fled will come storming back, restoring our great city to glory."* He threw his arms out with this final pronouncement.

"So now you see," Arnaud said as Budge began to take questions.

I swallowed and tried to find my voice. "Yeah, but he spoke of monsters, not wizards."

"You know as well as I that he's not going to distinguish between the two. Not after what befell his wife."

"No thanks to you."

"Be that as it may, the question now is how you plan to negotiate the new terrain."

I looked down the bar to where the bartender had wandered

over. He and the patrons were huddled in conversation. As I turned back to Arnaud, my head ached with the beginning of a migraine.

"I feel an offer coming," I said.

"Or perhaps a mutually beneficial arrangement."

"Let me guess, a new pact between wizards and vamps."

"Aligning to defend our rightful place in the city," he said.

I shook my head. "I'm not getting mixed up with you again."

"I don't see that you have a choice, Mr. Croft—that is, unless you elect to flee. But I sense that would be difficult for one whose power derives from the unique energies of the city."

He was correct to the extent that a wizard's power adapted to the environment where he practiced, to the particular pattern of ley lines. One could relocate, sure, but it took time to shape the new energies fully to his purposes—especially for a relatively new practitioner like me.

"If you do remain," Arnaud continued, "I am the only one with a fortification and sufficient personnel to defend it."

"Then why do you need me?"

"Because in the fever of war, favors are called in, strange alliances take shape, the opposition swells. Just look at any of history's great conflicts. We might soon find ourselves at a disadvantage."

"And you think I can do, what?" I said. "Round up the local wizards and march them to the Financial District? Tell them, hey, we're joining Team Vampire?"

Though I picked up magical auras around the city, I didn't know who and who didn't belong to the Order. My organization was highly compartmentalized, either to protect its secrecy or to decrease the chances of magic-users banding together to rebel. Both explanations made sense. I was sure I wasn't the only one to have questioned the Order's authority.

"It's above my wizarding level," I said.

"Very well," Arnaud replied curtly. "I suppose it will take circumstances to convince you. Until then..." He finished his drink, dropped a twenty in front of me for the promised cab fare, and slipped off his stool. Before I could say anything, the door to the bar opened and closed in a flash of sunlight, and Arnaud was gone.

I moved my untouched drink around a small pool of condensation, the class I was supposed to teach on the bottom rung of my concerns. On the television above me, Budge rattled off more details about his eradication program—dollar amounts, federal funding. Arnaud had forecast the development, sure. But that didn't mean I had to rush into an alliance with him, did it?

No, I decided. *I only need to inform the Order and await instructions. Which I'll do right after my class.*

I stood from my barstool, collected the twenty, and turned, only to be met by a meaty hand against my chest. I fell back onto my stool. The bartender rose over me, two of the patrons from the other end of the bar on either side of him. I looked around for the third guy but couldn't see him.

"Who was your friend?" the bartender asked.

I glanced toward the door Arnaud's blood slave had departed through. "Friend? I hardly knew the guy."

"Well, you came in here with him," the bartender said.

"Your powers of observation are astounding," I told him.

"I've never seen anyone move that fast," he said.

"Yeah," one of the barflies put in, a man with a trucker hat and thick beard.

"Really?" I said. "It probably just seemed that way because the rest of us were moving so slow."

The patrons' brows beetled as they tried to puzzle that out. The bartender's eyes didn't shift from mine, though. He loomed nearer.

"The boys and I have been consulting," he said. "We think he might be one of those supernatural freaks the mayor's talking about. And you know what? We think you're one of them too."

"Me?" The metallic bite of adrenaline filled my mouth as my gaze jumped between them. Who were these losers—one with a head shaped like an eggplant—to call me a freak? Power stormed toward my prism.

But when I caught a whiff of leather and musk, I realized what Arnaud had done. He'd exuded an aerosol that was releasing hormones into our systems: raw fight or flight. It was the same reason he'd manhandled the bartender into changing the channel instead of using his vampiric powers of persuasion. Arnaud wanted to incite a confrontation, to underline his point that the city was aligning against us. Though my heart pounded with an urge to clash, I settled back into my seat. I'd played into Arnaud's hands once. It wasn't happening again.

"Look guys," I said, forcing a calming breath. "I'm flesh and blood, just like you. I didn't come in here to cause trouble—which would be pretty hard for someone like me anyway." I held up my cane as proof of disability.

"Hey, Bill!"

I looked over to see the third barfly, the one I'd lost track of, emerging from the back of the bar carrying a shotgun. The stock end of the gun dripped water. "It was sitting in the crapper. That joker must've dropped it in there when he came in earlier to use the bathroom."

Bartender Bill scowled. "Bring it here."

"This cane belonged to my grandfather, actually," I said, pushing energy into my wizard's voice, willing their attention back to me. "Part walking aid, part novelty item. Can you make out that stone?"

The three barflies looked at one another, then at the white opal.

"What about it?" Bill growled. He had seized his gun and begun wiping the stock dry with his towel. I noted the tremor in his hands, the quavering edge to his voice. Arnaud's toxin was still pumping through him. He wasn't going to allow me out of his bar without a fight.

"If you look closely enough," I said, "you can make out Playboy's Miss June, 1948." Gathering energy, I watched Bill's eyes. When at last they squinted toward the opal, I shouted, *Illuminare!*

An intense light flashed against their faces. Shouts went up from the recoiling men. I climbed onto the bar to escape their semicircle. Bartender Bill groped toward me, but I was already into the first steps of flight. Ashtrays and beer bottles flew from my feet. The shotgun went off, and a shelf of liquor bottles erupted. Glass and alcohol rained over my back.

At the far end of the bar, I jumped down. Bill swung his shotgun toward the sound.

Vigore! I shouted, using a force invocation to shove two

of the stumbling barflies into Bill. The bartender lumbered backwards, the shotgun blowing fire into the ceiling. Chunks of plaster rained over them.

I opened the door onto the bright blur of the West Village and then sealed the door behind me with a locking spell. Hailing a passing taxi, I climbed in, my back wet against the seat.

"Where to?" the cabbie asked.

"Midtown College," I panted. "I'm late for a class I'm supposed to teach."

"Looking like that?"

I followed his squinting gaze to my liquor-soaked shirt. Great. Blood from the exploding glass stippled through the fabric over my left shoulder. My back was probably bleeding too.

"Just drive," I said. "Fast."

As the cab pulled away from the curb, I peered around to ensure Bill and the others hadn't escaped the bar. But more generally, I was looking to ensure the eradication program wasn't underway. What that would even look like, I had no idea. An increased police presence? Mystics and diviners rousted from their shops? Magic-users in arm and leg shackles, tape over their mouths? I scooted to the middle of the backseat, out of view of a city that suddenly felt hostile.

Goddamn you, Arnaud.

4

Following a change of shirt and a quick grooming, I stole from the faculty bathroom and, seeing that the coast was clear, made a run for my classroom, leather satchel slapping my hip.

I turned a corner and nearly plowed into Professor Snodgrass. The diminutive chairman of my department staggered in a circle and would have fallen if I hadn't caught him. With a huff, he slapped my hands away and straightened his small glasses. He peered up at me, eyes sharpening.

"Professor *Croft*," he exclaimed, cheeks reddening in anger.

"Oh, hey, sorry about that," I said, showing an apologetic hand as I made to scoot past him. Ever since my hearing the year before, where Snodgrass had motioned to have me fired, I'd managed to stay off his radar. Part of that had entailed getting to my classes on time. The other part had meant avoiding him whenever possible. I'd just managed to blow both.

Snodgrass checked his watch. "Don't you have a seminar this hour?"

"Right, I'm headed there now."

"Ten minutes late, I see." He stepped nearer, sniffing the air. "And what's that I smell?"

I met his snooty gaze. "Alcohol."

He blinked twice in surprise before his lips pinched into a smile. "So you admit that you've been drinking, that you were preparing to instruct your students in an inebriated state?"

"Do you want the truth?"

"Please, Professor Croft." He stood back, hands clasped behind the back of his tweed suit. The man could barely disguise his glee. He would finally have a bulletproof case for my termination. The prestigious college would not tolerate a drunkard for a professor.

"All right," I said with a sigh. "I ducked into a West Village bar to watch the mayor's press conference."

"And how many drinks did you have?"

"Drinks? None, actually." I watched Snodgrass's smile fracture. "The bartender threatened me with his shotgun, so I jumped onto the bar and made a run for it. He started shooting. Bam! Bam! Glass and liquor flying everywhere, like something out of a damned Western. I'm fine, obviously—I know that has to be a relief for you—but I did get soaked." I chuckled. "Hence the smell."

Snodgrass's lips trembled. "I can see this is all one big joke to you, Professor Croft, but I assure you, the board takes the matter of alcoholism *very* seriously."

"As they should," I said. "But absent proof, you'd just be wasting their time. Again."

The final jab was probably one too many, but with my nerves still raw from the mayor's announcement, not to mention Arnaud's harsh toxin, I wasn't in a good place to be fucked with. I stepped past Snodgrass, but I had only gone a few paces when he called to me.

"You might be interested to hear that I've done some investigating," he said.

"Congratulations," I called back.

"I admit, it baffled me how you were able to get your arrest record expunged by this Detective *Vega*." He said her name with bitter scorn. "A few inquiries later and, lo and behold, I discover you're working as a consultant to her department. On *supernatural* cases," he added.

I stopped and turned. "What's your point?"

"Oh, no point." He adjusted his bowtie. "Just that I find it all very interesting. A professor of mythology and lore—one who had been serving a probation, no less—suddenly in the pay of the NYPD. That would require a very compelling skill set, I should think. A compelling *expertise*."

"So I've taken an academic interest in the supernatural," I said, a little too defensively. "Big deal."

"Are you sure that's all it is?"

Panic sped my breaths. "I don't know what you're getting at."

"Given your grants, the board might be willing to overlook certain ... *tendencies*. But I doubt the same could be said for the parents who are paying their children's tuition. Especially now that the city has declared war on those with said tendencies."

"You're still speaking Urdu, and I'm late for my class."

"If history has taught me anything," Snodgrass shouted after me, "it's that when the leaders fail to act, you go straight to the people."

I reached my classroom to find the oscillating fan blowing a rattling circuit across the ring of desks—all empty. *Dammit.* By the college's rules, students only had to wait ten minutes for a tardy professor. I consulted my watch. My own students appeared to have followed that law to the second.

"Thanks, gang," I muttered.

I tossed my satchel and cane onto my desk and unbuttoned my shirt to my chest. Taking the fan cage in both hands, I leaned down until the lukewarm rush of air bathed my face and billowed my shirt.

As much as I hated to admit it, Snodgrass's words had rattled me.

There's no way the man knows about my wizarding life, I reassured myself. *He may have his suspicions, but that's all they are. Snodgrass isn't going to risk his reputation by calling up parents and making wild accusations. That would only put his own job in jeopardy.*

But I had to wonder. With the mayor's announcement sure to alarm the public, would merely *insinuating* someone was a supernatural be enough to alienate him? I considered the ring of empty desks. Of course none of it mattered if I couldn't get to my own classes on time.

I smiled bitterly, remembering an era when I would have arrived to find Caroline lecturing in my stead. Afterwards, she would have scolded me, insisting it was the "last time"—like she did every time. I had started calling her "Sub," short for substitute, a joke she eventually warmed to.

Closing my eyes, I imagined her faerie-scented skin from our night together, her soft whispers, her golden tendrils of hair spilling around me. I remembered the way our bodies, our magic, had moved against the other's. Had that night even happened? A night that was becoming more ethereal with the passing months? But there it was: the ache around my heart, the bruising emptiness, like what I'd felt when I'd awoken alone the next morning.

Yeah. It had happened.

The fan blades chopped up my forlorn sigh and blew it back in my face.

"Is this a bad time?" a woman asked from behind me.

I hurried to button my shirt back up and tuck my coin pendant away. The noise of the fan had washed over the voice, so I wasn't sure who it belonged to. Someone from administration, with my luck. Maybe Snodgrass was already sowing the seeds of suspicion. But as I turned and the woman in the doorway came into focus, my arms fell slowly to my sides.

"Professor Reid," I said.

"Professor Croft," Caroline replied, her lips pressing into a smile.

5

The last time I had seen Caroline was the night she'd come to my apartment. She disappeared the next morning without a trace. When classes resumed after the spring break, I learned she had put in for a last-minute sabbatical. She wasn't supposed to return until the fall semester, if then. After several calls that went straight to her voicemail, I gave up on trying to reach her.

Now, I took a moment to absorb the impact of her sudden manifestation. Caroline was dressed professionally—white blouse, khaki skirt, thin gold jewelry—but she carried the charged air of the fae, still subtle, but stronger than what I had felt around her the last time. The oscillating fan stirred her hair, which had been straightened, I noticed, and trimmed to her shoulders.

"What are you doing here?" I asked.

Caroline stepped from the doorway until she was standing in front of me. Her blue-green gaze settled on my chest, and she slid the top button of my shirt free. My breath went shallow, but I realized she was only fixing my shoddy redressing job. When she finished, she smoothed my shirt collar and rose onto her tiptoes. The kiss against my cheek was light, cordial.

"It's good to see you, too, Everson."

"You know what I meant." I tried not to stammer as my face warmed over. "I thought you were going to be away until the fall."

She took a seat in one of my students' desks and gestured to my desk across the ring from her. She wanted to talk but at a distance. Whether because she didn't trust me or herself, I couldn't tell. I complied, affecting a casualness that felt all wrong. Caroline smiled sympathetically. I moved my leather satchel in front of me and propped my arms on it.

"I owe you an apology," she said.

"How about an explanation?"

"That too." She clasped her hands on her desk. "The night I came to you, Everson, I was a bit of a mess. This, becoming a faerie, returning to that world ... it happened so suddenly, and I ... I didn't handle it very well. When I went to your apartment, it was to talk, to find my center. You're my closest friend, the only one who would have understood what I was experiencing. But your feelings—they hit me hard." She studied her hands for a moment. A silver band glistened on her left ring finger. "I'm afraid I let them overwhelm me."

"So that night was a mistake," I said numbly.

"That's not what I'm saying. I went along with what happened.

I *wanted* what happened." When she looked up, her eyes wavered with emotion. "But it was irresponsible. Worse, it was unfair to you. That's why I left like I did. As much for the loyalty I owed Angelus as his wife as for the loyalty I owed you as my friend. I needed to—"

"I'm sorry, Caroline," I interrupted, "but what I felt from you that night went waaay beyond friendship."

"I know. But it can't anymore. That's what I'm saying. I have duties now, responsibilities."

"Bigger than this, than us?" Having her answer that terrified me, but I needed to know.

"Yes," she said. "Bigger than us."

I sensed there was something she wasn't telling me. "Are you sure?"

Caroline hesitated before nodding.

"Then I guess we're done here." I angled my body toward the door, but Caroline made no move to rise from her desk.

"I didn't just come to apologize," she said.

"Gee, what else can I look forward to?"

"I've been in the faerie realm for much of these last months," she said. "At times it's felt like visiting twelfth-century Europe. The realm parallel to New York is a patchwork of feudal kingdoms, with all of the emphasis on lineages, territories, and certain decorums one would expect. Interestingly, the royalty there consider our modern world to be brutish and dirty."

"Then why spend time here?" I asked bitterly.

"Because of the portals."

"What about them?"

"They're vital to the kingdoms that control them."

Though I continued to hold myself at an angle to Caroline, I considered the implications of what she was saying. From the way she'd explained it earlier, distances scaled differently between our realms. A trip from Battery Park to the Bronx would take about thirty minutes in a cab, whereas in the faerie realm, the corresponding trip might take weeks, and often through hostile territories. "So that explains the fae's interest in the city," I said, straightening.

Caroline nodded. "Wars have been fought over those portals, treaties written. Marriages arranged," she added with lowered eyes. "Angelus's family has a kingdom in the north, a region that corresponds to a section of upper Manhattan. My mother's kingdom is in the south. Each kingdom controls a portal. Maybe you've noticed a new trucking line in the city?"

"Two Way," I said automatically. I had seen the green trucks trundling north and south all summer. "Wait, that's a fae operation?"

"The portals, and our ability to go between them, have not only established ours as the most influential kingdoms, but they've also engendered us with a responsibility to safeguard the greater realm. We have to move food, supplies, and forces when and where they're needed, and often quickly."

"Fine, but why are you telling me all of this?" I asked irritably. Her explanation of our night together had left me feeling like a cheap toy played with briefly and then tossed away. And now here she was, giving me a geography lesson on the fae realm as if I was one of her students. I wanted to go home and punch something. Instead, I used my fists to wipe the sting of sweat from my eyes. I noticed that Caroline's skin remained dry, as though wrapped in its own cool atmosphere. The oscillating fan shuddered another circuit.

"The portals have two sides," she said. "And though the fae are quiet about it, they are in constant negotiations with city officials to grant them exclusive access to the portals on this side."

"By *negotiations* do you mean bribes?"

"When they must."

I thought about the fae townhouse on the Upper East Side, the one I'd tried to force my way into in the spring. I had detoured past it a few times since, in the hopes of catching Caroline coming or going. That must have held the portal to Angelus's kingdom. The portal to Caroline's mother's kingdom would be somewhere in lower Manhattan.

"Ours is beneath Federal Hall," Caroline said with a tired laugh, as though picking up my thought. "You can imagine the kinds of strings the fae have had to pull over the years."

I grunted.

A stone's throw from Wall Street, Federal Hall stood on the site of the first capitol of the United States, where George Washington himself had been sworn into office. The building had been a national monument until about a decade ago when the city wrested it under municipal control—and then promptly shut the site down for repairs. Probably the fae's doing.

"I still don't see what this has to do with me," I said.

"Because of my connections to City Hall, I've been in talks with Mayor Lowder. He's—"

"Wait, you're talking to Budge? Even as he's planning to wipe us out?"

"He's not planning to wipe us out. Just listen," she said when

I started to interrupt again. "Budge saw you and me together at the gala that night back in April. He's told me about your confrontation in his mansion. I've assured him that you're not a threat, that you'll be no further trouble to him."

That damned professorial tone again. Indignation broke hot inside me.

"Thanks, but I can fight my own battles."

"Not if Penny wakes up," Caroline said.

"What do you mean?"

"Budge isn't sure he can control her."

"We already took care of that," I said.

"If you're talking about the information you have on them ... Look, Budge covered his bases well. The sympathy campaign protects his wife while she's comatose. Reveal anything about her werewolf nature now, and the public will eat you alive. That goes double when the eradication program gains momentum. The public will see it as a slander campaign. Meaning if and when Penny wakes up, she'll have carte blanche to go after you."

I had already been down that line of reasoning, but I refused to show any more weakness. "I'll cross that bridge when I come to it," I said.

"For your safety," Caroline went on, "I think you should come to the faerie realm for a period, as our guest."

"*Our*, as in your and Angelus's?" I shook my head. "Forget it."

"Just until we can assess the situation, see where the eradication program leads. The fae don't typically intervene on behalf of non-fae, but I've worked out an exception for you."

I waved my hands for her to stop.

"You're welcome to bring your cat, of course," she said.

"Look, Caroline. I get that you feel bad about what happened between us, that you want to try to make it up to me. But I'm not a charity case. I can take care of myself."

"Not against the kinds of forces that might be gathering."

The gravity in her voice matched the weight of her gaze: whatever it was she wasn't telling me. I wanted to press her, but my pride wouldn't allow it. I stood from behind my desk.

"Thanks for stopping by," I said.

"Everson..."

I strode to the classroom door and opened it. After a moment, she rose and walked toward me. "At least promise me you'll think about it. You still have my number. Leave me a message."

"I left several back in April," I said coldly.

She made a tentative move to hug me, but I backed away a step and stared at a spot just above her head. After a moment, Caroline relented and walked out of my classroom and most likely my life.

Good riddance.

"My ice bags are all soggy," Tabitha pouted as I hung my cane on the coat rack and locked the apartment door behind me.

I looked over at where my cat lounged on her divan, a box fan blowing orange hair from her squinting eyes. Her perch was a cooling system I had fixed up for her: a plus-sized cat bed set atop gallon bags of ice. The bags were water-filled now, one fallen to the floor and leaking.

"Yeah, yeah," I sighed. "Hop up, and I'll change them."

"This heat is *insufferable*," she complained as she stood from the cat bed and stretched. "Can't you do anything about it?"

"I told you, we're on a waiting list with the HVAC people."

She stopped and eyed my approach. "You look like walking death."

"Just a tough morning at the college."

"Oh sure," she said. "Telling stories to an audience of impressionable young women, mooning and batting their lashes up at you. Must be fucking torture."

"It has nothing to do with my classes, and watch your mouth." I picked up the dripping bags and carried them to the kitchen sink.

"Do tell."

"Thanks, but no thanks."

I could feel her sharp feline eyes on me as I emptied the bags and scooped fresh ice into them. The heat wave coupled with a dead air conditioner had made Tabitha more antagonistic than usual. She was looking for an opening to needle me. I wasn't going to give her one.

"Well, if you don't tell me what's wrong," she said, "how am I going to help you?"

"*You* help *me?*" I laughed once. "That's rich."

I returned with the ice bags and a fresh towel, arranging them beneath her cat bed. I used the old towel to wipe up the spill on the floor.

"Oh, come now, darling," she said in her hurt voice, curling onto the bed, ice crunching as she shifted her weight around. "I know I don't always show it, but it just kills me when something's bothering you."

"Yeah, right."

"I'm serious. Besides, who else do you have to talk to?"

She had a point. With no one to confide in, my encounter with Caroline was only going to play a numb loop in my mind. A part of me felt a cold satisfaction at having shown Caroline the door, but the heart-piercing truth was that she had walked out of it a long time ago. The four months since our night together would have been roughly two years in the faerie realm. More than enough time for Caroline to settle into her marriage, her new life.

"Fine," I said, aiming a finger at Tabitha. "But the second you say something catty, this conversation's over."

She widened her ochre-green eyes as though to say *moi?*

I sighed and lowered myself to the couch. "Caroline stopped by my classroom today."

Tabitha grinned at the delicious tidbit, but to her credit, she kept her mouth shut.

"She claimed she came to apologize," I continued, "and to explain what happened, you know, that night."

"Oh, I know *all* about that night," Tabitha purred, damned feline hearing.

"I mean, I see where she's coming from." I stood and began pacing. "She agreed to marry Angelus to save her father, which is admirable. It is. And her new role carries all kinds of responsibilities, not just to her—" I had to swallow hard before I could form the word. "—*husband*, but to that realm. Responsibilities that, believe me, I understand. But I felt something that night in the way we moved, in the way our magic melded. Something that..."

"Doesn't happen with just any old gal?" Tabitha asked.

She had one furry eyebrow arched, but not in sarcasm. It was an honest question. I considered it before collapsing back onto the couch and digging my hands into my sweat-dampened hair.

"Yes," I said.

Tabitha nodded in what appeared honest understanding. That had to be a first.

"And when we were talking today," I went on, "I kept getting this feeling that she was holding back. That there was something she wasn't telling me."

"Such as?"

"I don't know."

Tabitha appeared to be thinking as she licked a paw and combed it over an ear. "Well, if you sensed as much, I'm sure the reason will emerge eventually. Will you have occasion to see each other again?"

I stared at Tabitha a moment to make sure she wasn't mocking me before shaking my head. "Our meeting didn't end well. Though I do have a standing invitation to the faerie realm. Woop-de-doo."

"And what's the occasion?"

"Oh, earlier today the mayor announced a plan to eradicate supernaturals. We're all right as long as his wife remains comatose, but if she wakes up, Caroline thinks all bets could be off."

Tabitha scowled. "By *wife* do you mean that werewolf? I do wish you would have killed her. I never have gotten on with their kind, and living inside a cat's body doesn't exactly improve things."

"Half werewolf," I corrected her. "And yeah, I'm starting to wish I would've finished her off, too. Which reminds me, any sightings today?"

Since my encounter with Penny and her pack, I'd asked Tabitha to be extra vigilant for werewolves. Budge may not have issued a sic-'em order, but the pack was no doubt burning to avenge the attack on their leader and fellow pack members. After four months, nothing, but I wasn't about to let my guard down. Especially after the day's developments.

"No, darling, but let's not get off topic," she replied, no doubt to steer the conversation from the tours she hadn't carried out. "How did you reply to Caroline's invitation?"

"I told her no, of course."

Tabitha's lower lip pouted out. "But their realm is rumored to have the most *divine* delectables. Markets of plump, fresh-caught fish—not the farm-raised trash you buy. Succulent lamb. Goat's milk so rich it separates into a layer of cream thick enough to eat off the top." Tabitha's eyelids fluttered at the imagined foods. "It would be so wonderful, darling."

"Well, too bad," I said, "because I'm not going to hang around eating … *goat yogurt* while Caroline plays princess with Angelus."

Tabitha *tsk*ed as she shook her head.

"What?" I said.

"You clearly don't understand women. Don't you see? Caroline is using the excuse of some ill-defined danger to bring you into her world, to be closer to you. It's an age-old trick."

Hope flickered inside me. "Really?"

Tabitha darted out her tongue, too late to catch the trickle of saliva dribbling off her chin. I sighed. Her counsel no longer had anything to do with Caroline. She was thinking about the faerie food.

"All right," I said, slapping my thighs, "we're done here."

Tabitha returned from the fantasy, eyes sharpening. "Won't you even consider the offer?"

"No." I stood and retrieved my cane from the coat rack.

"Wait. Where are you going?"

"To learn about my mother."

6

Though the sun had just set, the dimming West Village streets continued to radiate late July heat. I hurried down the steps to Lady Bastet's basement-level business—minutes from learning the fate of my mother—only to find the door locked.

I knocked, waited, and then knocked again, harder.

Still no answer. *Must have stepped out.*

I was debating whether to wait for her, assuming she would even be back tonight, when something scratched the other side of the door. A cat's cry followed, the tenor low and strained. An alarm bell went off in my head. Without forethought, I drew my sword and aimed it at the lock.

"Vigore!" Energy coursed down the blade. The lock trembled and burst. When I pushed the door open, something lithe and black and wearing an odd collar darted past me and up the steps. *Crap.* I was preparing to retrieve Lady Bastet's escaped cat, when I picked up a familiar scent.

Blood.

I threw myself against the brick wall beside the door. Using my sword blade, I tested the threshold. The protective glyphs were down. Either Lady Bastet had inactivated them, or a powerful presence had broken through. In readiness for the latter, I summoned a shield of light.

I peeked around the corner—no one inside—and eased into the main room. The lights had been left on. Ahead, one of Lady Bastet's cats lay on its side, partly hidden behind a colorful hanging rug. In two more steps, I saw that the body was headless, blood pooling near the neck.

"Oh, Jesus," I whispered, bringing the back of a hand to my mouth.

More cats littered the floor, all decapitated by a ripping force, hair everywhere. One severed head seemed to be watching me, the mouth opened in a frozen cry. I cut my gaze to the back room. From my angle, I could see a slice of the stone table and the shadow of someone sitting at it.

Heart slamming, I eased toward the room at an oblique angle, sword and staff at the ready. I peeked around the doorway and froze.

No.

Lady Bastet was slouched back in her chair, eyes wide but not from entrancement. I entered the room. Spilled blood wrapped her neck like a wine-red cravat. I stepped closer, my breath stuck in my chest. Someone or something had slit the mystic's throat.

"Lady Bastet?" I whispered.

No answer.

My eyes fell from her bloodstained peasant's blouse to her wrists and ankles. No bindings. No signs of struggle. The gold band in her hair hadn't even shifted—which didn't make any goddamned sense, not for someone so powerful. Had she been caught deep in spell work?

Beyond my crackling shield, I took in the overturned shelves, shattered spell items, and scattered cat parts. The scene had the markings of a werewolf attack. Penny *had* been planning to order wolves here to find her daughter, but that had been before I'd put Penny in a coma. Had the mayor ordered the attack? Or was I looking at some kind of rogue event?

I circled the room, opening my wizard's senses. Lingering energy showed in fading, multicolored hues. The energy appeared to have originated from Lady Bastet in the course of her divination work. Magic-wise, I wasn't picking up anything foreign, or even violent.

I dispersed my shield with a sigh and drew a dog-eared business card from my wallet. I flicked it with my thumb a few times before nodding.

"Did you touch anything?" Detective Vega demanded.

Beneath midnight hair that had been stretched back into a ponytail, her professional eyes assessed the scene. She hadn't been happy to hear my voice when I rang her from a payphone. To Vega's credit, though, she hadn't hung up. Now, she acted cold and clinical, as if we'd never worked together, never helped one another out. That stung in ways I hadn't expected.

"Touch anything?" I echoed. "No."

She stooped toward Lady Bastet and examined the neck wound. "You said the door was locked when you got here?"

"Bolted. But her defenses were down."

Detective Vega seemed to ignore my last remark as she moved around the room, careful not to step on anything. "What were you doing here?" The question bordered on accusing.

"I asked Lady Bastet to perform a reading on something I dropped off earlier today." As I spoke, Vega continued to survey the scene. "I was returning to see if she'd finished with it."

"What was the item?"

"A strand of my mother's hair."

Vega mumbled something about crime scene contamination, but she shifted her line of questioning. "And she was sitting here like this when you arrived?" she asked, standing to one side of Lady Bastet. "You didn't pick her up off the floor or straighten her or anything?"

"No."

"When you dropped off the hair earlier, did you come into this room?"

"Yes."

"Can you tell if anything's missing?"

I looked around the trashed room. Was she serious? "Listen," I said, stepping toward her and lowering my voice, even though we were alone. "Those werewolves we fought at the mayor's mansion? I think they're the ones who did this. Penny and her husband knew Lady Bastet put Penny's daughter in someone's care, but they don't know whose. This could've been—"

Vega shook her head irritably. "Just answer the question."

I gathered my nerve. If there was a time to have it out, it was now.

"For what it's worth, there's not a day that passes that I don't regret what I did," I said, "that I don't think about the danger I put your son in. So here it is again: I'm sorry. I really am. But can we set that aside for right now?" I cut my eyes toward Lady Bastet. "There's a good chance we're looking at the work of wolves. Which puts us in danger too."

Vega faced me, hands bracing her hips. "This is an official investigation, under the jurisdiction of the NYPD." Her eyes bored into mine. "Other than the fact you were the first witness to the scene, there's no *we*. Got it? Now, can you tell if anything's missing or not?"

There was no compromise on her face. I blew out an exasperated breath as I turned from Vega to the table. The scrying globe was in front of Lady Bastet, the covering cloth folded neatly to one side. I scanned the table's stone surface for my mother's hair. Not there or on the floor around the table. My eyes ranged across the room's wreckage once more.

"Nothing obvious," I said.

"Holy *shit*," someone exclaimed from the main room, no doubt finding the dead cats.

I turned as the person scuffed toward us, his body soon filling the doorway—its width, anyway. When he saw me, he scrunched up his face like someone had punched him in the nose. I squinted back in disbelief.

"Hoffman?" I said. "What in the hell are you doing here?"

"It's *Detective* Hoffman," he answered. "And I could ask you the same. Thought we eighty-sixed your contract."

I turned to Vega. "But he was selling info to Moretti!"

"Yeah, or maybe I was setting him up," Hoffman shot back. "Ever think of that, smartass?"

By Vega's narrowing eyes, I guessed that she had reported her partner only to see him slapped on the wrist and sent back to work. It was tough times for the department—personnel cuts, waning public trust. The last thing they could afford was another investigation into police corruption.

"Is the door secured?" Vega asked him.

Hoffman gave me a final scowl. "Yeah, got a couple of uniforms out front. What's going on?" He looked down at Lady Bastet and grinned around the gum he was smacking. "Someone get upset over his fortune?"

Vega observed my balling fists and stepped between us. "We'll call if we have any more questions."

I continued to glare at Hoffman, who ambled around the scene, still wearing that stupid smacking smile. Vega's words only sank in when I'd forced a calming breath. "Wait, that's it?" I asked her.

"You're dismissed," she affirmed.

I made sure Hoffman was out of earshot before lowering my voice. "Look, I think we need to collaborate on this one. Find out if it really *is* the work of wolves and, if so, what they're up to."

"I said you're dismissed."

"Allow me to translate." Hoffman sauntered up behind her and jerked his thumb toward the door. "Take a hike, jackass."

I searched Vega's face for any sign that she might want to tell me something away from her partner. But her visage remained hard, hostile. Could she still be that angry with me?

"Fine," I said, "but if you have any questions—"

"I already said we'd call you." Vega turned away.

When Hoffman did the same, I unsheathed my sword and flicked my wrist. The path of the blade cut just behind Hoffman's left ear. I caught the tuft of hair that fell from his curly brown wreath.

Might come in handy.

7

It was full dusk when I reached the sidewalk. Headlights swam up and down the street as my cane tapped a hollow rhythm beside me. I needed to be back there, helping with the investigation. I needed to be doing *something*, dammit.

But Vega wouldn't allow it.

I racked my brain for a spell I could cast, one that would point to the killer. But lacking a target item, I came up blank. Did I even need a spell? I wondered. The crime scene had Penny's wolves written all over it. That filled in the who. But ignoring the why for a moment, how would they have breached Lady Bastet's defenses? How would they have overpowered her?

"Mr. Croft," a deep voice called.

I peeked back. The broad-shouldered man was mostly in silhouette, but I could make out the dull glint of a badge, and it wasn't NYPD. Shit. Penny's pack worked in government security, and there wasn't a chance in hell this man appearing on the heels of Lady Bastet's murder was a coincidence. I lifted my shirt away from the revolver holstered above my hip. For the last four months, I hadn't left home without it, a silver bullet in each cylinder.

"Mr. Croft," he called again, walking faster. "Need to have a word with you."

"I don't know any Mr. Croft," I called back. "You've got the wrong person."

My heart thumped as I moved my cane to my front and readied a shield invocation. I could probably take him, but I wanted to reach the next intersection, where traffic flashed past. The wolf would be less likely to shift in the open, giving me an advantage.

He wasn't going to let me get there, though. The man bounded past and wheeled, a feral light burning in his eyes.

"Protezione!" I called, throwing a shield of light between us and drawing the revolver.

He tilted his nose up and sniffed the air. "Yeah, it's him," he called past me.

Huh?

I was halfway into my turn when a blow from a second wolf crushed the side of my head. My legs jiggled for a moment, and I fell to the street, revolver tumbling from my grip as the light shield rained over me.

Voices, low and murky, seeped into my hearing. I squinted my eyes open. I was sitting in a padded chair in a small room. A warehouse office, judging by the corrugated metal and piles of old file boxes. Moths batted around a dangling bulb, some as large as sparrows. When one fluttered too close to my face, I tried to swat it away, but my arm wouldn't budge.

Head throbbing, I looked down at my wrists. Plastic zip ties secured them to the armrests. A second pair bound my ankles to the chair's legs.

Well, shit, I thought groggily.

I listened to the voices. I couldn't make out words, but they were coming from beyond the office door. Men's voices. Two sets. Probably the werewolves who had ambushed me. Meaning if I didn't want to end up like Lady Bastet, I needed to get the hell out of here.

And without making a lot of noise.

My cane was nowhere in sight, my coin pendant absent from my neck. I trained my attention inward, to my casting prism, and found it fractured and wrapped in fog. When I tried a centering mantra to restore it, my lips wouldn't separate. A strip of tape held them closed.

Great, someone knows who they're dealing with.

After attempting to create a pocket inside the tape using my tongue, I gave up and studied the chair's armrests. The foam padding around the right one had disintegrated down to a hard edge of metal. Sharp enough to cut through the plastic restraint? I moved my right arm back and forth in a minute sawing motion, a few millimeters each way, all the restraint would allow.

The voices drew nearer, their owners now casting shadows against the doorframe.

Crap crap crap crap.

I relaxed my arm as the werewolf I'd met in the alleyway entered, still in human form. He had dark red hair and arms the size of my thighs, though better sculpted. He was followed by a second hulking werewolf, no doubt the one who had smashed me in the head. They looked like brothers, especially in their matching security guard uniforms. I took an immediate dislike to both of them.

"Sleep well?" Brother One asked, smirking as he adjusted the belt holding his service weapon.

"He's up," Brother Two called to someone behind them.

I had been puzzling over who had ordered Lady Bastet's murder. Now I had a gut-wringing feeling I was about to find out.

"What's this?" a man's voice demanded. Between the brothers' shoulders, I caught a flash of lenses. A moment later, a pudgy figure shoved his way past the wolves. "Is he alive?"

It was Mayor Lowder.

Sorry to break it to you, sweetie, I thought to an imagined Caroline. *But contrary to your assurances, I'm not only a target of the mayor's eradication program, but part of phase one testing.*

"He didn't cooperate," Brother One said.

"Did he attack you?" Budge asked.

"He pointed a Smith and Wesson at him," the wolf replied, nodding at his brother, "packed with silver."

"We confiscated it," Brother Two said with a grin. "Then ran it over."

The revolver had cost me a small fortune, but its condition was the least of my worries at the moment.

Budge stopped in front of me, hands on the hips of his baggy trousers. He studied the right side of my face, the side that had absorbed the brunt of my fall. It felt stiff with blood. Budge sighed and looked over the rest of me. "Well, untie him, for God's sake. He looks like an Italian sausage."

Not the next words I'd been expecting.

The wolves looked at one another before stalking forward, fierce yellow nails emerging from the ends of their fingers. The same nails that had sliced Lady Bastet's throat?

They wedged their nails under the restraints and ripped away the plastic ties. Within seconds, I was free—but not free from danger. The wolves loomed over me, hatred shining in their flaming irises. I was the killer of their brethren, after all, maimer of their leader.

I leaned back as Brother One reached for my face. With a flick, he snagged a corner of the tape and tore the whole thing from my mouth. I licked lips that felt raw and swollen.

"Don't just stand there, Flint," Budge snapped. "Go get him a drink."

"A drink?" Flint asked.

"There's an old vending machine around back," Budge said. "See if there's anything left inside. You too, Evan."

The two wolves growled down at me before pacing away.

"You'll have to forgive them." Budge dragged another office chair from the side of the room and sat on the front edge of the seat. "Big dummies. I just wanted them to pick you up so we could chat."

"In a warehouse?" I asked skeptically.

"Yeah, well, this is sort of off the record. I couldn't have you coming to City Hall. Not without upsetting the rest of the pack."

He dipped his head so he could see my downcast face better. "Hey, I really am sorry about the rough treatment. You gonna be all right?"

Though the mayor was playing Mr. Nice Guy, I knew his game. He wanted to extract some sort of information before giving the kill order. Like he'd no doubt done with Lady Bastet.

"What do you want to talk about?"

Budge leaned to one side as though taking his measure of me. "Look, I'm not gonna bullshit you, Everson. I've got a list of reasons to want you gone, the top one being that you damned near killed my wife."

"Well, you damned near killed me. Makes us even, right?"

Budge smiled. "I have a private firing range I go to every Saturday, ten a.m. Over two hundred rounds a visit. Been doing that for at least twenty years now. I'm a damned good shot from fifty. You were about, what, twenty feet away when I pulled the trigger that morning? What I'm saying is that if I'd been shooting to kill, you'd be worm food right now."

A ghost pain throbbed in my right chest where the bullet had entered. I touched a hand to the spot and gauged Budge's distance. Even if he was packing, he was close enough that I could reach him before he drew. Pound him to the floor. The problem would be the wolves. With their preternatural senses, they would hear the commotion. I was in no condition to outrace them—and without my sword, gun, or magic, in even less condition to fight them.

"The truth is, Everson, I like you," the mayor went on. "No, I'm serious. You helped my stepdaughter, and you seem like a genuinely decent person. Plus, you've got some good people out there vouching for you."

Caroline, I thought with mixed emotions.

"I also happen to know you do a lot of good work for the city." He tipped me a conspiratorial wink. I stiffened when I realized he was referring to my duties with the Order: banishing nether creatures, closing their portals to our world. But who in the hell could have told him about that? Not even Caroline knew the extent of my work. We hadn't gotten that far.

"It's all right," he said, showing a hand. "Your secret's safe."

The wolves returned, Flint holding a green can. He was slightly bigger than his brother, and I pegged him as the older one. "There was only one drink left in the machine," Flint said, "diet ginger ale."

"Fine, fine." Budge took the soda and shooed the wolves back out of the office. "Here." He cracked the tab and handed the can to me.

The aluminum was hot in my grip, and the ginger ale went down warm, but I was too thirsty to care. Who knew how long I'd been conked out and pouring sweat before the mayor showed up? I drank down half the ginger ale, then lowered the can to my knee and burped.

"Better?" Budge asked, in a concerned voice.

"I would be if I knew what the hell you wanted."

"I'm getting to that."

I couldn't stand the dancing around anymore. "Did you know Lady Bastet was killed earlier today?" I said.

"The mystic in the Village?" The mayor's face scrunched up as he loosened his tie and used his collar to fan his neck. "She was the one who changed my stepdaughter back, right?"

I nodded slowly. I was usually good at reading false emotions on a person's face, but the mayor appeared surprised by the news, saddened even. Maybe a group of Penny's wolves *had* gone rogue.

"Any suspects?" Budge asked.

"None that I know of," I answered carefully.

"Damned shame." Sullenly, Budge wiped his brow with a forearm. "Too much of that sort of thing happening in the city. I'm not sure if you caught my press conference earlier today."

"I did," I replied. "Round up the supernaturals, throw them in an oven, save the city."

The mayor gave an embarrassed chuckle. "Well, those kinds of announcements are always one part policy, two parts theater." His mouth straightened as he rested his forearms on his knees. "The truth is, the problem is much more complex than that. Not only because my wife is, well, a supernatural, but because there are genuinely good supernaturals in this city. The diviner I consult in Chinatown, for example. Lady Bastet. The fae. *You.* Don't worry, Everson. I know that about my city. For the eradication program I'm proposing, I want to target the bad ones. The worst of the worst. The goddamned ghouls in the subway lines. The creatures making a bone yard of Central Park. Those are the ones I want gone."

I squinted at Budge, trying to figure out his angle. He was in a mayoral race that, by all rights, his opponent should have been running away with. That Budge was even close was owed to his wife's condition. But sympathy was only going to carry him so far. Enter the eradication program—or at least an expedited operation or two that would show dramatic results.

"All so you can announce 'mission accomplished' in October," I said, "sweeping you to victory in November?"

Budge grimaced before breaking into a you-got-me smile. "I have to keep reminding myself that you're a college professor, not one of my typical voters. Yeah," he conceded, "you're more or less in the ballpark. Which means I have three months to do what I announced. Not much time at all."

I studied his imploring gaze.

"Look," he said, "the federal government spotted me an advance, so the team I'm putting together is ace. But most of them are new to this supernatural thing. You know the ins and outs. Hell, I've seen you in action. You're good. Damned good. Plus, you've advised the NYPD before. It's just a matter of renewing your contract."

I couldn't believe what I was hearing. The man didn't want me dead. He wanted my help. I thought about Caroline's warning before answering. "What would your wife say?" I asked.

Budged looked toward the door and lowered his voice. "What *can* she say? By the time she awakens, the program will have wrapped up. I'll be in my second term, and I'll have you in part to thank. We both will."

"You sure about that?"

He nodded, his eyes moving back and forth over mine. In exchange for helping him, he was offering a kind of amnesty. No more looking over my shoulder to see whether Penny's pack was stalking me.

"Are any wolves going to be involved?"

"God, no," Budge replied, keeping his voice low. "Just NYPD officers and specialists."

"Detective Vega," I said.

Budge's brow furrowed in question. "What about her?"

I was considering what Caroline had said about how the information Vega and I wielded over the mayor and his wife would no longer be a deterrent. "I want the same deal for her."

Budge's face smoothed. "Already done."

"And there has to be discretion. I don't want every New Yorker and their grandmother knowing what I can do."

"Hey, mum's the word." His eyebrows rose above his glasses. "So?"

Even with my throbbing headache, the calculation was a simple one. Whether or not Budge *could* control his wife were she to awaken, I would be safer inside the eradication program than outside of it.

"I'll have to clear it with my higher ups," I said. "But as far as I'm concerned, yeah, I'm on board."

Budge's face lit up as he slapped my knee.

"Attaboy!"

8

I plodded up the final steps of my apartment building, cane and necklace back in my possession, casting prism restored, and reviewed the deal I'd made with Budge. If nothing else, it offered Vega and me another layer of protection. The only question was how robust that protection would be. I didn't know how much control Budge wielded over Penny's pack.

I unlocked the three door bolts and prioritized my next moves. First, heal up. Second, contact the Order about my participating in the eradication program. And third, start figuring out why the wolves had murdered Lady Bastet. That would tell me what kind of danger Vega and I might be in.

The apartment was dark when I entered. I was reaching for the light switch when, from the direction of Tabitha's divan, came a strangled moan. I stopped and yanked my sword from my cane, the bloody image of the decapitated cats searing through my mind's eye.

"Tabitha?" I called.

A pair of eyes flashed from the divan—but not the ochre-green of my cat's. These were yellow.

"Protezione!" I called.

Sparks burst from my orb as it manifested a shield of white light. In the sudden glow, the being on Tabitha's divan took shape. Not a wolf, though. A squat man in a corduroy sports jacket with elbow patches was sitting there, the pointed toes of his green leather shoes just touching the floor. Beneath a mop of gray hair, the man's eyes squinted back at me.

"Chicory?" I said.

The last time I'd seen my mentor had been ten months earlier, when he'd rescued me from the druids in Central Park and then forbade me from pursuing the demon cases. I dissolved my shield with another Word and hit the flood lights. Chicory lowered his hand from his brow.

"At ease," he said in his Irish brogue.

Tabitha was on his far side, purring and moaning as Chicory scratched the hair around her ears. They had always gotten along well, despite my mentor's disapproval of her succubus nature.

I sheathed my sword. "You scared all hell out of me."

"Ah, yes, I let myself in," Chicory said. "I hope you don't mind. I'd almost forgotten about your companion. She's quite a beautiful thing, isn't she? Though a little starved for attention, I should say."

I watched Tabitha moan and twist her neck as Chicory scratched around it.

"Not anymore," I muttered, walking toward them.

I searched my mentor's face, with its bushy brows, squash-shaped nose, and curmudgeon's lips, for some indication of why he'd come. His visits rarely heralded good things.

"So, what's up?" I asked.

Chicory gave Tabitha's head a final pat. "There you are, love." He wiped his hands together and stood to face me. Behind him, Tabitha curled onto her cat bed and passed out.

"Did you summon a gatekeeper from the In Between?" he asked pointedly.

Crap. "Well, I wouldn't go so far as to say *summon*. I had a brief chat with one, if that's what you're getting at. Emphasis on brief."

"And what did he say?" Chicory asked.

"Not much, to be honest."

"They rarely do, unless it's in the act of claiming your soul."

"Yeah, well, I'm not careless enough to let *that* happen," I said, recalling the sensation of dangling into the frigid void, my fingers clenching the mirror frame.

Chicory let out a *humpf* as he lowered himself to my reading chair. "You know the Order's policy on summonings."

"I told you, it wasn't a summoning. It was more of a ... leaving the back door open. I didn't force the gatekeeper to come through."

Chicory's eyebrows crowded his dark eyes. He wasn't buying it.

"Look," I said, "I was just trying to find out some information on my mother. I went to the Order first, I'll have you know."

"Then you should have awaited their response."

"Oh, yeah? And when would that have been? The next fossil age?"

"Everson," he said sternly, "I needn't remind you that there are penalties for wayward wizards."

"No, you *needn't*." I sat on the couch with a hard sigh. "I just find it funny that whenever I ask for a hand, the Order seems to fall off the face of the Earth, but when I commit a minor infraction—bam!—you're suddenly up in my face."

"You shouldn't expect your priorities and the Elders' to align. But preventing wizards from turning to the dark arts is a priority we all share. There's a reason there's only been one rebellion against the Order in its centuries of existence."

"Rebellion?" I said, sitting upright. "I've never heard anything about a rebellion."

Chicory, who had been pulling a smoking pipe from his jacket, paused to frown, as though he'd let something slip. He regarded the bowl of packed leaves for a moment before nodding. "That's not a story we tell our novice practitioners, but perhaps it's time you heard it."

I bristled at the word *novice* before reminding myself that, though I'd been wizarding for more than a decade, I remained an infant in the eyes of those who'd been practicing for hundreds, even thousands, of years.

Chicory drew his wand from another pocket, touched it to the pipe, and puffed until the leaves began to crackle. When he moved the stem from his lips, a sweet fragrance of tobacco drifted over the room. "The First Saint from whom we're all descended had nine children," he began.

"I already know that part of the history."

"Are your own students this impertinent?" Chicory asked with a frown. "If you want me to tell you the story of the rebellion, I need to start at the beginning."

I showed a hand to say *fair enough* and nodded for him to continue.

He took two quick puffs. "Now, the Order began informally, as you know. A way for Michael's nine children to train their own children in the art of magic, battling dark creatures, so on and so forth."

"Sort of like community homeschooling," I said.

"Very much so," Chicory decided after a moment's pause. "But like with any growing organization, as the practitioners multiplied and spread around the ancient world, the training became more formalized. Michael's children called themselves the First Order. They appointed regional heads, whom they called the Second Order. Later Third and Fourth Orders were added. Decisions made by the First Order were disseminated down the ranks. Over time, the Diaspora came to be known as the Order of Magi and Magical Beings."

This was still a review from my training under Lazlo, but I didn't say anything.

"Now," Chicory continued, "around the time of the late Roman Empire, the First Order attained a level of magic that transformed them. Some would say they became gods or at least god-*like*. Though they continued to exist on the physical plane, they inhabited more ethereal planes as well."

"The Elders," I said, scooting forward. Though I *had* heard all of this before, the thought of attaining that state—as indeed I might one day (if I managed to stay alive)—fascinated me.

"Precisely," Chicory said, the smoke that rose from his pipe seeming to bend reality. He aimed the stem at me. "Now here's what you *weren't* told. Of the original members of the First Order, only eight attained that godlike state. No one can say why the youngest did not."

"Runt of the litter?"

Chicory shrugged. "Perhaps he didn't inherit as much power from his father as the others. But it wasn't for lack of practice. This ninth sibling was intent on perfecting his magic, of transforming that art into science. Indeed, Lich—for that was his name—Lich devised the regimen for fledgling magic-users, penned many of the world's first spell books. You might imagine his disappointment, then, when his siblings ascended and he was left behind."

I caught myself nodding.

"But Lich was determined to join them," Chicory continued. "The legend goes that he practiced more fervently than he ever had before, the effort nearly killing him, until one day, after hundreds of years, his efforts opened a deep, deep fissure in the fabric of our world. Through it, he heard the whisperings of a being more ancient than the First Saints and Demons."

I leaned further forward, the rest of my apartment seeming to disappear.

Chicory nodded gravely. "By eavesdropping on the being's whisperings, Lich learned secrets that could elevate him to the level of his siblings and possibly beyond. From those secrets, he cultivated power. And with that power, he confronted his eight brothers and sisters, demanding his rightful place among them. They questioned the source of his magic. When he told them, they attempted to close the fissure to the Deep Down. Lich fought back."

"What happened?"

"A horrible battle. Indeed, the Order almost fell. But in the end, they destroyed Lich and sealed the opening to the domicile of the being who came to be known as the Whisperer."

I had always considered the Elders invincible. To hear that they'd been pushed to the brink sent a guilty jolt of pleasure through me while filling me with a deeper anxiety. "The Order almost fell?"

"The Elders took steps to ensure nothing like that would ever happen again." Chicory leveled his gaze at me. "*Including* creating a penalty system for wizards who insist on summoning beings they shouldn't."

"I told you, it wasn't really a summon—"

"Silence, Everson."

I watched him watching me, the smoke from his pipe enshrouding him in a sinister mist. Story time was over. Time to dole out the punishment. A heavy stone rolled around my stomach. Chicory set his pipe on an end table and folded his stubby fingers over his small paunch.

"Though you committed an infraction, that's not why I came," he said.

"It's n-not?"

"I'm here on another errand. When I let myself in, I *happened* to sense the remnants of the summoning spell, which you've all but confessed to. There are penalties for such actions, Everson. But given that you banished a demon lord last fall, I'm only going to issue a warning this time. *This time,*" he emphasized, raising an eyebrow. "You'll see no such leniency the next."

"I understand," I said, touching my clasped hands to my forehead. "Thank you."

"I'm here about your mother."

I lowered my hands.

"In response to your multiple inquiries into the circumstances surrounding your mother's death, the Order has sent me to address them."

"That's why you're here?"

"The answer, I've been told, is no."

"No?" I said. "What do they mean *no*?"

"They have no more information for you."

"They have no more information period, or no more information they want to tell me?"

"They hope this brings the matter to a close."

I couldn't believe what I was hearing. "Brings the matter to a close? The hell it does! All it tells me is that the Order is hiding something." I flattened my shaking hands against my thighs and took several deep breaths. "I'm going to ask you something, Chicory—*you*, not them—and I want the God's honest truth." I took another breath as I considered the question I'd been brooding over for the last four months. "Did the Order execute her?"

The room seemed to waver around us.

"I can tell you unequivocally that they did not."

I took a moment to decide whether or not I believed him. Chicory waited, a sober honesty standing in his eyes.

"But there's more," I said. "There has to be more."

"If there is, the Elders have chosen not to disclose it. We must accept whatever wisdom guides their reasoning."

"But it's my mother," I said.

"I know, Everson."

"Can you at least tell me whether she was a magic-user, a member of the Order?"

"She passed away before my transfer here," Chicory said. "But I don't think the Order would object to my telling you there's no record on her. None that I could locate, anyway. Not every generation manifests the power of Michael's lineage. While your mother carried the genes, the genes may not have found expression in her. They found expression in you, though—something the Order was unaware of until your adventures in Romania."

"Can you ask them?" I pressed.

Chicory sighed heavily.

"Please."

He move his head side to side as though deliberating. At last, he nodded. "I'll see what I can find out. But I can't tell you when to expect any information," he added hurriedly. "I have a full caseload right now."

"I understand. Anything's better than nothing."

"Very well." He stood and returned his pipe to his pocket. "Was there anything else?"

"Actually, the mayor is planning a program to eradicate ghouls and lesser creatures in the city. He wants me to act as a consultant. I told him I had to clear it with my higher ups." Not wanting to convolute the request, I said nothing about the werewolves or Lady Bastet's murder.

"That sounds fine," Chicory said. "It's why Michael sired children, after all. Just don't let it interfere with your other duties." Chicory shot me a final reproving look. "And no more summonings—or *leaving doors open*, as you call it. Not from the In Between, not from anywhere."

"No more leaving doors open," I agreed.

Chicory's cocked eyebrow issued all the warning I needed. Not only would I face extreme punishment, but I could forget about learning anything more about my mother.

"G'night, love," he said to Tabitha, giving her a final scratch behind the ears.

Tabitha shifted and purred in her sleep.

9

I met with the mayor twice that week, official meetings in his City Hall office. No more being beaten and grabbed off the street. For Budge's part, he acted as if that episode had never happened. We spent most of the first meeting discussing the supernatural geography of the city, narrowing in on the ghoul-infested subway lines and the wilds of Central Park.

Budge frowned down at the map spread over his desk. "Which one should we nail first?"

"Well, if the goal is to get the most bang for your buck in the shortest amount of time..." I tapped the defunct Broadway line in lower Manhattan. "...I'd go after the ghouls. With them gone, murders and disappearances will drop immediately. A hard stat you can point to."

"I like the sound of that," Budge said.

"Not to mention you'll be able to restore service to that line, something the public's been clamoring for."

"Great minds think alike." Budge checked his watch. "I've got a meeting with the MTA boss in a couple minutes. Sort of a blow hard, but that's between you and me. In any case, let's sit down again tomorrow, same time. I want you to talk Captain Cole and me through the nuts and bolts."

We shook on it. As had been the case all meeting, I couldn't find an ulterior motive. The eradication program seemed to be just what Budge had said it would be: a high-profile injection of money and resources into the problem of marauding monsters. If the program produced the results Budge needed, he had a chance of eking out a win in November.

I spent the rest of that day in my library/lab. I gathered all of the information I could on ghouls, distilled the information down to its essence, and then devised a way to eradicate them en masse. I studied maps of the subway lines. I tested various defensive sigils and magical incendiaries. Satisfied, I typed out a plan and carried it to the mayor's office the next day.

Lance Cole, the man appointed to head the Hundred, was sitting in a chair facing the mayor's desk in his captain's uniform. He greeted me with a nod that was hard to read amid the age lines creasing his dark face. As I went over my strategy with Budge, Cole sat back and listened.

When I finished, Budge turned to him. "What do you think?"

Captain Cole pressed the dark gemstone of a fraternal ring to his mustache and reread my proposal. When he reached the bottom of the page, he gave a single nod. "If you can cover the lights, and Everson here this part"—he brushed the bullet points with the pinky ring—"we can take care of the rest."

"How soon?" Budge asked.

"I can have the team ready inside of a week," Cole answered.

"How's that sound, Everson?"

"Works for me."

Budge beamed at both of us. "It's why I hired the best."

"Um, just one more thing," I said. "I'd like to have Detective Hoffman from Homicide advising as well."

Captain Cole's forehead wrinkled. "We already have Detective Vega helping out."

"Right, but Hoffman's worked on supernatural cases too," I said. "And he brings a different perspective." Which was to say he remained a stubborn-ass skeptic about the supernatural despite any and all evidence to the contrary. But that's not why I wanted him.

Cole appeared to chew on that for a moment before nodding. "Fine. I'm going to have you present your plan to the Hundred on Thursday. I'll make sure both detectives are there."

Excellent, I thought. *But it doesn't give me much time.*

I stopped at a camera store on my way home. In the vintage section, I found and paid for an old Polaroid camera and several packs of film.

Back in my apartment lab I placed the tuft of hair I'd cut from Hoffman at the crime scene into my silver casting circle. On the floor beside it, I created a second, larger circle. Inside that one, I set a mound of wet, gray clay that I kept in a plastic garbage container. I then sprinkled the clay with black ash, grated mandrake root, and two tablespoons of my own blood.

Pulling a spell book from a shelf, I consulted a set of Coptic instructions. For spying, there was scrying, projecting, and summoning lesser beings. But I needed recorded evidence, and that meant animation. I winced at the memory of my last attempt, the result a screaming golem that had run around punching himself in the jewels before I force-blasted him out of existence. Clay had rained everywhere and taken me weeks to clean from my rugs.

Impure clay, I reminded myself, hoping that had been the reason for the masochistic display. I aimed my staff at the mound of high-grade clay and recited the incantation, careful to pronounce each syllable precisely.

"Vivere ... pulsare ... respirare ... levarsi..."

Energy coursed through my mental prism. I pushed that energy, along with some of my own essence, into the clay. After a minute of nothing, the clay began to squelch and fold in on itself. The blood thinned into a network of vessels. Within moments, a shape became evident: a tadpole-like creature with large pods for eyes. It writhed and flopped on the floor, its shrinking tail soon replaced by sprouting legs. Arms pushed from beneath a head that was becoming less embryonic, more human. The eyes shrank and migrated inward until I was looking at an infant. The infant opened its mouth in a silent cry as it elongated, its C-shaped back becoming more lordotic. It was a boy. With growing limbs, the golem began pushing himself upright, tottering as dark hair sprouted from his molding head.

By the time the golem steadied and opened his hazel-colored eyes, I was at face level with a crude likeness of myself. I waited a moment, a force invocation on the tip of my tongue, but the animation didn't start screaming or swinging his fists. He only watched, waiting for my command.

"Dress," I said, spreading a pile of clothes at his feet.

The golem stared at the clothes before something took hold in his rudimentary mind. He reached for the plaid boxers first, stepping into them stiffly—left leg, then right—and pulling them up. Next he donned the socks in the same left-right order. It was how I dressed, which made sense, considering he was operating off a dimmer version of my own knowledge and memories.

He finished by putting on a necklace that featured a copper amulet, one I had infused with energy to sustain the being for the next several days. He even tucked it inside his shirt as I did with my own coin pendant.

"Ready to get to work?" I asked.

The golem regarded me with an expression not unlike a clothing store mannequin's.

"That's the spirit. But first we need a name for you. How does Ed sound?"

"Ed," he repeated in monotone.

"You like that, huh?" I chuckled and clapped his shoulder. "Well, I've got a job for you, Ed."

I trained my attention on the silver circle, where I'd set Hoffman's hair. Incanting, I drew the detective's essence into my staff and then directed the essence into Ed's amulet, turning it into a homing beacon. I waved Ed over to where I had set the Polaroid camera on the end of the lab table.

I spoke slowly. "Load the camera with film and take my picture."

Ed fumbled with the film's metallic wrapping, eventually shedding it and slotting the film into the camera. I smiled broadly as the golem raised the Polaroid to his right eye and clicked. A white-framed photo emerged from the camera's mouth.

"Good," I said, pulling the photo free.

As the image of me developed, I considered what I was doing. In the last couple of days, I had begun to see the eradication program as an opportunity to not only protect myself, but to get close to the Lady Bastet investigation. I needed info on who was behind the hit and why. I also wanted to recover my mother's final hair. Obtaining either from Vega would be next to impossible but Hoffman was another story. Mr. Moretti had already proven the man could be bought. I had considered waving some cash under Hoffman's nose, but blackmail felt like a surer bet.

Plus it was cheaper.

"All right," I said to the golem, who had been facing me patiently. "You're going to tail Hoffman for the next few days. Any time he meets with someone other than fellow NYPD, I want you to snap a picture. Above all, be discreet. If he spots you, run." I handed him several folded-over twenties and watched him insert them into his pants pocket. "That will cover cab fares. You'll stop back here once a day to drop off the pictures and pick up fresh film. When you feel the amulet's energy running low, I want you to return here for good. Understand?"

The instructions were rudimentary, intended to ensure we were on the same page. If I had performed the spell correctly, enough of my own intelligence now echoed inside Ed's head to steer him.

"Understand," he repeated in a blocky voice.

I looked my creation over once more. He was too clunky to appear fully human, but that was hardly a deal breaker in New York. I placed a Mets baseball cap on his head, pulling the bill low to cast a shadow over his face. Then, wheeling him around, I swatted his clay butt.

"Go get 'em, tiger."

10

I looked from my notes scattered over the lectern to the packed auditorium. The men and women sitting ramrod straight in dark blue uniforms had been selected from the NYPD's elite tactical teams, the best of the best. True to Mayor Lowder's word, they were all human. No werewolves. Even so, the Hundred was the most intimidating audience I had ever lectured to.

Sure ain't Midtown College, I mused, thinking of my six students.

I tapped my notes into a pile and, assuming a professorial air, leaned toward the mounted microphone. The sound system whined feedback until I remembered my wizarding aura and backed away.

"Good afternoon," I said.

The Hundred stared back with hard eyes and set jaws.

"Great. How about we dive right in?" I signaled to a technician. The lights dimmed, and everyone's eyes shifted to the digital screen behind me. I didn't need to turn to see the image of the gray monstrosity glaring back at them. I was pleased to catch a few winces.

"Ghouls," I began. "They range in height from six to eight feet tall and can weigh in excess of four hundred pounds. But don't let the size fool you. In addition to super strength, they're twice as fast as all of you here. Note the razor-sharp claws and canines ... A ghoul's preferred diet is rotting flesh, but they'll take whatever they can find, living or dead. When they hunt, it's almost always in packs. For years they've gone after low-hanging fruit: drunks and junkies, mostly in the East Village and Lower East Side. But they've grown bolder in recent months, coming up earlier in the evening and venturing farther afield."

I had the technician advance to an image of a bloody crime scene on a narrow street.

"Two weeks ago, scraps of an NYU student were found on Bond Street. Friends say she was walking home after a late-night party. The entire process from pursuit to capture to devouring probably took the ghoul pack less than a minute. Even armed with a snub-nosed pistol, the young woman had no chance."

The audience eyed the image in rapt attention. I could feel their minds wrapping around the idea that they would be facing an opponent most of them had dismissed as fiction until only recently. Captain Cole, who had introduced me minutes earlier, leaned against a wall to my right.

I signaled for the tech to skip ahead several screens. I'd made my point.

"All right, so here's the defunct Broadway line and its east-west services," I said, turning toward the map of subway routes in lower Manhattan. "Most of the ghouls are concentrated inside that red box, south of Fourteenth Street and west of Brooklyn. A couple of hundred, probably."

"If these things even exist," someone asked, "what do you need a SWAT team for? Why not just gas the lines?"

I focused on the back row until I could see the speaker, one of two plainclothes cops in attendance. "If it were only that easy, Detective," I replied, suppressing a smile. Hoffman had come. "Ghouls can go for days without air, making them immune to the kinds of gases you have in mind. I should add that their regenerative abilities also make them immune to most weapons."

"So what does that leave?" he asked. "Kryptonite?"

"Sunlight and fire," I replied.

"Sunlight? In the tunnels?"

"Let the professor talk," Captain Cole said sternly.

Hoffman scowled and settled back in his chair. I slid my gaze over to Detective Vega, who was sitting beside him. She looked back with a sour expression, clearly irritated by my inclusion in the eradication program.

"Thank you," I said to Cole, lifting the long pointer I'd set against the lectern. "Sunlight won't kill a ghoul, but it does weaken them. We can't introduce actual sunlight into the tunnels, no. But full-spectrum, industrial-strength spotlights will do the job. Equipped with these spotlights, armed teams will drop into the lines here, here, and here." I tapped the map at three of the line's branches. "The teams will converge toward the Canal Street station, driving the ghouls out ahead of them. Lights will also be shone down through the vents to keep the ghouls from escaping up to street level. Once at the convergence point, we'll seal the station, trapping the creatures inside. We'll then ignite a powerful incendiary, transforming the station into a crematory. They'll be reduced to ashes within minutes."

My research had shown that ghouls could be killed one of two ways: decapitation or extensive brain trauma. Because the first was too labor intensive, not to mention dangerous, I had recommended to the mayor the second. The plan would mean considerable damage to the station, but Budge had reiterated his support. "Better property than people," he'd said.

"Are there any questions for the professor?" Captain Cole asked now.

A burly woman raised her hand. "Are we sure the spotlights will be effective? What's to stop the ghouls from turning around and attacking them?"

"In a word," I said, "cowardice." I had the tech return to the image of the creature. "Appearances to the contrary, ghouls are pretty gutless. It's why they prefer scavenging to pursuing live prey. If the ghouls *were* to turn on any of the teams, sustained gunfire would steer them straight again."

A young man raised his hand. "With the ghouls possessing the kind of strength you're talking about, how can you be sure you'll be able to contain them at the Canal Street station?"

I had descended into the station the day before with an armed backup force and several full-spectrum lights. Despite my chest-squeezing phobia of being underground—and that the space reeked of ghoul—I took my time etching defensive sigils over the station's tunnels and exits. I planned to infuse the sigils with a high dose of energy, manifesting a field to contain the ghouls. But the Hundred didn't need to know the magical details.

"I'm sure," I replied.

"Well, what are you using for an incendiary?" the young man pressed. "Napalm? Thermite?"

Dragon sand, actually. Something else you don't need to know. "A substance that will be harder to detect," I replied. "Ghouls have a keen sense of smell." When I looked around for any other raised hands, I noticed that the seat Vega had occupied was now empty.

Yeah, she hates me, I thought.

"Thank you, Professor," Captain Cole said, approaching the lectern. I gathered up my notes and stepped from the stage as he addressed the auditorium. "The operation is scheduled to commence this Sunday at oh-seven-hundred. We'll be conducting full-gear simulations at the Tactics Range in the Bronx every day until then, starting this afternoon."

As the captain talked, I made my way to the back row and took the seat Vega had vacated. Hoffman shifted his bulk around to face me.

"Gotta hand it to you, Merlin," he whispered. "You've kept this con going longer than I would've thought possible."

"Con?" My temper flared, in spite of myself. "What do you call that thing we battled in the storm lines this past spring?" I asked, referring to the werewolf-vampire hybrid.

"You talking about that albino woman?"

"Oh, is that what she was? Okay, forget the creature. How about how I yanked you out of harm's way from thirty feet away?"

"Cheap trick. Any stage magician could've pulled that off."

"And enclosed the creature in a light shield?"

Hoffman scrunched up his face as if whatever more I had to say wasn't worth hearing. I had to remind myself that convincing him of my authenticity wasn't why I was talking to him. I drew a deep breath and let it out through my nose along with the pent-up tension.

"Still working the Lady Bastet case?" I asked.

He eyed me with suspicion. "So what if I am?"

"Any leads?"

"Like I'm gonna tell you."

I reached into the front pocket of my shirt and pulled out several Polaroids. My golem, Ed, had struck gold on his second day. I spread the shots over the chair's table arm. "You sure?"

He frowned at the images. The top ones showed him chatting with one of Mr. Moretti's men as he accepted an envelope. Subsequent photos showed him repeating the ceremony, this time with a representative of Mr. Brusilov, head of New York's Russian crime family.

"Looks like we caught you on payday," I said.

"Who in the hell took these? You?"

"Smile, you're on Candid Camera." I gathered the pictures up, tapped them into a neat stack, and slid them into my shirt pocket. "And there's more where those came from."

Hoffman leaned toward me until I could see every oily pore on his scrunched-up nose. "I'm gonna tell you two things," he whispered, "and you better listen to both really fucking good. First, I'm in the middle of a sting operation. That's what you're photographing, you idiot. Second, what you're doing here is attempted blackmail. I'm gonna let that go, 'cause frankly you're not worth the paperwork. But I see you or your camera anywhere near me when I'm working, and I'm taking you in. You understand me? That's five years on obstruction and another five on the blackmail. Let's see how smart you think you are then."

"A sting operation?" I said in mock surprise. "Oh, gee, the last thing I want is to interfere. A hundred apologies. Let me just turn these over to Captain Cole so he can discard of them properly. I'd hate for these to end up in the hands of an ambitious reporter."

As I went to stand, Hoffman clamped my forearm, his fingers digging into the fleshy underside. I winced and tried to pry his fingers away. Captain Cole stopped talking and frowned up at us.

"Is there a problem, gentlemen?" he asked.

I looked at Hoffman, eyebrows raised. After a moment, he released me and shook his head. "No, sir," he said. "No problem."

I lowered myself back to the chair as Captain Cole resumed talking.

"What the hell do you want?" Hoffman asked in a fierce whisper, facing forward.

"What can you tell me about the Lady Bastet investigation?"

"Nothing," he said.

I started to stand again.

"What I mean is we don't have anything yet," he said quickly. "We recovered some trace evidence from the scene. Hair, fibers, that sort of thing. But it's a business, people coming and going all the time. We have to crosscheck the evidence against her known clients. Even against *you*."

"No eyewitnesses?" I asked.

"If so, no one's talking."

"What about the cats?"

"What about 'em?" he sneered. "You think one of them saw something?"

"No, smartass. Any bite marks? Anything to suggest how they were decapitated?"

"Well, it wasn't from a blade. Those heads were torn off." He glanced over at me, his jaw working as though deciding whether or not to tell me something.

I tapped my shirt pocket with the photos.

"We found something odd in the fur," he said at last.

"What?"

"Some sort of residue. Lab says it's mostly sulfur."

I kicked that around. Sulfur could mean a demonic presence. Had someone aided the wolves?

"So, we good?" Hoffman asked, his temples shiny with sweat.

"Not quite. I need a couple of things."

Hoffman's lips pressed together. "What?"

"First a sample of the residue."

"What else?"

"You should have a piece of hair in evidence. Light brown. About this long." I held my two index fingers a foot apart. "I want that, too."

"You're asking me to tamper with evidence?"

"Like you've never done that before," I said dryly. "This time, you'll actually be doing the investigation a favor. The hair belongs to me. Well, not *me* me, but someone I know. I brought it in for Lady Bastet to do a reading on. It would've ended up right around the murder scene. I want it back. Look at it this way. It'll be one less lead to track down."

"Anything else, Columbo?" he asked irritably.

"Yeah. Keep me up to date on the investigation."

"And you'll hand over the photos?"

"Every last one," I promised.

11

"*They're slowing,*" a team leader's voice crackled over the feed.

In the tent serving as our command center, black-and-white monitors showed subway lines from the perspectives of the three below-ground teams. The message had come from the southbound team. Like the other two feeds, theirs depicted a graffiti-tagged tunnel narrowing into darkness. Save for the occasional bone pile and mound of excrement, the tunnel had been empty, the ghouls keeping well ahead of the rolling spotlights. Now, hulking shapes took form.

"How many?" Captain Cole asked into his headset.

"*Their numbers have been building,*" the team leader

answered, his slow steps rocking the feed from his helmet-mounted camera. *"Right now we're probably looking at a hundred or so. And they're getting louder."*

Grunts and whooping cries echoed through the feed.

Cole turned and looked at me. Beside him, the GPS map showed the three teams converging on the station below our feet. We were roughly fifteen minutes from a completed mission and with zero casualties. *How do we preserve this?* the captain's eyes were asking me.

I estimated the ghouls to be a hundred feet ahead of the southbound team. Not enough of a buffer.

"Have them turn up the lights and continue advancing," I advised. "But slowly."

"Did you catch that?" the captain asked through his headset.

"Roger that," the team leader replied. *"Lights up!"* he called.

The feed flared white before the camera adjusted and restored the grainy image. For a moment, the ghouls were exposed, hands and forearms guarding their eyes. They scrambled over one another to escape the full-spectrum light. My released breath relaxed my shoulders. If the ghouls had charged, the southbound team would have been in big trouble.

"Go ahead and have the other teams do the same," I said, "to be safe."

Cole gave the order. My heart lurched as the other two feeds lit up to show even larger crowds of ghouls. *Damn, more down there than I thought.* I was praying my defensive sigils would be up to the job, when the leader of the southbound team's voice returned, his tone urgent.

"One of them's stopping."

On the feed, an especially large ghoul had lingered behind the others. He stood in a half crouch, an enormous knuckled hand shielding his face. Members of the team began to shout and squeeze air horns as they'd been instructed. But though the ghoul flinched, he didn't retreat. Beyond him, other ghouls began to slow, their misshapen heads turning to watch.

Their numbers are starting to embolden them, I thought.

"What's the call?" the captain asked me.

"Stop advancing, but continue with the noise," I said.

With the lights blinding their infrared vision, the ghouls didn't know who or what was bearing down on them. I needed them to think it was a larger, more terrifying force—despite that the ghouls held a ten to one advantage. The rest of the Hundred were acting as an aboveground backup force, ready to drop in if needed. I hoped it wouldn't come to that, but this idiot wasn't helping. The ghoul squinted above his hand before taking a sidestep toward the stalled team.

"Prof?" the captain prompted.

"Yeah, yeah, I'm thinking," I said.

Each team was armed with automatic rifles and pistols, as well as concussion grenades—any one of which *might* do the job. But they could also throw the ghouls into a panic, sending the creatures stampeding toward the team. A warning seemed the safest move, something to inflict pain while being clear where the source of that pain had originated.

"The flamethrower," I said. "Just a burst, though. Enough to get it moving."

"Hit it with the flame," the captain said. "To injure, not kill."

"Roger that."

On the feed, a team member moved to the fore, a small flame dancing at the end of a flamethrower's barrel. I held my breath, more sweat spreading over the back of my work shirt. Either the flamethrower idea would work, or things were about to get really, really nasty.

"Be ready to drop in," Cole radioed to the backup team.

With a harsh whoosh, the feed turned bright white. A primal scream sounded as flames washed over the ghoul. A battle cry? But when the flames relented, the ghoul was loping away, the jacket of fire over its head and back guttering out. The ghouls that had stopped to watch fell into his bellowing wake until they were beyond the reach of the spotlights once more.

Thank God, I thought.

"Resume the advance," Cole ordered.

"The teams are ten minutes from the target area," a tech said from in front of the bank of monitors. "We're already seeing some arrivals."

I raised my eyes to the images of the abandoned station. The eerie infrared feeds showed the first ghouls shambling into view and then wheeling around in the face of ghouls arriving from the other directions. Several climbed onto the platform. Sensing they were being corralled, they scrambled over turnstiles and hammered their fists against the steel barriers beyond.

"I'm going to step out and ready the shields," I told Cole. "Have them use the flames on any more stragglers. Let me know when the lines are clear."

"Will do," he said.

I stepped from the tent, squinting in the sudden light. In the center of the road, halfway between the station's two entrances, I planted my feet. Eyes closed to the flashing police cordon several blocks ahead, I aligned myself with the defensive sigils I'd etched the day before. I reinforced the two shields over the subway exits to street level and then I shifted my focus to the sigils at the mouths of the three lines feeding the station.

"Southbound line is clear," a tech called from behind me.

"Cerrare," I said. Energy flowed down my legs, through the street, and into the sigils. I felt a robust shield swell into place between the retreating southbound team and the station.

"Ditto the westbound line," the tech called a minute later.

I repeated the Word, walling in the station from the east.

One to go.

At that moment, the droning of a fast-approaching vehicle broke through my concentration. *What the...?* I wheeled around to find a white news van squealing to a stop behind me. A camera crew poured from the van's side door. They weren't the only ones. More news vans appeared, parking at odd angles over the closed-off road, ejecting crews who proceeded to unspool cables, off-load equipment, and aim cameras at the subway entrances.

A blond woman, whom I recognized as an anchor for one of the local news networks, appeared in a bright red dress and matching pumps. She primped her feathered hair and, mike in hand, nodded at her cameraman.

"We're reporting from the Canal Street Station, where Mayor—"

"Hey!" I shouted. "What in the hell do you think you're doing? We're in the middle of an operation." I turned toward the tent. "Captain Cole!'

The anchor frowned and made a cutting motion across her neck to the cameraman.

"Do you mind?" she said to me.

"Do I *mind?*" I pictured the hundreds of ghouls pouring into the station right below us. I needed to concentrate, dammit. I thought I'd made that clear. Why wasn't anyone ushering these clowns out of here?

She planted a fist against her waist. "We're about to go live."

"Live? Here?" I couldn't believe what I was hearing. "Who gave you authorization?"

The woman was opening her mouth when a black Escalade rolled into the mix. The anchor and cameras turned toward it. When the Escalade stopped, a bevy of security personnel emerged, one of them opening the passenger door. Budge's smiling face appeared.

"I don't fucking believe this," I muttered.

Budge climbed from the Escalade and tottered toward the blond anchor. "Courtney, honey, how are you? Not still knocking around with that bum from Channel 4, I hope."

Courtney's lips pursed into a flirty smile. "Ancient history."

"Good," Budge said. "'Cause you're way out of his league. Better anchor, too."

I charged toward him. "Sorry to interrupt your little chat, but you let them through?"

Budge stumbled around until his watery eyes fixed on mine. "Well, sure," he said. "Someone has to document the moment of triumph." When he laughed, I caught a waft of alcohol.

"That wasn't the plan," I said through clenched teeth.

"And who's this?" Courtney asked Budge.

The mayor pushed his way past his security detail and grabbed me around the shoulder. The cameras followed him. "This," he said, hugging me to his side, "is my secret weapon."

"Let's keep it down, huh?" I whispered.

"Everson Croft!" he proclaimed. "New York City's greatest wizard!"

I felt the color drain from my face as I looked wildly from camera to camera.

Courtney squeezed in beside me and motioned her cameraman into position. He pointed at her to go. "I'm standing here with Mayor Lowder," Courtney said, "and who he's calling his 'secret weapon' in his campaign to rid the city of evil creatures, wizard extraordinaire, Everson Craft."

"Croft," the mayor corrected her.

"He's only joking, you know," I said.

"I'm sorry. Everson *Croft*," she amended. "Can you tell us in what capacity you're helping the mayor, Mr. Croft? Are you employing standard magic, or have you cooked up something special for the campaign?" She tipped the microphone toward me, eyes glittering in fascination.

As far as the Order was concerned, we revealed our magical identities at our own risk. And in a city like New York, risks ran aplenty. Especially now, with public outrage over supernaturals growing by the day.

"Mr. Croft?" Courtney prompted.

With energy I couldn't afford to expend, I swelled my wizarding aura. One by one, the blinking lights of the cameras went dark. Courtney's cameraman lowered the contraption from his shoulder and looked at it.

"Something inside just blew," he grumbled.

"Well, grab the backup," Courtney snapped. "Hurry!"

"Northbound line is clear," the tech called from the tent.

I wriggled from between Courtney and the mayor. "I need everyone to get back," I called. "Way back."

Budge gave an embarrassed laugh. "That's not necessary, folks."

"Yes, it is," I told them. I lowered my voice so only Budge could hear me. "If you don't want this operation turning into a shit show on live television, you're going to get them out of here. Now."

The mayor's face sobered. "Will a block be enough?"

"Yeah, sure," I said. "Just get them out of my hair."

"You heard him," Budge said, pushing his hands toward the crews. "Back it up a block. The man needs to work." The mayor's security detail formed a line and walked them back.

"You too," I told Budge as I stepped past him.

God, what a frigging nightmare.

With the intersection to myself again, I drew a calming breath and aligned myself with the final sigils.

"Cerrare," I said.

A shudder rose through the pavement as the final shield manifested. The station was boxed in. I could feel the ghouls ramming against my magical defenses, trying to escape. I pushed more energy into the shields as I awaited the final word. It came only a moment later.

"All teams clear," the tech called.

I shifted my focus from the shields to the dragon sand scattered over the station floor. Four hundred ghouls versus a two thousand-degree inferno? I was putting my money on the inferno.

"Fuoco!" I shouted.

In an explosive instant, the dragon sand ignited. The intersection shook. Up and down the street, red-orange flames

93

jetted from vents. And now a roaring chorus took up, the dying cries of ghouls.

But I couldn't relax just yet. I'd felt the shields bow out with the explosion. If even one of the defenses failed, the ghouls could escape the inferno and regenerate. I went sigil to sigil, reinforcing the enclosure with spoken Words.

North and southbound lines ... check. Westbound line ... check. West entrance to the station ... check. East entrance to the sta—

Something rammed into my side, spinning me in a half circle. I lost my balance and fell to the street. I also lost the Word, having only uttered half of it. I looked around for my assailant and found one of the cameramen running toward the subway entrance. His half-exposed belly swung side to side as he moved in for a better shot. That's what had felled me.

Swearing, I realigned my thoughts with the sigils over the station's East entrance. *Oh, crap.* My fragment of a Word had not only failed to reinforce the shield; it had dissolved it.

"Cerrare!" I cried.

The shield crackled and spread back into being, but I felt it crunch through bone. Ghouls had already begun to escape. I opened my eyes to the station's east entrance. The shadowy pit swelled with fire.

The cameraman had reached the sidewalk and was aiming his backup camera down the station's steps. He couldn't have known what he was looking at. He was still filming when the first blazing ghoul appeared. With a fiery slash, the ghoul opened the man's stomach. The man dropped to his knees, his innards gushing out, then collapsed beside his smashed camera. Three more ghouls scrambled over him, igniting his hair and clothes.

Behind me, members of the news crews began to scream.

"Get back!" the mayor was hollering. "Everybody back!"

Driven to blind rage by fire and pain, the four ghouls oriented to the panicked sounds—and charged.

12

"Vigore!" I cried.

The force that shook from my sword slammed into the lead ghoul. He roared as he was blown backwards, red fire pluming upon his collision against the metal entranceway that framed the stairs to the station.

A moment later, he was back on his feet.

With a shouted *"Protezione!"* I threw up a shield across the street. Because of the energy I'd just expended, the manifestation was weak. The charging ghouls crashed through it.

What now? I thought as I backpedaled.

The ghouls were close enough for me to smell their burning flesh. Flesh that, beneath the thinning flames, was beginning to regenerate. I cast my staff aside and gripped my sword in both hands. Attempting to decapitate four rampaging ghouls was tantamount to suicide, but there were innocents behind me.

Automatic gunfire chattered from either side. The ghouls flinched from the impact of bullets. Armored vehicles were rolling in, backup members of the Hundred firing from the vehicles' sides.

"Their heads!" I shouted in reminder. "Aim for their heads!"

If the hollow-point bullets could penetrate the creatures' dense skulls, they might inflict enough brain damage to drop them. At that thought, two of the ghouls' heads exploded in rapid succession. The flaming creatures collapsed to the street. A third ghoul joined them. The ghoul I'd knocked into the station's entranceway did not, however. With a bellow, he lowered his head, impervious to the bullets blowing bits of flaming flesh from his hide.

My backward jog turned into a backward run, until I rammed into the mayor.

His broad back remained to the ghouls as he pushed his arms toward the news crews, yelling for them to disperse. He ignored his security detail, one of whom had wheeled the Escalade around while another was trying to pull him toward the vehicle's open passenger door. I could see on Budge's corpse-white face that he believed he was watching his campaign swirl down the drain in front of the very opinion shapers he'd invited to the event.

I regained my footing as a foul heat seared the side of my face. Shoving Budge forward, I spun with my sword. The blade flashed, catching the ghoul's incoming arm at the wrist. A flaming hand dropped to the street, not far from where Budge and the security man had tumbled down.

The ghoul jerked back his spouting arm and let out a window-shaking howl. The gunfire had stopped, I noticed, the ghoul too close to the mayor for the Hundred to risk another fusillade.

"Christ Almighty!" Budge exclaimed, seeing the creature up close for the first time.

The ghoul, who had been thrashing in a circle, oriented to the sound and lunged. I reacted, swinging my sword like a golfer teeing off. I saw immediately that I'd gone too wide. The blade cleaved into shoulder but then rang off a knot of bone, implanting itself in the ghoul's thick neck.

Yes!

The ghoul stumbled to his knees. I twisted and sawed, trying to complete the decapitation, but the blade became wedged between a pair of vertebrae. I grunted with effort as flames and noxious fumes burned around me.

Without warning, pain exploded through my left calf. I looked down to see the flaming hand I'd severed seizing my lower leg. The detached appendages of ghouls, as well as various undead, could do that, but it was one of those things I always imagined happening to someone else.

I kicked my leg, but the fingers bit fast, nails sinking through skin and muscle. I shouted and reversed course, trying to yank the blade free now. But the vertebrae held it like a pair of pincers. Behind the ghoul's melted lids, the bulbous orbs of his eyeballs shifted. The thing was coming to. His good arm reared back, black claws level with my face.

"Forza dura!" I shouted.

A force exploded from the sword, freeing the blade and throwing me to the ground. With a chopping downstroke, I hacked the severed hand from my leg. Above me, the ghoul wavered to its feet. Its flaming head lolled to one side, the spine barely supporting it.

"Christ Almighty!" the mayor repeated, still down.

I scrambled toward him on hands and knees and shielded him with my body. Turning to the gunmen, I shouted, "Finish it!"

The explosion was immediate. I twisted my head enough to catch the effect. Bullets chewed through what remained of the neck. Ghoul and head fell to the street, the second rolling toward the gutter.

The gunfire ceased. Except for the crackling of burning bodies, the intersection was quiet.

I rolled off Budge. We both sat up and looked around. The news crews that had retreated in panic crept forward, several cameras fixed on the headless body burning in the street.

"Is everyone all right?" Budge asked, gaining his feet.

Captain Cole emerged from the tent and gave him a thumb's up: the operation had succeeded. Budge nodded, swiped the hair from his brow, and hustled around until he was in front of the cameras.

"My fellow New Yorkers," he said, "you've now seen the horrible menace with your own eyes. You've also witnessed what happens when a determined leader mobilizes the best resources to confront that menace head on. We're not done yet, but we're on our way. Phase one of the eradication program is complete." He swept an arm out. "The ghoul threat to our great city is ended!"

I had to hand it to him. Whatever the man lacked in common sense, he made up for in political instincts. The picture of him in front of the creature carnage was going to look pretty damn impressive on tomorrow's front pages.

"I'll be more than happy to take your questions now," he said, then broke into his signature *aw-shucks* smile as the cameras and clamoring reporters pressed in. "One at a time, please."

I caught the coverage that evening on my portable television, an early rabbit-ear model that tolerated my aura better than most. The local stations devoured the story, devoting their entire news slots to that morning's operation, the coverage ranging from favorable to gushing.

"...an estimated four hundred ghouls eliminated," Courtney was saying as I shifted the pillows that propped up my wounded leg. *"And with that, the mayor claims he's on his way to eliminating all supernatural threats from the city, though he said that will require a second term."*

"Well played, Budge," I muttered to the television.

"Just a second term?" Tabitha yawned from the divan. "Does he have any idea how many of us there are?"

"He said *threats*. And he's only going after the worst of the worst."

"Well, there are plenty of those." Tabitha began ticking them off her paw. "Soul eaters, succubi, incubi..."

"Clear and present threats," I amended. "Ones that give the mayor the biggest political payout. He's not going to risk chasing beings that ninety-nine percent of the city can't even see." My head ached with the urge to be right. Or maybe I was determined for the vampire Arnaud to be wrong.

"Well, what about me and you?" Tabitha asked.

"What about us? We're not threats to anyone. Hardly anyone even knows we exist." A vein in my temple began to throb, as though I were making the argument to Arnaud himself.

I awaited Tabitha's response, but she was staring past me, a grin growing across her furry lips. I followed her gaze back to the television. A headshot appeared through the snowy reception, one I recognized.

"You were saying?" Tabitha purred.

"In the excitement of today's operation, an interesting figure emerged," Courtney said in a chirpy, you're-not-going-to-believe-this tone. *"His name is Everson Croft. He's a college professor, a consultant to the mayor, and a modern day wizard. I saw it with my own eyes, folks. Watch here as he battles a flaming ghoul, using only a sword and magical incantations."*

I'd thought all of the cameramen had been in retreat, but at least one had had the brass to stop and shoot. Shaky film rolled of the moment I caught the ghoul in the neck. I could see the severed hand crawling up behind me like a giant spider. Leaping, it affixed itself to my leg. The rest happened quickly. The shouted Word, the ghoul stumbling backwards, me hacking the hand away and shielding the mayor, and at last, the ghoul succumbing to the hail of bullets.

"How delicious," Tabitha said.

"Whatever his title," Courtney continued, *"I think we can agree that Everson Croft is a hero—our hero—and someone we'll continue to follow closely. From all of us here at TV 20, goodnight."*

I sagged back in my chair as the credits rolled over the dimming news set. I couldn't believe it. I was the night's feel-good closer.

"Well, this should make things interesting," Tabitha said.

"Yeah, no thanks to *Budge*." I limped over to the television and slapped the power button. "Invites every major network to the ghoul roast, then shows up drunk and starts blabbing about his secret wizard weapon."

"Not so secret now."

"No kidding. The jerk just made me a walking target."

"That's what you get for dealing with a politician. I've seduced many over the centuries. They're the same everywhere."

I hopped on my good leg to the phone on the kitchen counter. I'd infused the injuries from the ghoul-hand attack with healing magic, but the claw punctures had been deep and bacteria ridden, meaning a longer mend time.

"What are you doing?" Tabitha asked.

"What do you think? Calling the mayor to tell him I'm out."

I'd reasoned that my inclusion in the eradication program would make me safer. Right now, I felt anything but. My identity had just been broadcast to every New Yorker with a television, which was most of them. The morning papers would take care of the rest.

"Let's not be hasty, darling," she said. "The mayor's office is compensating you handsomely, after all. Your income from the college is nice, but it's hardly adequate to our lifestyles."

She meant her lifestyle, but I wasn't processing anything past "college." I dropped the receiver back in its cradle.

"Crap."

Tabitha gave a startled blink. "What is it, darling?"

"My chairman," I said. "Snodgrass."

13

I burst through the front doors of Midtown College, tucking my shirt in as I ran. I hadn't slept a wink the night before and so shouldn't have been late, but I made the mistake of buying several morning papers from the corner newsstand and carrying them back to my apartment to peruse. Time escaped me, and for good reason. All but one of the circulars mentioned my inclusion in the eradication program. A few devoted entire columns to the story of the New York wizard.

I huffed out a curse. *Snodgrass has been waiting for this,* I thought as I pulled off the fake beard and sunglasses I'd donned to avoid public recognition. *Waiting for something he can use to banish me from the college. And now he has it, dammit.*

He would make good on his threat to alarm the parents of my students, to get them to yank their children from my courses. "After all," I could hear him telling them, "you don't want him corrupting your daughter's mind with some enchantment or whatever else he decides to put in there. If he's kept his real identity a secret for this long, what else might he be hiding?"

No students meant no classes. No classes meant no job.

I skittered around the corner of the hallway and was met by a wall of noise. "This is a graduate-level seminar," I heard Snodgrass shouting as I drew nearer. "It *cannot* be audited."

Huh?

I arrived at my classroom and peered through the half-open door to find my chairman standing and waving his arms at a mob scene, his face turning the same dark burgundy as his bowtie. "Did you hear me?" he demanded. "This is a closed course. If you are not registered, leave *now*."

Was this my classroom? I leaned back to read the number over the door before looking inside again. This time I spotted my six regular students at their desks. But the remaining students, including the fifty or so jockeying for standing room, were completely new to me.

"There he is!" one of them shouted.

Heads swiveled toward me. A fresh clamor went up. The students surged in my direction, Snodgrass disappearing behind them. A multitude of mouths talked at once. "Is it true?" "Did you do those things on television?" "Are you a real wizard?" "Can I take your course?"

Several pushed newspapers and drop-add cards at me.

I held up my hand and cane in a warding gesture and backed

against the door. The students, most of them young women, formed a jabbering semicircle around me, admiration bright on their faces.

My God, they're serious.

Snodgrass fought his way through the crowd, fixing his skewered glasses as he arrived beside me. "Professor Croft," he shouted above the commotion. "A word outside, please."

I followed him into the hallway and forced the door closed behind me. He proceeded down the hallway a short distance, stopped suddenly, and wheeled on the high heels of his leather shoes.

"*What* in the devil do you think you're doing?" he said.

I looked from him to the students' faces crowding the classroom door window.

"Croft!" he snapped.

"I'm sorry ... what?"

"This is an academic institution, not some camp for teeny-boppers. Is this a stunt to improve your enrollment?"

"Stunt?"

"Did you compel those students to attend your class through some inducement?"

A realization struck me. As impossible as it seemed, Snodgrass had yet to hear the news. I walked backwards until I reached the classroom door and opened it to a surge of noise.

"You," I said, pointing to a young woman. "May I borrow your paper?"

With all the reverence of a virgin making an offering to a god, she stepped forward and handed me her copy of the *Gazette*. As she retreated back into the masses with a mad giggle, I closed the door and returned to Snodgrass. He accepted the paper as though I was up to some trickery.

"Page one," I said.

I watched his eyes fall to the lead headline:

CITY: 1 MONSTERS: 0
MAYOR'S PROGRAM OFF TO A BLAZING START

The photo underneath showed members of the Hundred firing on the final flaming ghoul while I covered the sprawled-out mayor. Snodgrass's eyes skipped to the sidebar: "LOCAL WIZARD STARS IN EFFORT." My smiling headshot had been lifted from the college's online directory.

I still wasn't thrilled about the exposure, but it appeared to have boosted my status with the students—something that was dawning on Snodgrass as well. I couldn't pass up the opportunity.

"Those *tendencies* of mine you mentioned last week?" I said as he read. "Well, they're out there, and guess what? The students of Midtown College are *loving* it." I embellished the word with a lascivious flick of my tongue.

Snodgrass's eyelids blinked rapidly. At last, he folded the paper with a sniff.

"This changes nothing," he announced tersely. "I still plan to phone parents. I would be remiss as department chair if I didn't. In the meantime, I want those students out of your—"

At that moment, the chairman of the college board, Mr. Cowper, rounded the corner with the seven other board members. Cowper pulled up when he spotted me and smacked his flabby lips.

"Ah, Professor Croft," he said. "We were just discussing you in our meeting."

"Oh, yeah?" I tried to read the sagging folds of his face to discern whether that was a good thing or a bad thing. Maybe I'd turned on the cocky too soon.

"Yes, we've received a positive *avalanche* of inquiries this morning about your fall courses," he said. "We were wondering if you might consider increasing your offerings. You'd be compensated, of course. And it couldn't hurt your application for tenure."

"Y-yeah, of course," I stammered. "I'll see what I can come up with."

"Please do," Cowper said. "It will really help out enrollment. Especially in *this* department." He looked pointedly at Snodgrass before issuing a final lip smack and moving off with the others.

I grinned down at my department chair. "It just keeps getting better."

A tremor moved across Snodgrass's blanching face. "I don't care *what* you are," he said, shoving the newspaper against my chest and pointing past me. "I want those cretins out of your classroom. Now."

"What's the matter? Afraid your department will be overrun by ancient mythology and lore majors?"

"It's a—a—a—" His lips sputtered, unable to spit out the word.

"Tell you what. While you're figuring out what *it* is, I'll go ahead and start my lecture."

I pivoted on my cane.

"This isn't over, Croft!" he shouted at my back.

I waggled my fingers behind me in farewell before opening the door and wading into my new fan base.

After class—a two-hour session that featured a lecture on the ghoul myth across cultures, a long Q&A about my role in yesterday's operation (which I played *way* down), and ended with me adding twenty-two new students to the course—I called Hoffman and arranged to meet him at a deli down the street from the college.

The detective arrived, shaking his head. "Must really think you're hot stuff, huh? 'Local Wizard Stars in Effort,'" he said, reciting the *Gazette* headline. "What a bunch of crap."

I shrugged in answer. Hoffman tossed a pile of paperwork onto the far end of the booth seat and collapsed opposite me. His tie was loosened and the sleeves of his sweat-stained shirt bunched up to his elbows.

"Tough morning on the bribery circuit?" I asked.

Hoffman's cheeks clenched at the dig. "I saw your little photographer buddy earlier."

I straightened and peered around. It had been several days since I'd last seen Ed. When he didn't come home for good, I assumed the spell had expired and he'd collapsed into a clay mound somewhere. I'd been planning a hunting spell to retrieve the amulet. "Where?" I asked.

"I was gonna give him a fat lip," Hoffman went on, "but the weasel took off. Ran like a little girl."

"And yet it was enough to outrun you," I pointed out.

Before Hoffman could respond, the waitress arrived with the two coffees I'd ordered. As she walked away, Hoffman leveled a thick finger at me through the steam.

"I'll say it again. Those photos don't show what you think they do. I'm just going along with this 'cause I don't want you making a goddamned mess of my operation. Do you have the photos?"

"The info first," I said.

Hoffman peered around, then hunched over the table. "The lab's still going through the trace evidence. So far it all matches up with the woman's clients. We're interviewing them. No suspects yet."

"Any of them work in security?" I asked, thinking about the werewolves.

"The clients?" He snorted. "They're about the farthest thing from security you can get. They were seeing her for potions and palm readings. Bunch of fruitcakes if you ask me."

That didn't make any sense. The wolves had to have left *something*.

A Ziploc bag landed in front of me. Inside was a clump of gray hair.

"Your residue," Hoffman said. "Techs still don't know where the stuff came from."

While Hoffman gulped his coffee, I held the bag up to my eyes. Squinting, I could make out a fine yellow dust on the ends of the cat hairs. When I unsealed the bag, the faintest odor of rotten eggs leaked out. Definitely sulfurous. I resealed the bag, folded it over, and placed it inside my leather satchel. I would run some spells on the residue back at my apartment.

"How about the human hair I asked for?" I said.

"Not in evidence."

"What?"

"You said light brown and about a foot long, right?"

I nodded, remembering the final hair I'd drawn from my mother's brush.

"I checked the log," Hoffman said. "Nothing like that was collected. They found a little shriveled-up piece of hair on the victim's lap, though. The DNA was too corrupted to test."

"Her lap?"

Heat shriveled hair, but so did intense magic. I recalled how I'd discovered the mystic: slumped in her chair, arms at her sides. She had probably been yanked into that position from behind, the hair she had been handling falling onto her lap. Had Lady Bastet completed the reading before her murder? Had she seen who killed my mother?

Hoffman's voice broke through my racing thoughts. "We done here?"

I collected myself. "One more question."

"That's all I know about the case."

"Not about the case. It's about, um, Vega."

"What, you got a little thing for her?" He smirked. "I'll tell you what, buddy, she sure doesn't like *you* anymore."

"Did she say why?"

I got that we had hit a nasty bump in the spring, but that had been four months ago. Could she still be that upset? I considered how she'd treated me at the crime scene, the look she'd shot me at my presentation on the ghoul operation. There had to be another reason.

"Hey, your problem, not mine," Hoffman said with a harsh

laugh. "Ask me, she recovered her senses." He finished off the rest of his coffee and held out a hand. "The photos."

I pulled a stack of Polaroids from my satchel. "These are most of them."

"What do you mean, 'most of 'em'?" Hoffman snatched the photos away and flipped through them like they were playing cards.

"I'm keeping the rest. You can earn them back by finding me suspects."

The thick flesh of Hoffman's brow collapsed down. "Listen, you little smartass—"

His voice broke off as a large shadow fell over our table. We both looked up. The redheaded werewolf brothers loomed over us.

I reached for where I kept my revolver before remembering those two had destroyed it. For a moment, I reflected on how Grandpa's possessions had existed in twos. In his tool shed, he'd kept two sets of everything—hand drills, claw hammers, awls— and always the same kind. Ditto his night robe and slippers, his pocket watch, his fedora. I snuck into his bathroom once and discovered two identical shaving mirrors beside two identical straight razors with bone handles. When I asked my grandmother about this, she told me he had always acquired things in pairs. His reasoning? If something broke or went missing, he had an immediate replacement.

Too bad I hadn't adopted the habit. With the inflating cost of firearms, I wasn't sure I could afford a replacement now.

Muscles swelled beneath the wolves' security guard uniforms, but I was preoccupied by the burn in their irises. Left to their pack instincts, the brothers would tear me apart. Hoffman must have sensed the potential for violence, too.

"Been nice chatting," he said, scooting from the booth. "Gonna leave you to your friends."

"Mayor wants to meet with you," Flint said to me.

"We make appointments for those now." I blew on my coffee and raised it to my lips. Werewolf or not, I didn't care for his threatening tone.

Flint thumped the mug with a finger. It flew from my grasp and shattered against the tile wall. Hot coffee rained over the table. I looked down at my dripping hand, then over at Flint.

"Problem?" I asked.

"Next time, it's your head," Flint growled.

"Is that what you told Lady Bastet?" I asked, testing him.

The muscles around his nose bunched up. "Don't know what the hell you're talking about. Now let's go."

I searched Flint's and Evan's eyes. If either had been involved in Lady Bastet's murder, they were disguising it well. I pulled several napkins from the dispenser and began drying my hands.

"Fine," I said. "But I'm not riding with you. I'll catch a cab."

Flint snarled and lunged toward me. Evan caught him by the arm and grimaced, clearly fighting his own inner beast. Whoever was running the pack in Penny's stead had forbidden them from exacting revenge against me. But who would that be? Budge? As a mortal, he wouldn't wield that kind of power. There had to be a second in command somewhere.

Flint controlled himself and straightened. "One o'clock," he growled. "Or we come back."

I'd been anxious to return to my apartment to begin work on the sulfur residue, but I'd get nothing done with a pair of pissed-off werewolves in the back of my mind. Plus, I still intended to resign from the eradication team—something I could do in person. Though the press coverage had improved my position at Midtown College, any further attention would only hurt. I consulted my watch.

"Tell the mayor it's a date."

14

The cab dropped me off at the checkpoint outside the plaza that fronted City Hall. The guard, another werewolf, studied my ID with a snarl while a second wolf gave me a bruising pat down. They returned my ID and shoved me through. I limped over the plaza, squinting from the bright concrete.

"Everson."

I looked up to find Caroline descending from City Hall's columned portico, one hand forming a visor above her eyes. She was dressed in business attire and carrying a black leather briefcase over one shoulder. She looked like a lobbyist, which I supposed she was. Among other things.

I met her halfway up the steps.

"You came," she said.

"Yeah," I replied, not sure what she meant. "I'm supposed to meet with the mayor."

She angled herself so the sun was no longer in her face and lowered her hand. When her blue-green eyes searched mine, a keen pain pierced my chest. I looked back at her neutrally.

"My offer still stands," she said.

"You mean the vacation in the faerie realm? I'm handling things pretty well up here, thanks."

"That could change."

"So you've said."

Her lips pressed together. "Everson—"

"I've worked out something with Budge," I said, cutting her off. "I help him, he helps me. And as much as I dislike the press attention, it now means he hurts me at his own risk. Same goes for Penny, if she ever wakes up." Though the rationale sounded good, I still intended to resign. I just wasn't going to tell Caroline that—for no other reason than to challenge her.

"*Were* things to go wrong," she said, a thin comma forming between her eyebrows, "do you have somewhere you can go? Someplace safe?"

I thought of Arnaud's offer of a renewed alliance.

"It won't come to that," I said.

"I see a lot more than you can."

"Care to share?"

A breeze blew a strand of hair over Caroline's cheek. I had to restrain myself from brushing it back behind her ear. Too much had happened since the night we'd held each other. She fastened the hair away herself, eyes flicking to the bottom of the steps. My gaze followed. A tall, striking figure in a Cambridge suit leaned against a flagpole, his copper hair shining in the sun.

The sight of Angelus kicked me in the heart with both legs.

"You should probably go," I said, already starting to leave. "Don't want to keep hubby waiting."

She seized my arm, the force turning me so I was facing her again. "You're standing on a precipice, Everson. And it's crumbling." The aggression in her voice and grip surprised me.

"What are you talking about?"

"You're not as safe as you think you are." She released me. "Let me *help* you."

A determination in her eyes seemed to be masking a deeper conflict. For a moment, I thought she was going to lunge at me—though whether to strangle or kiss me, I couldn't tell.

I glanced over at Angelus, who was still watching us.

"I don't need your help," I said, and paced up the steps.

This time, Caroline let me go.

I groaned when I spotted the werewolf brothers waiting for me beyond the scanners inside the City Hall building. "What are these two?" I muttered. "Part retriever?"

"You're late," Flint said. "Follow us."

"Thanks, but I know the way to the mayor's office." I stepped around them toward the elevators.

"We're not going to the mayor's office." Flint grabbed my right arm above the elbow. Evan took my left, and the two began marching me down a long hallway. I twisted my shoulders, but their large hands held me like a pair of manacles, fastening me between them.

"Where are you taking me?" I demanded.

Flint touched an earpiece. "We've got him."

Who was he talking to? The pack's second in command?

Evan drew a key and unlocked a door that opened onto a narrow, empty corridor. The wolves turned their wide frames such that Flint was pulling me, Evan pushing me. They hadn't confiscated my weapon, which seemed odd. Still, Caroline's warning flashed hot in my mind.

You're not as safe as you think you are.

"*Respingere!*" I cried.

From the opal in my cane, white light detonated. My arms wrenched violently as the force blasted Flint down the corridor and Evan back into the door we'd just entered through. The pain in my left shoulder registered a moment later, as well as the familiar clunk of dislocation.

Dammit.

Supporting the infirm arm at the elbow, I ran back toward the door. It had collapsed out into the main hallway with Evan's impact, along with Evan. But in the next instant, Evan sprang up and activated his earpiece. If he was calling for backup, the hallway would soon be swarming with wolves. He pawed for his holstered firearm. Another deal breaker.

I stopped and reversed course. Down the narrow corridor, Flint was slower to recover. He staggered to his feet, blood on his brow. If I could get past him, I could search for a rear exit. When he saw me coming, he sank to his haunches, a deep growl growing from his chest.

Have to keep going. Have to hit him hard enough to make him stay down.

Fumbling my cane apart, I held the staff weakly in my left hand. Manifesting a shield, I used additional Words to shape it into something resembling a battering ram. I sensed Evan bounding up from behind. With my right hand, I aimed the sword behind me at an acute angle to the floor. I'd managed this once before in a car but never while running.

"Forza dura!" I shouted.

The power that stormed from the sword hit the floor and launched me forward like a rocket. I hurtled down the corridor. Flint tried to throw himself out of the way, but in an explosion of sparks, the battering shield rammed into him and left him tumbling in my wake.

The floor rose quickly as the blast from the sword petered out. My front foot caught the carpet, and I was thrown into a bruising roll that shot fresh pain through my shoulder. My head absorbed some solid shots as well.

I stood and staggered in two nauseating circles to collect my weapons and orient myself. My casting prism was shot, but behind me, Flint was still down. I turned back toward the end of the corridor, where a door with a red crash bar read: EMERGENCY EXIT.

Just need to get out of here.

I shambled toward the exit—and nearly collided into a side door that swung out in front of me. A man wearing a headset and Prada sunglasses peered out. "There you are!" he exclaimed in a prissy voice. "Get *in* here!"

I stared for a moment, trying to figure out if I should know him. The man's frosted hair stood in a voluminous coif, while his black designer shirt opened on a thin, hairless chest. The shirt's sleeves flapped as he motioned for me to come. Though the eyes beyond the tinted lenses were animated, I could discern no werewolf in them. A touch of faerie, maybe.

"Come *on!*" He seized my wrist with dainty, but insistent, force.

I glanced back at the wolves. Flint was struggling to his hands and knees, and Evan had disappeared from view, probably to intercept me on the other side of the emergency exit. In my still-woozy state, I allowed the man to pull me after him. He led me through a warren of corridors.

"I'm Marcus, by the way—goodness!" he exclaimed, glancing at me over a shoulder. "You look absolutely hideous."

"Huh?" I was still struggling to work out who the man was and what he wanted.

"I have him, but he needs work. Can you hold them off for another ten." I realized Marcus was talking into his headset. He let out a dramatic sigh. "I need to *work* on him, Dwayne. He's an utter disaster."

I pulled against him. "Look, this is where we're going to have to part ways."

Marcus pushed me into a brightly lit room and looked me up and down. "Wrong hair, wrong fashion, wrong, wrong, *wrong!*"

He stamped a foot for emphasis, making me jump back. I bumped into something at thigh level and lost my balance. A padded chair caught me. Marcus swiveled the chair until I was staring at a dressing-room mirror. He frowned studiously over my right shoulder as he turned the chair each way and then began finger-teasing the hair on the sides of my head.

"Ugh. I can't work with this," he decided.

Before I could stand from the chair, it collapsed backwards and I was looking at the ceiling. Warm water gushed against my brow. In the next moment, Marcus was massaging cold conditioner into my hair. "I want elegant for you," he said, "with a touch of rakish, a touch of ... *le mystérieux.*"

I struggled from Marcus's fingers and threw myself over the side of the chair. I landed on my hands and knees, sputtering as conditioner streamed down my face and into my eyes. Someone jerked my cane away, and a pair of hands seized me roughly by the arms. I was lifted into the air and slammed into the chair with enough force to relocate my left shoulder.

"Stay put until he's done," a gruff voice ordered.

I squinted my stinging eyes open to find Flint and Evan standing in the doorway, wearing pissed-off expressions. But they weren't coming at me. I looked from their earpieces to Marcus's headset. Was this who they'd been trying to deliver me to?

Marcus sighed as fresh water showered over my face and hair. "Are *all* wizards this difficult?"

With the werewolves standing guard, my cane in their possession and my casting prism offline, I had no choice but to let Marcus complete his work—to what purpose, I still had no idea.

Following a quick washing, Marcus scrubbed my hair with a towel and used a brush and blow dryer to give it a feathered look. He moved to makeup next, smearing a base layer over my face. He then came at me with various stencils, brushes, and lip glosses— "Or else the lights will reduce you to a corpse," he said. Rather than explain further, he talked into his headset in emotional bursts, demanding a few more minutes from this Dwayne.

"There," he said at last, standing out of my view of the mirror.

I hardly recognized the face staring back at me. "What in the hell?"

"Don't touch it!" Marcus squealed, swatting my hand down.

I pursed my lips to make sure the copper-colored reflection was mine. In addition to the fake tan, Marcus had drawn over my eyebrows, making them more dramatic, with little curls on the ends. The harsh rouge along my cheekbones complemented the bright red of my lips.

"There's nothing elegant or mysterious about this," I said, searching around for something to wipe it off with. "I look fucking ridiculous."

Marcus nodded at Flint and Evan, and they pulled me from the chair. Marcus reappeared with a black cape. "Here," he said, fastening it around my neck. "There's no time to change you out of that shirt, so keep the cape closed. Oh, and let's get this on you." He turned and reappeared with a leather hat with a huge brim and tall bulbous crown, which he set atop my head.

"Now you look the part," he said.

"For the hundredth time, what's this for?" I demanded.

Marcus tilted the hat slightly. "He's ready," he said into his headset.

Flint and Evan escorted me from the dressing room and up a short flight of steps to a door. Flint knocked, and another man with a headset answered—Dwayne, I presumed.

"Great, thanks, guys," he whispered to the wolves.

The wolves slammed the cane against my chest and shoved me into the dark room after Dwayne.

"Don't worry," Dwayne said in a breathless voice, "you're not going to have to speak. After your introduction, you're to stand behind the mayor, a bit to his right. We've marked the spot with tape. Try to affect a mysterious look. Better yet, brooding. They'll eat that up."

"Who?" I asked.

"Ooh! They're ready for you."

Dwayne led me around a corner until we were peering out onto a small stage from the side. The mayor, who stood at the podium where he gave press conferences, glanced over at us.

"And here he is, ladies and gentlemen," Budge announced. "The man—or rather, wizard—of the hour, Everson Croft!"

Oh, hell no.

I tried to turn around, but Dwayne blocked me and pushed me out onto the stage. I emerged into the packed press room to a detonation of camera flashes and shouted questions. Budge seized my hand and pumped vigorously. "Thanks for coming," he whispered. The handshake went on for several seconds as he smiled toward the cameras. He finally released me, nodding toward the X taped on the floor behind him. Stunned by the sudden attention, I dutifully took up my position and faced the press in my makeup and hat.

"Mr. Croft!" a reporter shouted. "Where did you learn your magic?"

"I, ah..."

"C'mon, guys," Budge answered for me. "You know a good magician never reveals his secrets."

"How powerful are you?" someone else shouted.

Budge laughed. "What do you think? I went out and found some weakling wizard? He's the most powerful in New York. And he's working for me and my administration."

I grimaced at the lie—I may not even have been the most powerful on my block—but I saw what Budge was doing. He was fanning the positive interest in me in order to claim the glow for himself.

"Can you give us a demonstration?" another reporter asked.

An excited chorus of "yeah"s followed.

"No, no," Budge said, waving his hands, "there'll be none of that. Everson needs to conserve his power for the next phase of the eradication program. And if you thought the ghouls were something, wait till you see what's coming up."

"If he's so powerful," a female reporter cut in, "what's to stop him from turning on the city?" I saw the anxiety in the young woman's eyes—exactly why I kept a low profile. The mood of the assembly seemed to pivot as several reporters around her nodded.

I watched the mayor for his response.

"Look, I've known Everson a long time," he lied. "Besides being a potent wizard, he's a man of integrity. A man of morals. And hey, he's a fellow New Yorker. We have a mutual interest in protecting the city that raised us."

"But there has to be *some* constraints on him," the reporter pressed.

"Well, sure," Budge said, sweeping an arm out. "All of *you*. If I've learned anything in my years of public service, it's that the press can lift the lowliest to the heavens and drop the mightiest into the gutter. If Everson gets out of line, why, just crack him with a column or two. That'll straighten him up."

Relieved laughter broke around a fresh burst of questions. But when Budge turned enough for me to see his face, there was no humor in his eyes.

15

"Thanks for being such a good sport," Budge said, settling behind his office desk. "Can I get you anything?"

"How about some makeup remover?" I grumbled.

I dropped the hat and balled-up cape onto a coffee table and sagged into a deep leather chair across from him. The press conference had gone on for another thirty minutes. Thirty interminable minutes in which I'd stood there, a stage prop, while Budge rattled off superlatives about his program.

It only strengthened my determination to resign.

"You wanted to talk?" Budge pulled out his smartphone and began thumbing through the messages.

"I'm out," I said.

"Hm?" He raised his eyebrows without looking up.

"I'm resigning from the program."

The mayor's eyes joined his brows. "Resigning? What are you talking about?"

"I asked for discretion. That was one of the conditions for my participation. You nodded and said, 'Mum's the word.' Do you remember that? Well, mum apparently left the building and got run over by a truck."

"Hey, I'm sorry," Budge said, showing his hands. "I got a little enthusiastic."

"A little enthusiastic? You outed me to every major news network in the metropolitan area. And what was that little stage production just now?"

"I was trying to take the pressure off you."

"By making me a Broadway extra?"

Budge set his forearms on the desk. "Look, I should've warned you I was bringing in the news crews yesterday. And, yeah, things got a little dicey there with the ghouls getting out and all—but listen to me. Capturing that final battle on film? You can't pay for coverage like that. And it's exactly what New Yorkers need to see—that there *are* monsters out there, and we're fighting 'em. Did you catch today's poll numbers? I jumped four points overnight. Four points! The race is a statistical dead heat." He laughed in disbelief.

"Good, so you don't need me anymore."

"Don't need you?" His mouth straightened. "You're the face of this thing."

"No, I'm not."

"You heard the press out there—they love you."

"Right, and that's the whole point," I said. "I don't want the attention."

"What about our deal?"

He was referring to the protection from Penny, should she awaken. But as I looked on Budge's wavering brown eyes, I knew I'd been kidding myself. The man didn't wield that kind of power. Penny would have her retribution whether I helped the mayor win or not.

"I'll take my chances," I said.

"Well, gosh." Budge sat back. "I'd hate to think what would happen if the press decided you weren't working in the public's best interest, that you *were* dangerous."

Heat prickled over my face. "Is that a threat?"

"Hey, I just know reporters. They're a bunch of jackals. You stop giving them what they want, and pretty soon they start digging for the bad stuff. Past arrests. Shady associations..."

The son of a bitch *was* threatening me. He was saying that if I didn't remain on board, he would make sure the press knew about my indiscretions, including my arrest for murder two years earlier. And as went the press, so would go public opinion. Fear and anger stormed inside me.

"Well, maybe they'll learn some interesting things about the mayor's office, too," I said through gritted teeth. "Such as Penny's true nature."

Budge shrugged. "It'll be your word against ours. And my wife can't very well speak for herself." He nodded past me. I turned my head and observed a back wall heaped with floral baskets and bouquets. "Those arrived today. All for Penny. The volume's down from the spring, but we still can't get them to the Dumpster fast enough. That Caroline is brilliant. Too bad you let her slip away."

"Caroline?" I said in confusion. "What does she have to do with this?"

"You didn't know?" he said, sweeping hair from his glasses. "She's been advising me."

"Advising you?"

"Yeah, ever since Penny's hospitalization."

That explained what she'd been doing at City Hall, what she had meant by *You came*. I knew she had been negotiating with the mayor for the fae's access to the portal in lower Manhattan, but advising him? I looked back at the pile of flowers and weighed the mayor's remark.

"Wait," I said, "the sympathy campaign was *her* idea?"

"And it's worked like a charm," Budge said. "She came up with the eradication program, too."

"The eradication program?" I stood and paced a circle around the chairs in front of his desk. The revelations were coming in too hard, too fast. By my second circuit, I started molding them into something sensible. The fae kingdoms Caroline served were anxious to maintain control over the lower portal. If Budge's opponent in the mayoral race, Abby Azonka, couldn't or wouldn't cotton to the idea, the fae had to ensure Budge's reelection. Whoever advised him would need an expertise in New York politics as well as a strong connection to the mayor's office—Caroline offered both, the second through her father, one of the mayor's attorneys.

In essence, *she* was the reason the information Vega and I once wielded over the mayor's office was no longer effective. "Was hiring me as a consultant also Caroline's idea?" I asked bitterly.

"She was against it, actually," Budge said. "Didn't say why, though."

I gave a begrudging nod, remembering her warnings, including her most recent one about seeing a lot more than I could. I assumed she'd been referring to her fae powers, but now I wondered. As advisor to the mayor, had she already worked out the contingencies? Seen a looming threat?

"So why did you come looking for me?" I asked.

"I went to that detective first. What's her name?" He circled a hand. "The one who was with you when you visited my mansion in the spring?"

"Vega?"

He snapped his fingers and pointed at me. "Yeah, that's the one. Anyway, I was told Vega ran a supernatural unit in Homicide. She was the one who insisted you be brought in."

I stopped pacing. Why in the hell would Vega want me involved in the eradication program? I remembered the dismissive way she'd dealt with me at the crime scene, the bitter look she'd given me in the auditorium.

"Did she say why?" I asked.

"Well, she said she'd help out however she could, but for the scale of the operations we were talking, we really needed someone of your caliber. You know, a magic-user who understood the threats, knew the monsters' weaknesses, how best to go after them, so on and so forth."

So *Vega* was the one who had told the mayor about my work.

"But to tell you the truth," he continued, "I think she just wanted to make sure you got the same deal."

"What deal?"

"Extra protection in the event someone woke up." He laced his fingers behind his neck and grinned, evidently pleased at how the conversation had come full circle. "Funny how you asked the same for Vega."

I sat down again, my head starting to throb.

"Look at it this way," Budge said, buddy-buddy again. "You've got one friend who came up with the idea for the program and another who insisted on you being a part of it. Both of them are drop-dead gorgeous to boot," he added with a laugh. "How can you say no to that?"

"Just shut up for a minute."

I massaged my closed eyes. I had to think, but the only thing striking through was Budge's threat to use the media to turn public opinion against me. And with the city's growing bloodlust for nasty supernaturals, I'd be a walking target. Unless, of course, I aligned with Arnaud or took up Caroline's offer to hide in her world. Both nonstarters.

"Fine," I said, opening my eyes. "I'll stay in the program."

At least until I can figure out something else, I thought.

"You're making the right decision."

"But on one condition," I added.

"What's that?"

I picked up the cape from the coffee table and wiped my brow, smearing copper makeup over the fabric. I moved on to my nose, cheeks, and finally my lips and jaw before tossing the soiled cape onto the mayor's desk.

"Keep me out of your damned press conferences."

16

"When in Diablo's name is someone coming to fix the air conditioner?" Tabitha asked, sauntering into my lab and hopping onto the table.

"We're still on the waiting list," I answered distractedly, motioning for her to move away from the casting circle. I squinted at the circle from another angle and added more silver filings to the far side.

"That doesn't answer my question," she said.

I had returned to the apartment, relieved to find Tabitha fast asleep in front of the box fan, her belly swollen from the tuna steak I'd set out for her earlier. Now I regretted not spiking her lunch with Xanax.

"If not this weekend then next, all right?" I said with a sigh. "The brownout fried a ton of AC systems in the neighborhood. Now can you leave me alone? I have something important to do."

Tabitha made a dramatic noise and plopped down at the end of the table. Shed hair blew off in tufts around her. "Have you given any more thought to Caroline's offer?"

"No," I said thinly, picking strands of orange hair from the casting circle.

"Just think. We could be in that wonderful realm right now instead of melting in this hell hole."

I ignored her, my eyes moving between the casting circle and an illustration in the book I'd propped open. The book was a crumbling tome that protected a caster against powerful demonic attacks. Not knowing the origin of the sulfurous residue Hoffman had given me, I couldn't afford to take any chances. The casting circle featured two concentric circles with extra sigils of protection. I stooped and fixed a blemish in the outer circle.

Tabitha made a scoffing sound. "Men and their wounded egos."

She was still talking about Caroline. I bristled. "This doesn't have anything to do with my ego."

"Ooh. Touchy, touchy."

"Just let it go," I said. "I need to concentrate."

"You saw her today, didn't you?"

I glanced over, in spite of myself. "What makes you say that?"

"I know that hot and bothered look."

"I saw her briefly," I admitted, hoping that would be enough to satisfy Tabitha. I should have known better.

"I told you she's trying to get up close and personal."

"It was a chance encounter outside City Hall," I said. "She was leaving a meeting with the mayor as I was arriving."

"And what did she say?"

"Same old, same old."

Even as I waved a dismissive hand, Caroline's warnings continued to echo in my head. *You're standing on a precipice, Everson. And it's crumbling.* As one of the chief architects of Budge's reelection campaign, she was seeing something that I couldn't. But what?

"Hmm. Perhaps I was wrong," Tabitha said in a musing voice.

"About what?"

"While I wouldn't put it past her to claim you were in danger in order to get closer to you..."

"You don't even know her."

"...her persistence in the face of so hopeless a case makes me wonder now." Tabitha propped her chin on a curled paw. "Perhaps you should take her at her word. You might *actually* be in danger."

"We're not going to the faerie buffet."

"It's not about food," she said, then added, "not entirely."

I met Tabitha's gaze. Was my cat right? Was refusing to listen to Caroline my way of retaliating for her choosing a life with Angelus and the fae over me? Was I jeopardizing my safety to prove to Caroline that I could take care of myself, that I didn't need her help?

"All right," I admitted, "maybe ego has a tiny bit to do with this, but it's not the whole story." I lifted my satchel onto the table and pulled out the evidence bag with the cat hair. "I need to stay here to figure out the whos and whys of Lady Bastet's murder. The answer might not only have implications for me, but also

Detective Vega." I was still puzzling over Vega recommending me for the eradication team. Had it been to protect me, as the mayor suggested?

"Well, the *whos* are the wolves, correct?" Tabitha asked.

"Huh?" I said, emerging from my thoughts. "Oh, I'm not so sure. I had a little run-in with them earlier, and they showed impressive restraint. They would rip me to shreds if left to their instincts, but someone's got a tight hold on their leashes. And they have a hell of a lot more reason to kill me than to kill Lady Bastet."

"What about the mauled cats?" Tabitha asked.

I considered the mystic's disabled warding glyphs, the lack of signs of struggle. At last, I considered the evidence bag in front of me: sulfur lifted from the torn necks of her cats. "I'm starting to think the real killer *wanted* the murder to look like the work of wolves."

"What in the world for?"

"That's what I'm hoping to find out," I said. "So either keep quiet or go back to your cat bed."

Muttering something about crappy ice bags, Tabitha remained in a languid heap on my table. She lowered her head to her paws. I waited another moment to ensure she would stay silent before I opened the plastic bag and emptied the contents into the casting circle. Stepping into my protective circle on the floor, I drew my staff and called energy to my prism.

"Cerrare," I said.

Energy infused the sigils and moved around the concentric circles, closing them. Brow furrowed, I concentrated toward the cat hair. My first spell would be a simple detection spell to determine the nature of the residue, to learn what sort of being had deposited it.

"Rivelare," I said, staff pointed at the circle.

The hair swirled and amassed at the circle's center. In the next moment, small popping noises sounded, and a yellow smoke drifted from the clump of hair. The sulfurous smell intensified, but now it carried something else: a distinct odor of ozone. That went with casting.

"The residue originated from a spell," I said.

"And not from a demonic spell," Tabitha put in.

"No?" I hadn't progressed that far.

"I have a nose for my own. That carries the taint of human."

"Black magic, then." I gave another sniff, opening my wizard's senses further. "Cast from elder wood."

I withdrew energy from the detection spell. *A fellow magic-user.* And if he or she had disabled Lady Bastet's glyphs and killed her without a struggle, then we were talking about a powerful one. Personal enmity between the mage and the mystic? Maybe, but I didn't like the timing.

"Let's do a little hunting," I said.

"Knock yourself out," Tabitha murmured.

With a spoken Word, I shifted half the hair to one side of the circle as a reserve and kept the other half in the circle's center. I aimed my staff at the small pile and incanted. After several moments, a subtle pull took hold on my cane as it began to absorb the residue's essence. The pull grew stronger, which was a relief. I'd feared the mage had covered his tracks and that the spell would crap out. That he hadn't cast a spell to avoid detection suggested the mage either wasn't as powerful as I'd thought or so powerful that he didn't care.

"I see you."

I jumped at the distorted voice. My gaze searched the circle, but there was no one and nothing there. To the circle's right, Tabitha had shuffled back into a threatening crouch. Her hair was puffed out, ears flat to her skull. But her dilated eyes weren't aimed at the circle. They were glaring at me.

"Yes," she said, "I see you, *Everson Croft*."

"Tabitha?"

But it wasn't Tabitha. A hunting spell worked like a plumbing snake, reaching through the essence of something to hook a target. But that conduit ran both ways, enabling an adept target to lash back and hook the casting circle. Which was exactly what had happened. The minute I knew we weren't dealing with a demon, I should have reconfigured the circle. Not only that, but I'd been careless in removing Tabitha's errant hairs. A few must have remained inside the circle, allowing the mage to take possession of my cat.

I cycled through Word after Word to break the hunting spell, but Tabitha's lips only forked into a grin.

"Who are you?" I demanded.

"I *was* of no concern to you, Everson Croft," the mage said through Tabitha.

"How do you know my name?"

"I know a lot about you. I own something vital of yours."

The confidence with which the mage spoke sent a cold shudder through me. What in the world was he talking about?

"Leave it, Everson," he warned, "or you will join others who have waded into matters beyond their purview. Indeed, crossing paths with me a second time would be *very* bad luck."

He was speaking as though in riddle. *Bad luck* and *crossing paths* called to mind black cats. And *a second time*?

In a sudden flash, I remembered the cat that had darted out when I'd blown open Lady Bastet's door. I had assumed the cat with the sleek midnight coat to have been the lone survivor of the massacre, but something told me the feline hadn't belonged to Lady Bastet.

Had I crossed paths with the departing mage?

To test the theory, I said, "You killed Lady Bastet."

Tabitha's black eyes moved back and forth over mine. At last, her lips grinned again. "You're more astute than you appear," the mage said. "But don't mistake astuteness for adeptness. You're still a babe in the woods."

The satisfaction in the mage's voice stoked a raw rage inside me. Without forethought, I called a tidal wave of power to my prism. *"Uccidere!"* I shouted, unleashing the power through the conduit, the force shoving me backwards. Tabitha recoiled too, eyes startling wide.

A moment later, though, her body shook with laughter.

"You're a tempestuous one," the mage said. "It looks like you require a more tactile warning."

Before I could raise my staff, Tabitha sprang, claws flashing. Her rear legs kicked me in the chest, toppling me backwards. Hot tines raked my right cheek. I landed hard, cracking my head against the edge of a bookshelf. The room blurred as I struck out my arms in defense.

"Are you all right, darling?"

I blinked over to where Tabitha was sauntering up. I started to shrink away before sensing she was herself again. A quick check showed me the hunting spell had been broken. The mage was gone.

Tabitha's pupils narrowed inside her green irises as she leaned down to inspect my cheek. "Who did you manage to piss off this time?"

"A mage," I replied, understanding that Tabitha had no memory of the possession.

I touched the knot on the back of my head and inspected my fingers. I wasn't bleeding there, anyway. My face was another matter. I looked down at the blood spattering the thigh of my pants. The claw marks felt deep enough to leave scars, even with healing magic. No doubt the mage's intention. I drew a handkerchief from my pocket, balled it up, and pressed it to my cheek. I then used the bookcase to pull myself to my feet.

"So the hunting spell was a score?" Tabitha asked.

"Not quite," I said. "The mage was too powerful. He let the spell go just long enough to issue a warning."

"Seems you've been getting a lot of those lately."

"No shit," I muttered. "This one was to keep my big nose out of Lady Bastet's murder—which the mage all but confessed to."

I limped back to my lab table and looked down at the smoking casting circle. I thought about the shriveled strand of hair the investigators had found on Lady Bastet's lap. If it had belonged to my mother, as I suspected, maybe it explained the timing of the murder.

I repeated the mage's warning in a whisper: "Leave it, Everson, or you will join *others* who have waded into matters beyond their purview."

"What, darling?" Tabitha asked.

...matters beyond their purview, I repeated to myself.

I turned toward Tabitha, speaking quickly. "All this time I've been thinking the murder had to do with the wolves or the mayor's office. But what if the mage killed Lady Bastet for what she'd learned?"

"What in the world are you talking about?" she asked in irritation.

I thought back to the murder scene. The toppled shelves, the decapitated cats, Lady Bastet's slit throat, and in front of her ... the scrying globe! If Lady Bastet had been killed at the conclusion of the divination session, the final images she received might still be in the globe.

I slotted my sword into my staff, grabbed several spell items from my drawers, and made for the ladder.

"Where are you going?" Tabitha asked.

"To ignore a warning," I said.

17

I descended the steps to Lady Bastet's former business and found the door secured by a police padlock. I drew my sword and inserted the tip inside the shackle. With a whispered *"Vigore,"* I cracked one of the shafts from the body and slipped it from the hasp.

I opened the door. Inside, afternoon light fell through the high basement windows in dusty slants. The showroom was clean, the hanging rugs gone, probably in a forensics lab somewhere. For a panicked moment, I became certain the scrying globe would be gone too.

After sensing no one else inside, I sealed the door behind me with a basic locking spell and hurried to the windowless back room. I called light to my staff and exhaled. The globe was there, on the table. The rest of the room had been straightened, shelves righted, the items that had fallen from them swept into a pile. Blood stains still marred the floor, though.

I returned my gaze to the scrying globe. It seemed to absorb the light from my staff, giving nothing back. The orb simply stared, a gray, inscrutable eye.

The chair in which I'd found Lady Bastet was scooted out at a slight angle, as though inviting me to sit. I didn't sense any traps, but given the power of the mage, and that he seemed to have anticipated my hunting spell, I built a protective circle around the chair before lowering myself onto the seat.

"All right," I whispered, eyeing the globe. "Let's see if there's anything left in your memory."

I set my sword and staff on the table and pulled two silver candles from my pockets. I lit them and stood them on either side of the globe. Next, I extinguished my staff. As darkness collapsed around the candles, the marble-like surface of the globe shifted. Nothing appeared, though. Scrying required a level of intuition that I lacked, not only to perceive images but to interpret them.

Fortunately, I kept an Elixir of Seeing on hand. It had been drawn from a '48 batch, which was supposed to have been an especially good year. I pulled the flask from my shirt pocket and drank the bitter potion down.

It didn't take long to start working. Within minutes, I began to feel insubstantial, ghost-like. A dull pressure built between my eyes while, from the sides of my vision, a dark mist drifted in. The mist thickened until I could no longer see the candles in front of me. With a final, rude gouge, the pressure in the center of my brow relented, and a third eye opened.

The scrying globe hovered in front of me like a misty planet, larger than it had appeared to my physical eyes. Light from the candles glistened over a surface that had begun to swirl. Images flashed forth, talking to me in a strange language—one I could suddenly understand.

Oh, God.

The images were horrifying. But I was no longer just observing them.

I was living them.

I staggered in the center of a pillared room, a woman, pain seething in every part of my body. The metallic tastes of blood and fear stained my palate. Through hanks of sweat-soaked hair, I could see the burning candles that ringed me. Robed figures stood among them.

"Please," I managed, the word raw in my throat.

Their responding voices rose at once, a single word climbing above the others: "Traitor."

"No," I said, searching for a way out.

A force blast caught me in the chest and knocked me back. Breathless, I stumbled to keep my feet. Another blast nailed me between the shoulder blades, pitching me onto my hands and knees. My right collarbone cracked in a harsh flare, and I moaned. The figures swam toward me.

My son, I thought through the haze. *Need to stay alive for my son.*

"Did you really think you could keep up this shameful duplicity without me finding out?"

I squinted at the tall figure emerging through the others. The face beneath his hood was an ornate gold mask, the eyeholes dark and vacant, open mouth set in a frown. A mask of judgment.

"I did nothing," I said.

The mage's black gown shuffled to a stop in front of me. "Nothing?" he scoffed. "You joined the Front as a sworn rebel against tyranny. You pledged your allegiance, your *life*. Only for us to learn that you're a plant for the Order."

I shook my head. "That's a lie."

The mage drew a wand. I could smell the elder wood. "Then you shouldn't have a problem submitting to a mind flaying."

My insides twisted up. A mind flaying would entail a level of pain beyond anything physically imaginable. It would lay bare everything—not only my infiltration of the Front, but my true feelings for my son. I had acted as if he were a mistake, a nuisance to be tolerated.

Struggling to my feet, I faced the mage. "I will submit to nothing."

"Then you are admitting guilt."

"If that's what you want to believe."

"It's the truth, traitor," he said. "And you know the penalty."

I stared past the eyeholes of his mask, defiant. "Do your worst."

With a grunted Word, he thrust his wand toward me. The force threw me against a stone pillar, knocking the wind from me. He spoke another Word and vines snaked up through cracks in the floor. I was too stunned to move. Could only watch as the vines encircled my legs, my broken body, binding me to the pillar. They wrapped my throat and squeezed until I gagged.

The mage moved closer. "It didn't have to end this way, Eve."

From a great distance, I flinched at hearing my mother's name.

The mage turned toward the other robed figures, fellow magic-users. "Behold the penalty for treachery," he announced. I imagined a hard grin forming behind his mask. "Death by fire."

No, I thought.

Though my eyes remained fixed on the mage, I saw my son's face. He had just turned one. The week before, he had taken his first steps, spoken his first coherent sentence: *Mama, read me.* Such a smart boy.

A crushing sadness filled my heart at the knowledge he would never know me. Not really. I had already discussed the contingency with my parents. My mother would love him as her own. My father would protect him. The Order would look after him as well...

"Fuoco!" the mage shouted.

Dark red flames sprang up around me and glistened in the mage's gold mask until he looked like something demonic. Soon, the flames hid his face, and there was only pain.

I love you, Everson, I felt my mother's cracking lips whisper.

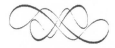

I landed against the cold floor with a gasp. The room was dark, my shirt soaked with sweat. I pawed around until I encountered the stone table and pulled myself to my feet. The globe stood from the darkness, its surface dimming. The candles on either side had burned to their nubs and gone out, the puddles of wax cool and firm when I touched them.

How long was I out?

I stared at the spent candles, remembering the fire from my vision. It had consumed me. No—consumed my mother. I had relived the agony and sorrow of her final moments, felt her vanishing love for me. The experience—too raw to put into words—tore around my insides.

Arnaud had been telling the truth. I believed now that my grandfather *had* gone to him after my mother's death and said the words, *They killed her. My God, they killed her.* My mother had been murdered by a rebel group she had managed to infiltrate. Had been burned alive by their presumed leader, a mage with a gold mask whose voice I recognized.

A scuff sounded from the showroom.

I seized my sword and cane from the table and spun. The sun had set while I'd been entranced; the showroom was now cast in dark shadows. Another scuff sounded: someone trying to exercise stealth. Either the locking magic on the front door had petered out or someone had dispelled it.

Heart slamming, I moved to one side of the door in the rear room and pressed my back to the wall. My mother's executioner was still alive. He had murdered Lady Bastet to keep his deed a secret. He had hijacked my hunting spell and spoken through Tabitha to warn me not to pursue the matter. That was where I'd recognized the mage's voice from.

Another scuff.

My lips trembled in fury as I summoned energy to my prism. *You screwed with the wrong wizard family, you son of a bitch. Whatever happens, you're going to know pain. Even if it kills me.*

A dark shape entered the doorway.

"*Entrapolarle!*" I bellowed, swinging my staff around.

White light burst from the opal, and a crackling shield encased the figure. I slammed the figure against the near wall and raised my sword overhead. The sound of muted gunshots stayed my arm. As the shield dimmed, I found myself staring at Detective Vega. She stared back with startled eyes.

"Croft?" she shouted, eyebrows crushing down.

I released her and called light to my staff. "Wh-what are you doing here?"

"No," she said, emerging through the sparks of the dissolving shield, "that's *my* question."

I glanced back at the globe before meeting her gaze. "I was looking for something."

"You *broke* in here," she said.

"Yeah."

The confession seemed to catch her off guard. Her dark eyes searched my face, pausing on the healing claw marks.

"Do you want to tell me what the hell's going on?" she asked.

With a steadying breath, I sheathed my sword. "It wasn't the wolves."

"What?"

"The wolves didn't kill Lady Bastet."

"*That's* what you're doing in here?" She holstered her firearm and took a menacing step forward. "Listen to me, Croft, and listen good. You may advise the Hundred, but that does *not* give you jurisdiction to investigate any old murder you just happen to take an interest in."

Fresh anger burned inside me. "Any old murder? Let's see, a powerful mystic was executed on the same day I just happened to drop off something for her to read. Excuse me for taking a goddamned *interest*."

"I told you we'd be in touch."

"Yeah, to blow me off," I shot back.

"For your information"—Vega jabbed a finger against my chest—"I already eliminated the wolf angle. Nothing linked them to the murder. I moved onto a substance we found on the mutilated cats, but I guess your informant already told you that," she added with a sneer.

She knew about my arrangement with Hoffman. I steeled my jaw.

"I get that you think I'm a novice when it comes to the supernatural," she went on, "but I have other resources besides you. The substance came from magic."

I chafed at the idea of her consulting another magic-user. It felt like betrayal—something I didn't need any more of in my life. "And what were you going to do with that information?" I challenged. "Stick it in your Wizard Database and look for a match? You're out of your depth, Vega. You have no idea who or what you're dealing with."

"If you're suggesting you have info," she said, "you're obligated to share it."

I stared back at her. My emotions might have been all over the map, but I knew better than to say anything that would put Vega in the path of a powerful mage. And after what he'd done to my mother, he was *my* problem.

"Forget it." I stepped past her.

She seized my arm. "I'm serious, Croft. I already have you on breaking and entering."

My anger spiked, but I talked it back down, forced myself to relax. When at last I spoke, my voice was calm, quiet. "I understand

I have you to thank for getting me a spot on the mayor's eradication team. For protection, right? I appreciate that. I do. And if you want to continue to keep me at arm's length, fine. That's probably being a good mother. But I'm not going to stop pursuing Lady Bastet's killer. How you deal with that is up to you."

I drew my arm from her relenting grip and walked from the back room.

"The problem with you, Croft, is I never know who I'm dealing with."

I turned and found her standing in the back doorway, fists on her hips.

"What's that supposed to mean?" I demanded.

"It means that I was ready to put the past behind us—only to find out you're dealing with Arnaud again."

"Arnaud? I don't have a goddamned thing to do with him."

"Oh yeah? You didn't meet with one of his at a bar in the West Village last week?"

She was referring to the morning of the mayor's press conference. That had only been ten or so days ago, but with everything that had transpired since, it felt like ten months. I'd relegated it to the back of my mind. *Explains Vega's ball-breaking stance towards me, though,* I thought.

"Who told you that?" I asked.

"That doesn't sound like a denial."

I sighed. "It's not what you think. Meeting with him was part of a deal for him to stay out of my life."

"Yeah, I know all about your *deals*."

Of course she did. The last one had led to her son getting grabbed. I cursed my word choice, but there was way too much going on in my head right now. I needed to leave. I surprised myself by walking back toward her.

"Look," I said, "Arnaud is always shifting pieces around his little chess board, looking for advantages. It's how he's stayed alive this long. But I know his game. I gave him ten minutes of my time. That was all. True to his word, he hasn't approached me since. And if I know vampires, he won't."

Vega was looking at me as though trying to decide what to make of me. In hindsight, agreeing to meet with one of Arnaud's had been stupid. I glanced past her to the stains on the floor.

"It's not like I gave him my blood or anyth..." My voice trailed off as a horrifying thought struck me.

"What's wrong?" Vega asked.

"The blood in the room," I said, nodding past her. "You had it tested?"

She looked over her shoulder and back at me. "Yeah?"

"Did any of it..." I swallowed. "...belong to me?"

Vega's brow beetled as she shook her head.

The room seemed to reel as I recalled the mage's words: *I know a lot about you. I own something vital of yours.* The black cat that darted out Lady Bastet's front door hadn't been wearing an odd collar. It had been holding the clay tube with my blood.

"Shit," I spat.

18

I spent the next day in my apartment, afraid to leave my protective wards, not even sure they *could* protect me. The mage who had killed my mother had my blood, and that was bad. Super bad. With it, he could cast all manner of blood magic, up to and including a death spell.

I would be powerless to stop him.

I paced the length of my bookshelves again, eyes jerking from title to title, but I'd already pulled the relevant ones and read through them. They only reaffirmed what I already knew about blood magic.

I was fucked.

I sagged into my padded chair with a hard sigh and eyed the evidence bag beside the books on my desk. The bag held what remained of the cat hair and spell residue—my sole connection to the mage. I had mentally cycled through the spells I was capable of casting, but I was still too junior. None of them would enable me to find the mage or strike him without his knowledge. And if the mage was as adept as he seemed, he probably had a nasty counterspell in waiting.

That left communicating with the Order—and that was where I was stuck.

First, there were the questions. Why didn't the Order have a record of my mother? Were they trying to hide something? And why hadn't the Order done anything about her murder? The mage should have been toast. Was he that powerful, or was there something more going on?

Complication number two fell back on my blood. The mage had taken it without my consent, true. But that wouldn't earn me any pity points with the Order. The fact I had given my blood willingly, to whomever, was what mattered. If the mage used my blood in any kind of black magic, I would be considered just as guilty as he was. In which case, the only way I'd be spared the death penalty was if the mage killed me first.

I massaged my closed eyes, the final moments of my mother's life flashing behind my swollen lids. The pain, the blasts, the mage with the gold mask, the bitter exchange, the cruel fire—

The ringing phone made me jump.

I considered letting the call go to my answering service, but I was selective about who I shared my unlisted number with, and this could be important. I arrived downstairs and grabbed the receiver on the fifth ring.

"Yeah," I answered.

"Everson!" the mayor said. "Listen, I know we barely touched on it in our meeting yesterday, but I want you to go ahead and start drawing up plans for the next phase in the program."

"Central Park?" That had been slated for late August.

Budge lowered his voice. "Between you and me, I was hoping for a solid month of coverage on the ghoul operation, but the press is already running out of steam. We're looking at another week, tops. They want fresh stories on the program. Maybe we can divide up the park, do it in phases?"

"We'd have to," I said, considering not only its size, but its creatures.

"Yeah, maybe a series of grab-and-hold operations," Budge said. "We could even reopen parts of the park, host a big cookout with blankets, clowns, the works—you know, something tangible for the public. Don't get me wrong. Ridding the lines of the ghouls was great, but it's gonna take months to get those lines in good enough shape to run trains through again."

I caught myself nodding. Despite that Budge had all but blackmailed me into pledging my continued cooperation, I was thankful to have another problem to divert my thoughts.

"All right, but listen," I said. "This is going to be a lot different from the ghoul operation. For one, we're dealing with a different class of creature. Goblins, hobgoblins—bad, bad dudes. They might not have the regenerative powers of ghouls, but they're smarter, more tactical minded. Also, we won't have anything like the subway tunnels. This is going to be jungle warfare."

"Is that a problem?" Budge asked.

"It is if you're trying to avoid casualties."

"Hmm, good point," Budge said. "At this phase, though, I think the public would be willing to stomach a few losses, don't you? Shows them we're taking the problem seriously. Just so long as the losses are minimal and they don't include you. You're still the face of this thing, remember."

I let the remark go. "When do you need a plan by?"

"Have something Friday. If we want to maintain campaign momentum, Caroline's saying we need to get the ball rolling by the following week. Otherwise, I'm bleeding points again."

Mention of Caroline sent a raw charge of emotion through me. I wondered vaguely about the looming threat she was seeing. In light of recent developments, it didn't seem so pressing.

I cleared my throat. "Friday it is, then."

I still had the mage to worry about, and whether or not to tell the Order, but in my years as a scholar I'd found that shifting my focus to a secondary problem often yielded answers to a more pressing primary problem. Subconscious incubation, I'd heard it called. I hoped that would be the case here.

"The more spectacular, the better," Budge said, and hung up.

A week later found me pacing the command-and-control center's main tent, gripping a Styrofoam cup of bitter coffee. All around me, NYPD officers and technicians manned computers and communication equipment. For the second phase of the eradication program, we had set up in Grand Army Plaza, just outside Central Park's southeast corner. As before, Captain Cole wanted us close to the action. Only this time, there *was* no action.

Across the tent, he shot me a stern look that said, *Where are they?*

I dropped my Styrofoam cup into a trashcan. Above me, a series of monitors showed grainy green images of woods, overgrown paths, a derelict amusement park—but no creatures. On the GPS display, the numbered points indicated that the sweep, begun at midnight, was nearly complete.

"Well?" Cole asked, voicing his displeasure now.

"It's only the first action," I said defensively. We had divided Central Park into six sections with the plan to clear them in successive actions, south to north. Tonight we were tackling the southernmost section, up to the transverse road at Sixty-fifth Street. While half the Hundred performed the sweep, the other half were stationed around the perimeter in armored vehicles. No creature was going to get out alive. That had been the idea, anyway.

Cole walked up to me. "You said we'd get engagement."

"I said *maybe* we'd get engagement. I'm an academic, remember? Qualifiers are our stock and trade. I also said the heaviest concentration of creatures was going to be farther north. Either way, we secure the southern park and the mayor gets to throw his cookout. Everyone's fat and happy, right?"

"This is about liberating, not securing," Cole said in a menacing voice. "You don't liberate a place by strolling through it and shouting 'all clear.' The local Cub Scout troop could've managed that."

"Good," I said, turning away. "Consult their den mother next time."

Cole seized my wrist. "You know what I'm saying, Prof."

I felt my other fist balling around my cane. It was late, my nerves were stretched, and—qualifiers or not—the operation was *not* going as planned. And here Cole was trying to make me the scapegoat. Monitors flickered. Cole must have sensed the crackle of magic too because he released my wrist.

"Look," he said, "I hate the political B.S. as much as you, but it is what it is."

"Yeah, I get it," I said, a sigh dispersing the power that had rushed to my prism. "The press needs a monster count. Otherwise, this is going to look like an expensive publicity stunt—one the mayor's opponent will jump on as yet another example of his reckless spending."

"How dangerous would it be to send a team north to try to bag a few bodies?" he asked.

I followed his furrowed gaze to the map of Central Park. It was a large aerial shot that should have answered his question. The further north one ventured, the wilder and more rugged the park became—and thus, the more dangerous. I'd only ventured into those wilds once, and that was with a stealth potion. Even then, I'd nearly been flame-broiled by druids.

"Not worth it," I said.

"Team of five," Cole went on. "If they're killed in action, not a huge loss."

"It is if we have nothing to show for it."

But the stern line of the captain's lips told me he'd already made up his mind. He readied his headset to issue the command.

"We found something," a voice crackled over the feed.

Cole and I turned simultaneously. The GPS display showed team members converging near the park's southeast corner—a wooded area anchored by a horseshoe-shaped pond. My eyes cut to the nearby monitors. One of the feeds steadied on the base of a giant boulder. Several armored officers were clearing branches away from what I realized was the entrance to a tunnel.

"Careful," I muttered.

Cole nodded. "Drop in a couple grenades," he ordered.

As team members readied the grenades, I studied the tossed-off branches that had been used to screen the tunnel. Something about the concealment seemed too obvious. I eyed the GPS display. In the men's eagerness for action, they had converged too quickly, were too close together.

"Have them spread apart," I told Cole quickly. "There are probably other access points to the—"

The bangs of the exploding grenades cut me off. Fire blew from the hole, the retreating camera catching it as a white-green flare. The camera whipped around suddenly. I drew in a sharp breath at the sight of small figures blurring past the trees. Thunks sounded, and the camera fell to the ground. Out ahead of the camera lens, beyond a spray of twigs, I could see two downed members of the Hundred, the seams in their body armor bristling with arrows.

A blow horn sounded, followed by a chorus of garbled cries.

"Son of a bitch," I said, instinctively drawing my cane apart. "Goblins."

"We have engagement!" Cole shouted into his headset. "I repeat, we have engagement!"

19

Unlike many of the creatures in the city, Goblins were not undead. Neither were they descended from the original demons. They had come up from the faerie realm in an age before fae kingdoms controlled the portals. Passing for stunted humans, they were a mean, marauding race. They never adopted modern weaponry, however, and were eventually killed or driven into hiding. But their love of human treasure kept them close to urban centers.

Several of the monitors showed small figures cutting in and out of view, pursued by bursts of gunfire. Arrows flashed at cameras in a deadly hail. Though more likely to pilfer than plunder these days, the goblins' skill in battle had never left them.

"They're everywhere," a team leader called through one of the feeds. *"Coming from all sides!"*

"Everyone to the southeast quadrant," Cole ordered. "Perimeter team, move in."

"We don't know how many there are," I said. "There could be hundreds."

"That's not what you told us at the briefing," Cole growled.

I stammered for a moment, but he was right. I'd told him and the mayor that we could expect a few dozen creatures, a number I'd extrapolated from the statistics on murders and attacks in and around south Central Park.

When I found my voice, I said, "So we pull back, reassess."

"We've got personnel pinned down," Cole answered. "They need backup."

A nauseous heat broke out over my face. "There's no telling how far the goblin tunnels extend. You could be sending your forces into a bigger trap."

Cole ignored me, shouting more commands into his headset as he moved off.

I looked from my inert sword and staff to the frenzy of activity around me. On the monitors, more helmet-mounted cameras were staring at the ground or up into trees, their operators dead or dying. I'd underestimated the number of goblins. Underestimated their cunning. Once the sweep team had converged on the poorly hidden hole—a decoy, no doubt—the goblins had poured from surrounding holes and launched an ambush. And something told me the goblins had a second ambush in waiting for whatever backup arrived.

We were playing into their grubby little hands.

"Entering from Central Park South," I heard a familiar voice report over one of the feeds.

Vega?

I ran over to where Cole was standing in front of the GPS display, barking coordinates. "You sent Detective Vega out there?" I asked.

He pushed me aside with a forearm and leaned over one of the communication technicians seated at a computer. He said something into his ear that I couldn't hear.

"Hey!" I grabbed Cole's shoulder. "I asked you a question."

"She's on the perimeter team," he shouted. "We were short one."

I was about to ask why in the hell he'd put her on the perimeter team when I remembered something else I'd said at the briefing. The perimeter team would be unlikely to see major action. They would be in place as a containing force. I swore and sprinted toward the tent door.

"Prof!" Cole shouted. "I can't let you go out there!"

Yeah, I know, I thought cynically. *I'm the face of this thing. But I'm also the reason for the current clusterfuck.*

"Tell your team not to shoot at the white light," I shouted back.

I broke out into a humid, halogen-suffused night and took a moment to orient myself. Armed NYPD officers stood around the perimeter of the plaza. A block away, news vans huddled. Voices rose in earnest at my appearance, and several cameras aimed their lenses at me.

"How's it going so far, Mr. Croft?" a reporter called.

"Will you be joining the action?" another one wanted to know.

Awful, and I don't have a choice.

I wheeled toward the distant popping of automatic gunfire. Vega had said she was joining the combat from Central Park South, a street that bordered the bottom of the rectangular park. Police officers shouted after me as I left the plaza and accessed the street at a run. At the next block, I jumped a police barricade across a stone staircase and descended into the park itself.

"Protezione!" I said.

White light burst from my staff and hardened into a shield around me. I would stand out, but I would also be protected from both friendly and enemy fire—assuming the goblins weren't bearing magical weapons.

The steep staircase deposited me onto a busted-up asphalt path. Trees pressed in from all sides. More gunfire sounded ahead of me. Away to my left, I picked up a burst of goblin speech.

"Vega!" I called.

Arrows clattered off my shield.

Shit. I reinforced my protection and plowed into the woods ahead. Leafy limbs batted at my shield. I stumbled over something and went down. I knew without looking that it was a body.

Please don't let it be hers, I thought desperately.

I turned and held up my staff. White light illuminated a row of small sharp teeth and the staring squash-colored eyes of a goblin. Its muscled torso had been ripped open by gunfire. Beyond the black talons of an outstretched hand rested the creature's short bow. I hesitated for a moment, never having seen a goblin up close. Even in death it looked menacing.

Another hail of arrows got me moving. By the growing volume of goblin chatter, I guessed more were emerging from underground—just as I'd feared. Gunfire answered in staccato bursts.

"Fall back!" I shouted. "Fall back!"

But a fresh series of horn blasts obscured my cries.

I saw the next body before I could trip over it. One of ours this time. With a force invocation, I rolled the body onto its back, arrow shafts cracking beneath the weight. I let out a relieved breath even as my stomach clenched at the sight of the young man's lifeless face.

I pulled the helmet from his head, donned it, and activated the communication system. "This is Everson Croft," I said. "We're outnumbered. I'm ordering everyone to fall back. I repeat, I'm ordering everyone—"

Feedback blew into my ears, and the power box exploded. I swore and tossed the smoking helmet aside. Cupping my hands to the sides of my mouth, I shouted for Vega again.

Behind me, something broke through the brush.

I turned and nearly screamed. The hairy giant that loomed over me grunted, pointed ears flattening back from a short brow and huge red eyes. *Bugbear,* a voice stammered in my head. *It's a frigging bugbear.* Eyewitnesses frequently mistook the creature for a bigfoot—an easy mistake to make. Only a bigfoot didn't brain its victims and tear them limb from limb.

From a fanged mouth, the creature let out a horrid cry.

I raised my sword, but the shock of the encounter had cost me the precious second I'd needed to cast. Muscles hardened across the bugbears hairy torso and a club came crashing toward me.

I criss-crossed my sword and staff in front of me at the same moment the club collided into my shield. Sparks blew against my face, and the impact hurled me backwards. I ricocheted from tree to tree like a giant pinball. At last, I crashed to a stop. The woods reeled around me as I sat up, but the glimmering shield had held, sparing my life.

"Not gonna survive a second round, though," I mumbled.

I chanted quickly to reinforce the shield. The bugbear screamed again, limbs breaking with his next charge. Too soon, his fierce red eyes shone above me, club raised overhead.

"Respingere!" I called.

The pulse from my shield knocked the bugbear onto his heels. Without my feet planted, the counterforce sent me backwards. The shield and I broke through a sweep of reeds, and then we were ... bobbing?

Oh, you've got to be kidding me.

The shield fizzled and burst apart. Warm water soaked through my clothes. I splashed until I was standing shin deep in the muddy shallows of a pond, my sleeves dripping wet.

Beyond the tall reeds, the bugbear unleashed another scream.

I waded across the finger of water at the pond's tapering end and splashed onto the opposite shore.

"Protezione," I tried.

Brown light popped around the staff's opal before blinking out.

I peeked back through the reeds. In the faint moonlight, I could see the rustling trees that marked the bugbear's progress. I took several crouching steps backwards before the sounds of gunfire and goblin chatter stopped me. Escaping the bugbear meant fleeing into the heart of combat. Without my protection, I wouldn't make it ten yards before an arrow or bullet found me.

But I had to locate Vega. Had to get everyone out of the park.

Red eyes appeared above the reeds. They shifted from side to side before narrowing in on me. A low growl rumbled across the water. I readied my sword, but I wasn't dealing with a fire-soaked ghoul. This creature was at full strength and had all of his senses. I would get one thrust or swing. Anything short of a lethal result, and I was looking at an express train to the afterlife.

Yeah, screw that.

I turned and ran. I'd take my chances in the combat zone—and take Harry here with me. The bugbear crashed into the water at my back. With any luck, he would eat bullets before I ate arrows. Right now, I was eating a whipping series of tree branches, and they were slowing me down. I panted out a Word of protection, but no shield would take shape.

Something whistled near my head. An arrow.

"Vega!" I called, more from desperation now than anything.

"Croft," she shouted back.

My heart jerked as I veered toward her voice. She was alive! My new route took me around and down the hillock I'd been ascending. I scrambled and slid past massive boulders.

"Vega," I repeated.

"Over here," she said.

I found her in a protected pocket where three boulders came together. She was sitting against the far boulder, aiming an automatic rifle toward the opening. Her helmet was off, and I caught a shine of blood along her hairline. I glanced over my shoulder before crouching beside her.

"Are you all right?" I asked.

She winced. "Got clubbed in the head."

"By big, bad, and hairy?"

"I emptied my pistol at it. Not sure whether I hit it or just scared it off. What in the hell was it?"

"A bugbear," I said, looking back again. "And you're lucky. Not many live to tell the tale."

"Yeah, well, I'm not feeling very lucky." She rubbed her right knee, the leg straight out in front of her. "Twisted something when I went down. I can't put any weight on it."

"Where's your helmet?" I asked, searching around. "I need you to contact the others, clear them out."

"The blow cracked it in half. Communication's shot."

"Crap," I muttered. "How are you fixed for ammo?"

From feet away, a scream sounded. Terror threw me in a half spin. The bugbear's silhouette filled the opening to our sanctuary, red eyes pulsing. He screamed again and pumped his club overhead. I raised my sword in a sad effort to parry the inevitable blow.

A deafening burst of gunfire resounded through our space. The bugbear danced like a giant epileptic and fell backwards. He crashed to the ground with a solid *whoomp*.

"Holy crap," I whispered, watching the creature's chest deflate.

"Fully loaded until just then," Vega said, answering my earlier question.

I lowered my sword. "Nice shooting."

"Thanks, but we've got bigger problems."

"Yeah, I know. The goblin horde."

"Worse."

"Worse?" Something gave my gut a hard twist. "What could be worse?"

"Command and control was ordering our evacuation when I lost communication. Cole—"

"Wait," I interrupted. "He ordered your evacuation?" Even as I asked, I realized the only gunfire I was picking up now was sporadic and distant.

Thank God for that.

"He's ordering a napalm strike," Vega finished.

I choked on a fresh fit of panic. "A strike? When?"

But I could already hear the distinctive *bat-bat-bat* of rotary blades. Attack choppers were incoming.

20

I now understood why Captain Cole had tried to stop me from leaving the command-and-control tent. He had just ordered his helicopter division to drop a few hundred pounds of liquid hell. It didn't change anything, though. I still would have seen that Vega made it out of the park.

"If I support you, do you think you can stand?" I asked her.

"Not like I have a choice." Gripping the automatic rifle in her left hand, Vega let me underneath her right side and grasped my neck. I wrapped an arm around her upper back, and we stood together.

"The shortest way out is the way I came in," I said.

Vega drew a sharp breath between her teeth as she took her first hopping step. With me stooping and her limping, we made our way down the hillock. With each step, I braced for the sting of an arrow, but none came. I listened for goblins, searched the surrounding trees for their movement. Vega seemed to be doing the same, the rifle aimed from her abdomen. I guessed the thundering of the approaching helicopters had driven them back into hiding.

Vega and I were squelching through the mud around the pond when something heavy crashed away to the west. Another bugbear? The explosion that followed told me no. Fiery light broke through the trees, accompanied seconds later by an intense, oily-smelling heat. Crap, they were dropping the napalm.

"Path is just over there," I panted. "We'll take the stairs out."

The next explosion was closer, the heat like raw blisters over my skin.

Vega grunted as we burst onto the crumbling path. We were paces from the staircase when she staggered. I squeezed her perspiring body to my side to keep her from falling.

She swore. "My good leg's giving out."

"Muscle fatigue," I said, sweat pouring from my own body. I peeked back and beheld an apocalyptic scene. A large swath of park was in black-red flames. The helicopter's first pass had targeted the park's lower west side, but I could hear them circling, coming in from the east. They would drop their remaining tanks in the vicinity of where we were standing.

"Go for it," Vega said, already knowing what I was planning.

I stooped and placed my shoulder against her stomach. She folded over my back until I could get an arm around her thighs and lift her fireman style. I trudged forward, gaining speed, and hit the staircase at a jog.

"Shit!" she cried.

I thought the jostling motion had hurt her leg until I realized arrows were clattering against the steps around us.

Shit is right, I thought.

I glanced back to see the short, stooped silhouettes of two goblins at the bottom of the steps. I high-stepped as an arrow tore a chunk of fabric off my pant leg. I felt Vega moving her rifle around into a shooting position. I paused at a landing midway up the staircase so she could aim. At the same moment gunfire burst from my back, something knifed into my right calf. The pain felt like molton. I went straight down with a holler, Vega tumbling from my back.

"Nailed them both," she shouted above the roar of the choppers.

"And one of them nailed me." I turned my leg over until I could see the dark shaft of the arrow. It was in there good.

"We'll take care of that once we're out," she said, crawling toward the final flight of steps.

When she looked back to make sure I was following, the fire reflected in her eyes showed her fear—not for herself, but for her son. The idea of him growing up motherless. I nodded and crawled after her, remembering the fear and sadness my own mother had felt in her final moments.

Fresh detonations shook the earth. A chopper swept low. More napalm tanks crashed and tumbled into the woods behind us. Too close. We weren't going to survive their explosions.

I said a quick prayer and shouted, *"Protezione!"*

Light sputtered around my staff's orb, then, breaking from its water-logged lethargy, came brilliantly to life. The light wrapped us in a spherical shield as fire roared from the woods and engulfed us.

"*Respingere!*" I cried, channeling the force toward the landing downstairs from us.

In a whoosh of flames, the counterforce launched us into a weightless parabola. We cleared the park and were soon plummeting toward the street. The sphere shattered into sparks on impact. We rolled over asphalt, my sword and staff clattering in different directions.

Vega and I came to a rest near the far side of the street. I looked up, road-rashed and reeling. Beyond my splayed legs, fire consumed the lower park and presumably the remaining goblins and bugbears.

I let my head fall back again. "Holy hell."

Thelonious's creamy white light lapped around the edge of my consciousness, my incubus sensing weakness. I had expended all of my energy with those final invocations. I looked over to where Vega was scooting past me. Using her arms, she lifted herself onto the curb. She sat there without speaking, in shock, firelight glistening over the skin of her face.

"You all right?" I asked.

"I owe you, Croft," she said, her voice distant.

For a moment, I thought she said *I love you*. A conflicting brew of emotions swam through me, casting up strange vapors, until the words resolved into what she'd actually said.

"Let's just call it even," I replied.

"No. I mistrusted you ... one of the few good guys in the city."

From the direction of Grand Army Plaza, footsteps pounded up the street. I turned my head to find Captain Cole flanked by two NYPD officers. A block beyond them, more officers were working to keep the press in their cordoned-off zone. Half of the cameras were aimed at the inferno, the other half at me.

Cole arrived in front of us, his expression either one of concern or anger, I couldn't tell. Everything was going hazy. His gaze fell to the arrow in my leg.

"Ambulances are on the way," he said.

"How many did we lose?" I asked, not wanting to know, but needing to.

"You don't have to worry about that right now," he replied.

"How many?" I repeated.

"Thirty-six men."

Thirty-six. The number echoed numbly in my skull.

To shift my attention from the dark mage, I had buried myself in the Central Park operation. I had poured in everything—my resources as an academic, as a wizard—to assess the monster threat, to determine the safest, most effective way to combat it. But I'd been kidding myself. With specters of revenge whispering around me, I'd missed things that should have been obvious. The goblins' tunnel networks under Paris were storied. Why couldn't their race have done the same under Central Park? And now, because of such oversights, more than a third of the Hundred were dead. Men with wives and children...

"I've already spoken to the mayor," Cole said. "He's meeting with advisors to determine the next step."

The first ambulances rounded the corner and slowed toward us. Beneath the strobing lights, rear doors opened. Attendants in blue coveralls emerged. Thelonious's growing presence made me waver as I pushed myself to my feet. I couldn't even feel the arrow in my calf anymore.

"Her first," I slurred, nodding at Vega.

The attendants wrapped her in a foil blanket and, squinting from the heat, helped her into the closer ambulance. Her eyes lingered on mine until the doors closed. I bent to retrieve my sword and staff, slotting them back together. When two more attendants approached me, I turned away in a limping half circle, the creamy waves really storming in now.

I didn't fight it.

"Croft," Cole barked. "Where are you going?"

"To catch a cab," I said faintly.

21

Foul smoke laced the air outside my apartment the next morning. Hungover and sore, I limped up the street alongside a truck delivering morning editions of the *Gazette*. That the delivery was late told me printing had been delayed to carry the news of last night's operation. I didn't know how the mayor had spun the bungled job and didn't want to. Adjusting my sunglasses above my fake beard, I looked away so as not to catch any headlines.

I did the same on the bus ride to Midtown, averting my eyes from the spread-open papers. I didn't even want to glimpse the expressions of the commuters reading them. Smoke from Central Park drifted past the windows. North of Twenty-third Street, it became so thick that I started to see pedestrians in surgical masks.

I entered Midtown College through a back door and removed my disguise. I had nearly canceled my morning class, but it was almost finals week, and I'd already canceled last week's classes to work on the operation. The college was one bridge I couldn't afford to burn.

My right calf throbbed with magic as I climbed the empty stairwell. I'd awoken before dawn in a doorway in Times Square, a flat bourbon bottle between my legs and quarters everywhere. I did the post-Thelonious check, patting my pockets for wallet and keys. Both there. Clothing, cane, and necklace intact as well. I then craned my body around to read a flashing sign overhead. Thelonious had ended up at a peep show, which explained the quarters. His visit this time had been short and tame. Maybe he was tiring of using me as a vessel. For once, though, I hadn't minded the oblivion.

Upon returning home and treating the arrow wound, I had a sober hour to reflect on the horror of last night's operation. Of what I had allowed to happen. Thirty-six dead. Men who would still be living if I'd been thinking clearly instead of about what the mage had done to my mother, what he could still do to me.

I had decided then and there that I was no good to anyone until I hunted him down and destroyed him.

That would be my priority.

In that vein, if there were any potential positives to come from last night's operation, it would be my removal from the program. Budge's first act to save face. He didn't need a wizard now, anyway. He could simply napalm the rest of Central Park. He wouldn't get his cookout, no—at least not the kind he wanted—but neither would he suffer the fallout from further casualties. And he'd have dump trucks full of charred creatures to show for his effort.

"Sorry I'm late," I said as I stepped into my classroom.

Two students stared back at me: Denise and Brie. I checked my watch as I unshouldered my satchel and dropped it onto my desk. I wasn't *that* late.

"Where is everyone?"

"We didn't think you'd come," Denise said.

I squinted at the young woman before realizing there must have been something in the paper about my injuries. "Oh, that. No, no, I'm fine." I flexed my right knee a couple of times to show her.

"Is it true?" Brie asked.

The words seemed to tremble past her lips. I set my leg back down and studied her again. Was I missing something? The two young women were among my more enthusiastic students—both added after the ghoul operation—but now their faces were taut and pale.

"Is what true?" I asked.

Denise took a folded newspaper from her bag and pushed it to the edge of her desk as though it were an explosive device. I broke my rule by looking at it and nearly choked at what I saw.

Above the side column that featured my headshot was a single-word headline:

TRAITOR

I lifted the paper from her desk and unfolded it. For a dizzying moment, I was in my mother's staggering, bleeding body with that word, that awful word, being hurled at me from all sides.

NEW YORK - Everson Croft, the wizard consultant to Mayor Lowder's ambitious eradication program, gave faulty information that led to the slaughter of three dozen NYPD officers, a credible source claimed. The men lost their lives in last night's operation to clear the southern end of Central Park.

"Croft knew the Hundred would be overwhelmed by creatures," the source, who asked to remain anonymous, said. "Which was why he underestimated the threat. He wanted the operation to fail, and fail spectacularly."

According to Police Commissioner Warren, the operation did not fail, thanks to the decisive actions of Captain Lance Cole. "He made the right call, meeting the overwhelming force with attack helicopters and napalm," Warren said. "Indeed, Cole may be the only reason the Hundred wasn't reduced to zero."

As for Croft's motive, the anonymous source said the wizard is secretly working for the city's banking class.

"With Mayor Lowder close to securing the federal bailout, the city will no longer be in the thrall of the big firms," the source said. "The firms know this. They're fighting it. They need the mayor to lose his reelection bid, which means denying him any success. Croft was a plant to that end."

Though the large firms, including Chillington Capital, have contributed millions to Lowder's opponent, the source declined to speculate on whether Abby Azonka knew of the arrangement.

"But there's something Azonka should know," the source said. "She's accepting money from vampires, and I don't mean the figurative kind. Let's just say not all of the city's creatures hide underground."

When asked whether Croft was one such creature, the source said, "No, but he might as well be."

The mayor's office declined to comment on the story, declaring it under investigation.

In the meantime, the city is planning a dedication for the slain officers today at noon, and...

I returned the paper to Denise and stepped slowly backwards until I was leaning against my desk. The room revolved around me. *"...bad information ... wanted the operation to fail ... a plant..."* My two students looked on worriedly as I choked down a surge of liquor and bile.

Last night Cole had said the mayor was meeting with advisors to determine the next step. Was this what the fae had come up with? Was this their solution to the bungled operation? To throw me under the bus?

Impossible, I thought. *Caroline would never let that happen.*

But was it impossible? Given the insinuations against Budge's opponent, the anonymous source had clearly come from the mayor's office. And Caroline's allegiance was to the fae now, to securing the portal in lower Manhattan. In the eyes of her race, the fate of someone like me meant nothing.

Hence, Caroline's warnings, I realized.

But why make me a traitor? Why link me to the bankers?

Because the portal is located in vampire territory.

Securing Federal Hall, the building in which the lower portal was housed, was only half the battle for the fae. The other half was them being able to come and go as they needed. The vampires may have been making that difficult, demanding a hefty tribute or something. The solution? Poison my name to mitigate any political fallout from the operation and then put me in league with the vampire bankers, thus poisoning them too.

Two birds, meet one stone.

I raised my gaze to the students. "No," I answered. "It's not true."

Denise let out a relieved laugh. "We knew it."

Brie drew a finger through the mascara-tinted tears forming beneath her eyes. Her voice hitched as she spoke. "It's just, you're our favorite teacher, and—and—and everyone was talking like you'd done these horrible things. And—and we just refused to believe it."

"Thanks," I said, digging into my pocket and handing her a clean handkerchief. "That's really nice of you. Both of you. Class will be cancelled until we can get this sorted out."

I spoke calmly, but my mind was scrambling like a spider in a glass jar. I needed to get out of here, needed to get to a phone. I would call Vega, even Budge—someone who could tell me what in the hell was going on.

"Is there anything we can do?" Denise asked.

"Maybe don't mention I was here?" I suggested.

Denise and Brie nodded as though taking solemn vows. That would help, anyway. As they collected their bags, I slung my satchel over a shoulder and retrieved my cane. I would go out the way I came in, don the sunglasses and beard to disguise me from a public that wanted my head on a pike, and go straight to a payphone.

Someone cleared his throat.

I spun toward the doorway. At first I saw only the backs of my departing students, but when they stepped around a diminutive figure in a bowtie and three-piece suit, my heart plummeted into my stomach.

"Going somewhere?" my department chair asked.

"Professor Snodgrass," I said, then thought, *please tell me you didn't read this morning's paper.*

His triumphant grin suggested otherwise. "What did I tell you?" He took a jaunty step into the room. "I said this wasn't over, that I was going to be watching you. It appears I had good reason, Croft."

"It's Professor Croft," I answered testily.

"Not anymore." He stepped inside the room. "You're suspended."

"Based on an anonymous allegation?" I snorted. "We'll see what the board has to say about that."

"Oh, the board's spoken." He reached into his jacket pocket and handed me a crisp white envelope. I searched Snodgrass's face for a lie as I stood my cane against my desk. I opened the envelope and unfolded the letter. It was a suspension order, signed by Chairman Cowper.

"Effective *immediately*," Snodgrass said, stepping to my side.

My face smoldered at his undisguised glee. "I can read."

"Oh, and there's more."

"What, you're an admitted cross-dresser?"

Hands clasped behind his back, Snodgrass gave a forbearing smile. "Hold onto that humor, Mr. Croft. You're going to need it where you're going." He turned his face toward the door and called, "You can come in now."

Three bulky NYPD officers pushed into the room. I recognized them as members of the Hundred. One led with a pistol. The other two wielded black batons. Loathing creased their faces.

"It's a lie," I told them.

"Everson Croft," the lead officer growled. "You're under arrest for treason and accessory to mass murder."

Snodgrass retreated past the officers. "For the record, the college stands firmly with the NYPD. Use whatever force you deem justifiable, men. Rest assured, there will be no one here to witness it."

Without taking my gaze from the advancing officers, I unshouldered my satchel, reached for where I'd set my cane—and swiped air. When Snodgrass turned and stepped into the hallway I saw that he'd hidden my cane behind his back. *That son of a...* Grinning, he balanced my cane on an index finger and closed the door behind him. I retrained my focus on the advancing officers and tried to summon my wizard's voice.

"Look guys," I stammered, "you need to let me explain."

"Explain it to Charlie Dumars," the lead officer said, his voice low and steely. "Or how about Eddie Gleeson, Don Whitley, T Bone Jones. Explain it to the thirty-two others you murdered."

"I underestimated the threat," I admitted, backing away from them. "I screwed up. But not in the way it's being spun."

"Shut him up," the lead officer ordered.

The two flanking officers raised their batons and rushed forward.

22

Raw energy crackling against my prism, I aimed my palms toward the advancing officers, squinted my eyes—and at the last second, covered my head. Without my cane, I didn't have control. I could maim the officers, or worse. God knew, I didn't need more dead NYPD on my conscience. And it would make me look guilty, putting the remaining officers in the city on shoot-to-kill orders.

I would take my lumps, play possum, and then determine a non-lethal way out of this.

I squinted up as the officers descended on me.

Maybe easier said than done.

The first baton blow cracked my right forearm, the pain

shooting all the way to my shoulder. The second baton caught me across the diaphragm. The air left my lungs in a nauseating grunt. I dropped to my knees and folded over, arms wrapping my head.

The batons rained down on my back in deep, thudding blows.

Stay conscious, Everson, I thought through gritted teeth.

"Stop!" a woman shouted.

The blows tapered, then ceased. I fell to my side, my body one big, throbbing slab of pain. I could hear the officers breathing heavily as limping footsteps entered the classroom.

"I want three minutes with him," the woman said, "then he's all yours again."

I looked up, half-expecting to see a recovered Penny, but I found Detective Vega instead. Hardly a *whew* moment. Vega glared down at me, her lips a trembling line.

When the officers didn't move, she barked, *"Alone."*

The sharpness of the command got them moving. They filed out into the hallway, shutting the door behind them.

"Oh, c'mon," I grunted through the pain. "You don't believe that horseshit in the paper."

"You don't speak unless I tell you to." She drew her pistol and aimed it at my head. "On your feet."

"Apparently you do," I muttered.

"I'm not going to ask you again," she said.

"Oh, was that a request?"

Using the seat of a nearby desk, I pushed myself to one knee and then up to my feet. Amoeba-like spots swam over my vision. When they receded, Vega had stepped closer. She was wearing one of her all-black suits, a metal brace bracketing her right knee. Her knuckles were white around her pistol grip. I'd seen her angry before, but this seemed different, worse.

"You're a fucking liar," she said.

"Do I have permission to speak now?"

"You told me you weren't working with the blood-suckers, and you're neck deep in them."

"Your proof?"

"And *I'm* the one who vouched for you, you piece of shit."

"Exactly," I said, anger breaking through my voice. "So how in the hell could I be a plant?"

"I swear to God, I could kill you right now."

"Really?" I staggered back from her thrusting pistol, my palms showing. I glanced past her to my classroom door, where the officers were peering in through the mesh window. I half considered waving the three inside to resume beating me—I liked my chances better with them—but with my next stumbling step backwards, I was beyond their view.

"I'd be doing this city a favor," Vega went on.

"You're a detective," I said. "Exercise some logic, for Christ's sake. If I'd wanted the Hundred decimated, why did I risk my neck to get them out of the park? Why would I—"

"Shut up!" she shouted. But her eyes were suddenly out of sync with her voice. They seemed to soften as they cut to my right.

"Huh?"

"Shut it, I said!" Louder, and with the same eye motion.

I peeked over my shoulder. The window. Vega had steered me into the corner and out of sight of the officers for a reason. When I looked back at her, she nodded once, eyes insistent. I reached back and thumbed the latch open. That she didn't shoot told me I'd read her intentions correctly.

"You don't get it!" she shouted, clearly for the officers to hear. "You're scum to me! You're nothing!"

"Thank you," I said, and slid the window up.

"I can buy you a minute," she whispered. "No more."

I threw a leg out and, ducking beneath the raised window, brought the other leg out until I was sitting on the sill. I looked down at the one-story drop into an alley that ran behind the college.

"Vega, I…"

"Don't make me regret this," she whispered, and gave me a shove.

I plummeted the ten feet, arms pinwheeling. The instant my feet contacted ground, I folded my knees and crashed onto my side. Despite the pain, I was up quickly. I tilted my face to where Vega resumed yelling at the spot where I'd been standing, carrying on the charade.

She was risking a lot to give me a head start, God love her.

I took off at a shambling run down the alleyway. I needed to make every second count.

Paces from breaking out onto Forty-fifth Street I realized my disguise was still in my pocket. I stuttered to a stop, strapped the dark-brown beard around my head, and pushed on my sunglasses. I then peered around the corner. Several police cruisers were parked along the side of the college. More would be rushing in soon. I needed a better disguise.

I spotted an aging wino squatting in the alcove of a shuttered business, flies buzzing around his fishing hat. Despite the summer heat, he was wrapped in a dirty brown topcoat. Bingo. I just hoped he'd socked away enough brain cells to perform a simple transaction.

"Hey," I said, jogging towards him.

The rim of his stained fishing hat tilted up, and a whiskered face squinted from the shade.

"How much for the hat and coat?" I asked.

"How much ya got?" he asked back.

"How about a twenty?" I fished the bill from my wallet.

He chuckled and shook his head.

"Seriously?" I said, looking at the soiled articles. "That's being *very* generous."

"What? I'm supposed to jump up and shuck my duds at the first whiff of money? I've got more dignity than that. Besides," he said, his eyes taking on a dangerous intelligence, "I know that panting voice. You're on the run, my friend. Meaning I'm not just providing you goods, but a service."

"Service?"

"You don't want me to squeal to the boys in blue, do you? Give them an up-to-date description?" He winked as a yellow smile appeared inside his whiskers. "So let me ask you again. How much ya got?"

I swore as I leafed through my wallet. "About one-forty," I muttered.

He snatched the sheaf of bills, stuffed them away, and then shed his coat with exaggerated care. I looked over my shoulder, an anxious pressure ballooning my bladder. My minute was almost up.

"C'mon, already," I said, shifting from one foot to the other.

The man stood and insisted on helping me into the coat—an act he also performed as if he had all week. Finally, he pried his hat from an oily pile of hair and pressed it down over my head.

He looked me up and down. "Out of this world!"

"Yeah, I was thinking the same," I said, but referring to the coat's god-awful stench. "Hey, could you see it in your heart to give me back a twenty? I don't have anything for cab fare."

"Read the fine print." He clapped my shoulder three times. "All transactions final."

My face burned at the man's laughter, but I didn't have time to argue. A block behind me, shouts were breaking from Midtown College, and I knew what that meant. Without turning, I assumed the staggering walk of the homeless. Plenty of those in Midtown, which was unfortunate for them, but very fortunate for me. The police would be looking for a professor.

"Good luck," the man called after me, and laughed some more.

23

Police cars crawled past, canvassing the streets around the college. I continued my shuffling walk, eyes alert behind my sunglasses for signs of danger—such as the pair of officers up ahead, sticking their heads into businesses and taking a close look at the foot traffic.

Can't appear alarmed, I thought, my pulse racing. *Have to keep walking.*

When the officers were almost to me, I staggered toward a man in business attire and petitioned him for change. The man grumbled, and a quarter landed in my palm. The police officers glanced at the exchange but kept walking. I needed to get the hell out of Midtown.

But where to go?

I squeezed the quarter as I considered my options. The apartment was out; NYPD would be all over the building. Thankfully, Tabitha would be okay on her own for a few days. She couldn't get into the fridge, but she'd be able to access the pantry and run the water taps. Worst case, there were pigeons. She wouldn't be happy about it, but she'd survive.

I shuffled through a short list of alternate destinations.

The East Village again? I shook my head. The abandoned buildings might hide me from mobsters but not from a determined police force that numbered in the tens of thousands. That went for any of the crumbling neighborhoods. I didn't just need a hiding place this time; I needed protection.

I considered the two who had already offered me safe houses: Caroline and Arnaud.

I hated both options, frankly. The fae townhouse in the Upper East Side was closer, about thirty blocks north, but there was the *Gazette* article. If the fae had been the source of the fabricated story, regardless of Caroline's role, I wouldn't find safe haven among them now.

That left Arnaud and his fortified Financial District.

I swore at the fact I was even considering him. That would be another awful move, though. Besides the fact that Arnaud would only protect me to the extent he could use me, running to the vampires would slap a "guilty" moniker beside my name and ring it in bright red lights.

No, there had to be a third option.

More police cruisers appeared. Another foot patrol hurried along the sidewalk across the street from me. I continued my homeless shuffle, pausing to paw through a trashcan. Far down the valley of buildings, the smoky sky opened over the Hudson River, New Jersey on its far shore.

Something Chicory had told me years before suddenly came back.

If you need to flee the city for any reason, he'd said, *there's a spot on Gehr Place, just over the river. Little blue house on a short street. You can't miss it.* Chicory didn't elaborate other than to say the house was to be used in life or death situations only. This seemed to meet that requirement.

To get there, though, I'd need money.

I looked at the quarter I'd been handed. Well short of cab fare, but for a bus through the Lincoln Tunnel I'd only need a dollar fifty more. I knew where a stop was, too. Tacking north and west, I petitioned more pedestrians. Two blocks later, I had enough—and just as a Jersey-bound bus was pulling up to the stop.

Thank God.

I hurried toward the bus and boarded, two foot patrols converging on the sidewalk behind me.

I took a seat near the bus's rear door and looked out the grimy window. The police officers stopped to talk. A couple of them pointed back toward the east. With a grunt, the bus pulled from the stop in the opposite direction. I snuck a look around. The handful of passengers jouncing in their seats weren't interested in me. I relaxed back into the fumes of my coat.

Almost home free, I thought. *Thanks to Vega.*

She must have seen I was being set up and rushed to the college to beat the police there, probably after trying me at my apartment. When she found me in their custody, she had improvised, pretending to want some one-on-one time to tear into me. And, man, had she sold it.

If I ever got out of this, I owed that woman. Big time.

Right now, though, I had to consider my next move. After Chicory had told me about the house, I'd located Gehr Place on a map. I pulled up the mental equivalent. *Should be easy enough to reach,* I thought, working out the route for when I got off the bus. *Then I'll find the blue house and see what's what.* I couldn't imagine the Order would be upset. I had received permission from Chicory to participate in the eradication program, after all. The lie about working with the vampires could hardly be blamed on me. Then again, we were talking about the Order.

"Oh, fer chrissake," the bus driver complained above the sharp hiss of air brakes.

Seizing the pole beside me, I rose and peered out the front window. We had just crossed Seventh Avenue, and for the next block and a half, red brake lights stared back at us through the smoke. I peered beyond the backup and felt my heart climb into my throat. The police had set up a checkpoint.

I blew out a hard sigh. *Of course they did.*

Up ahead, officers were interrogating drivers and opening trunks and van doors. I pictured a large cordon around Midtown, the college at the epicenter. Probably had the subway stations manned as well.

But that wasn't the worst part.

As the bus inched forward, I could make out the uniforms of government security guards. The frigging werewolves were in on the hunt. Which meant that no matter how good my disguise or how foul smelling my coat, I wouldn't escape their detection. I had to get off. Now.

I pulled the yellow bell cord. A sharp ding sounded. When the driver didn't stop, I yanked the cord twice more.

"Heard you the first time, pal," he growled. "The stop isn't for another block."

"Here's fine," I insisted.

"Can't do it."

Another block would put me too close to the checkpoint. And depending on which way the wind was blowing... Crap. Outside my window, the triangular flaps from a theater awning were batting westward. If I disembarked any nearer, the wolves would definitely pick up my scent.

I slapped at the back door. "C'mon, man. I've gotta go."

"Cross your legs and clench."

Several passengers chuckled at the driver's quip, but it gave me an idea.

"Fine," I said, pretending to unbuckle my pants as I squatted. "It's your mess."

The ruse worked. The driver's eyes started in the rearview mirror, and he stomped the brakes. The back door flopped open. I wasted no time jumping from the bus, the driver's colorful threats trailing after me.

I waited until I was halfway down the block before peeking over a shoulder. At the checkpoint, one of the wolves had straightened from a car he'd been inspecting. His head was tilted back in a sniffing posture. Through the smoke and exhaust, a slip of my scent had reached him.

Swearing, I hastened my pace.

At the far end of the block, I spotted the four officers I'd seen from the bus. They were turning back in my direction, one of them speaking into his shoulder mike. Wonderful. The werewolf must have radioed to tell them I was near. I slowed as more officers appeared. They were stopping pedestrians now, herding everyone toward the checkpoint with shouts and pistol motions.

Several officers remained behind to watch buildings—no doubt until a wolf arrived to clear them. I took a hard right into a Korean grocery store. There would be a rear exit, maybe an alleyway, a fence I could jump. But I had barely made it past a stand of colorful snack bags when a squat woman charged from behind the register and blocked my way.

"You leave!" she shouted up at me. "No steal food!"

My disguise was a little *too* good, apparently. "No, no, I'm not here to take anything. I just wanted to see if you have a back door." My hope was to slip out before the officers could cover the rear of the building. I pointed past the woman and spoke slowly. "Back door?"

"No steal food!" she repeated, jabbing me in the stomach with a pair of fingers.

"Hey! Ow!"

All right, this wasn't working. Not wanting to draw any more attention, I retreated back onto the sidewalk. To one side of me, the police were continuing to drive the crowd forward. On the other, two wolves were approaching from the checkpoint, closing in on my scent. No way I'd be able to challenge them without my staff and sword.

Trapped mid block, I dug an arm into a trashcan, pretending to look for food. My thoughts scrambled madly. The second a wolf got close enough to ID me, I'd be grabbed. And given the severity of the accusations, the best I could hope for was life without parole.

Assuming I wasn't torn apart.

Need to calm down, I thought above my pounding heart. *Need to think.*

Shoes clanged over metal as the first wave of distressed pedestrians moved past, the herding officers at their rear.

I honed in on the clanging sound.

There's my escape.

I yanked my arm from the trashcan. Using the pedestrians as cover, I stayed low and wended my way toward the noise. Soon, a rectangular opening in the sidewalk appeared, covered by sections of metal grating. The final section rattled under the growing footfalls.

I hustled ahead of the barking calls of the officers, shouldered several pedestrians aside, and pulled the grate free. A few complaints went up around me, but I was quickly inside and hanging from a shelf beneath the lip of the opening. I pulled the grating back into place and looked down between my dangling feet. It was a decent drop, about twenty feet to the tracks below, but it could have been worse. Some of the holes went down five stories.

Still, going underground was going underground—something I hated worse than tax time. A pressure was already building against my chest, thinning my breaths. I closed my eyes.

Let's just hope a train isn't coming, I thought, and let go.

I swung my arms around until my palms were aimed at the up-rushing ground and shouted, *"Vigore!"*

Energy ripped through me and hit the ground with enough force to stall my descent. I landed in a crouch as though I'd only dropped five feet, pocketed my beard and sunglasses, and peered up at the shadows passing over the grate. One of the shadows stopped. A light glared and swept across my face.

"Hey!" an officer shouted. "Stay right there!"

Great, some goody two shoes must've alerted them to my plunge.

I hurried down the tracks until I was out of view of the grate. Jumping the thrumming third rail, I climbed onto a service walkway that paralleled the tracks. The tunnel stretched north and south into blackness.

I dug through the bum's coat pockets, hoping to find a lighter, but all I came up with was a sizeable collection of cigarette butts and a Honey Bun wrapper. That left my coin pendant. I loosened the coat and unbuttoned my shirt until the pendant dangled into view.

"Illuminare," I said.

Energy crackled around the coin. Moments later, a soft blue light suffused it, illuminating the space for several feet ahead of me.

I took a moment to get my bearings. That the rail was active told me I was in the Seventh Avenue line. Unfortunately it didn't feature any branches to Jersey. None of the subway lines did. Meaning I could either head north, in the direction of the Bronx, or south, toward lower Manhattan. I grimaced at the thought of entering Arnaud's district before understanding I wouldn't get that far, even if I wanted to. My pursuers knew I was down here. At this moment, officers would be descending into the stations on both sides of me, hemming me in.

As if to affirm the claustrophobic thought, to the north flashlights beams swam against a distant bend in the tunnel.

Adrenaline screaming through my body, I dimmed the light in the coin pendant and hurried south along the walkway. There were no light beams coming from the tunnel ahead of me—yet. But if wolves had joined the posse at my back, they would be on me in short time.

Think, Croft. Think goddammit.

The defunct Broadway line was only a block or so to the east of me, the stations all barricaded. If only I could find some way to—

There!

A metal door appeared in the wall to my left. I pulled the handle, surprised when a crust of rust broke off and the door swung open. A service tunnel plunged into darkness. I scooted inside and closed the door as a powerful flashlight beam shot past. The south-bound team had arrived.

I broke into a run, faded graffiti art on the tunnel's brickwork whizzing past. I'd gone about a hundred feet when a cinderblock wall reared up in front of me.

Wha—?

I got my arms up a split second before impact. The violent rebound threw me onto my back, head cracking against the floor. Stars wheeled around my staring gaze. I struggled into a kneeling position, then stood, catching myself against the wall. The cinderblocks glowed gray-blue in the light of my coin. When the Transit Authority had closed the Broadway line, they'd apparently sealed off all of the access tunnels. That could be remedied. Aiming my palms at the wall, I called power to my prism—or tried to. The collision had shrouded it in fog. I began a rapid centering chant to restore my ability to cast.

I didn't get very far. A deep growl rumbled behind me.

I spun, the mantra breaking off. A second growl sounded, this one from a different body. Down the tunnel, two sets of eyes shone into view, their orange irises fiery with anger.

Beyond them, a small army of footsteps echoed toward the service tunnel entrance. I pressed my back to the wall like a cornered cat and squinted as a flashlight beam hit me in the eyes.

"We've got him!" an officer shouted.

24

With one hand blocking the flashlight beam, I could make out the advancing werewolves. They were still in human form, but the chase had aroused their lupine natures. Beneath wrinkling nostrils, lips peeled from fanged teeth. Muscles bulged underneath their uniforms.

Just need some time, I thought.

Summoning what meager power I could to my wizard's voice, I shouted, "Stop!"

The wolves hesitated, startled more than enthralled, it seemed. Without taking my eyes off them, I removed my necklace, palming the large coin pendant, which continued to glow a pale blue, and held it out in front of me.

"This is silver," I lied, the iron cold in my grip. "If I cast through it, it will burn you alive."

When the wolves' nostrils flared, I drew the coin back inside the bouquet of my coat to cloak its scent. The wolves would pick out the iron eventually, but not before my prism was restored.

I hoped.

"I don't want to hurt anyone," I said. "I just want to negotiate the terms of my surrender." The pressure of being underground was stifling my voice, stealing its power. The words themselves would have to convince them.

"We don't negotiate with cop-killing pieces of shit," someone called back.

"Yeah, how about we just stick a few bullets between your eyes?" someone else put in.

I squinted toward the multiplying beams of light. Though I couldn't see the police officers holding the flashlights, it wasn't hard to imagine their hostile faces—or the guns they were aiming. If the wolves and NYPD had something in common, it was their belief that I had willfully murdered members of their brotherhood. Like blood spreading through water, a scarlet aura of vengeance united them. I would have to tread really damned carefully.

"I just have one request for my surrender," I said.

"Lower your weapon!" an officer ordered.

"That Detective Hoffman make the arrest," I persisted.

There was nothing special about Detective Hoffman. He just happened to be one of the few officers I knew by name, other than Vega. And I didn't want to get Vega any more involved than she already was. Requesting Hoffman was a stalling tactic, something to buy me a precious minute or two.

"We're not gonna warn you again, Croft! Lower your fucking weapon and get on the ground!"

I could practically feel the tension on their triggers.

I swallowed. "Just contact him, let me know he's on the way, and I'll do everything you say, I promise. No one gets hurt."

The wolves growled in the silence that followed. Like the officers, they had heard rumors of my powers, the feats I was capable of. Publicity had its perks. It was this more than anything, I suspected, that held them at bay. If they knew how defenseless I was, my face would've been eating concrete by now. I blinked sweat from my lashes as I chanted softly and awaited the verdict.

Hopefully it wouldn't come in the form of a firing squad.

The officers must have been consulting in whispers because one of them finally said, "We're calling him now."

My legs buckled in relief, but I steeled myself. I still had work to do. I closed my eyes to the wolves, the flashlight beams—pushed them to the back of my thoughts—and returned to my training with Lazlo.

This may be the most important lesson I ever teach you, my first teacher had said. *If you lose your prism, you must retain your focus. A wizard who cannot cast is a dead wizard.*

I remembered the way Lazlo's cloudy, wolf-torn eye had stared into mine.

In the tunnels beneath New York, I whispered and re-whispered the centering mantra.

Deep in my mind, the prism vibrated. Power eddied through my body. I repeated the chant until the prism's contours appeared through the fog, glowing as they returning to form.

"Hoffman's on the way," an officer barked. "Now surrender

your weapon and get facedown on the floor, like you promised." The flashlights advanced above a careful procession of footsteps.

I watched the wolves stalk closer too, the lead one sniffing the air.

"He's not packing silver," he growled, his advance becoming more confident.

The wolves were fifteen feet from me now, close enough that I could see follicles of hair growing from their foreheads and jowls. They couldn't hold their wolves inside any longer. The hunger for pack justice was too powerful.

A little closer... I thought.

"I'm warning you, Croft," an officer said.

I extended the coin out in front of me, its edges crackling with blue light.

"On my order," I caught the same officer mutter.

It had to be now.

"Illuminare!" I bellowed.

The energy that stormed through my restored prism emerged from the coin as a dazzling explosion of light. For an instant, the tunnel turned bright white. The wolves recoiled with snarling cries. I could see the officers now—eight of them—arms thrown to their faces.

A shot went off, ricocheting from the wall to my left.

"Vigore!" I cried.

Power branched from my other palm and slammed into the wolves. They cannoned into the officers behind them, flipping them like bowling pins. When they landed, several officers pawed around for their weapons, stunned and blinded. The men were harmless as long as they remained that way. The wolves, with their senses of hearing and smell, were another story. I spotted the two staggering onto their hands and feet, more wolf now than human.

Replacing the coin around my neck, I turned and pressed both hands to the wall.

"Forza dura!" I shouted.

In an explosion of mortar, the wall toppled away. I scrambled over the collapse and into the sewer-like stench of the Broadway line. Following the successful operation two weeks before, armed teams had swept the lines and destroyed the handful of remaining ghouls. Restoration work had already begun. I emerged through the dust to find a string of lights running along the tunnel above step ladders and large bundles of electrical wire. No workers, fortunately.

I dropped onto the tracks. A few blocks to the north, lights glowed where the Broadway line shared the Forty-Second Street station with the Seventh Avenue line. The station was inside the cordon and could still be manned by police. I sidestepped away from it and broke into a run.

I'd have to take my chances south.

My plan was to go about fifteen, twenty blocks, then climb one of the emergency staircases located halfway between stations. I'd blow open the hatch beneath the sidewalk and try to blend into the street scene, somewhere in the Twenties. From there, I'd work my way south and west toward the piers with Jersey-bound ferries. The last step—catching a boat—would be the most difficult, but I'd worry about that when I got there. Which was feeling far from certain.

It was my phobia, dammit. After only a hundred yards, my lungs were already heaving for air. My chest wasn't allowing enough oxygen in or poisonous Co_2 out.

Growls sounded from the service tunnel behind me.

And then there was the matter of the werewolves.

I'd read about the effects of bright lights on their brain synapses and had been counting on a longer recovery time. Now I listened in horror to the sounds of cinderblocks grating and toppling. So much for that theory. The wolves had just joined me in the line.

Ahead, a door to an emergency staircase appeared, but I was still inside the cordon. If any of the downed officers had recovered enough to radio out, the street would be covered. I shed my coat— the lion's share of my disguise—and slung it in front of the door. With any luck, the wolves would stop and sniff it and then expend time deciding whether or not I'd ascended.

I ran on. With each gasping breath, a cramp gored my side; spots danced around my vision. From around a bend, the yellow lights of another station glowed into view. *Crap.* I was coming up on Thirty-fourth Street, a station the Broadway line shared with an intersecting line.

But as I started to slow, I spotted a parked vehicle ahead.

What in the...?

The vehicle pointing away from me looked like a cross between a large dune buggy and a truck. A flatbed hitched to its back was loaded with equipment. I took quick stock of the large tires balancing the vehicle on the tracks, two sets of smaller metal wheels in place to keep it from derailing. It was an MTA maintenance vehicle, no doubt parked outside the station for easy access. Someone had spray-painted BERTHA on the side of the truck in big balloon letters.

A set of keys dangled from Bertha's ignition.

Oh, hell yes.

Heart slamming, I climbed through the crash bars and slid behind the steering wheel. Behind me I could hear clawed feet pounding the tracks. The smelly coat hadn't fooled the wolves. I seized the key in the ignition, said a quick prayer, and gave a twist.

No response.

"Oh, Bertha, please don't do this to me."

I could hear the wolves' harsh panting now, echoing down the tunnel.

I looked around the cab for something I might have missed. The automatic gearshift beside my right leg was slotted in Drive. I pushed it to Park and twisted the key again. Bertha's engine chug-a-lugged for several agonizing seconds before turning over with a throaty roar.

"Yes!"

I yanked the gearshift into Drive and pressed the gas. The metal wheels whined against the rails, and Bertha rumbled forward. I waited for the speedometer to edge past twenty before allowing myself a glimpse into the truck's side mirror. For a blessed instant, the tunnel curving away behind me was empty.

And then it wasn't.

The two wolves, in full wolf form, were speeding toward me like they were on a greyhound track, eyes burning with the hunt. In comparison, I felt like I was moving through thick mud.

"C'mon, c'mon, c'mon," I pled, putting more weight on the gas pedal, which was already to the floor.

The needle trembled to thirty, the vehicle rumbling as if it were going uphill. It was the load. Bertha was pulling several hundred pounds of equipment. I turned around, craning my neck to see the hitch to the trailer. I might have tried to crack it with a focused force blast, but without my cane, I'd be more likely to derail both truck and trailer.

I straightened and looked into the side mirror again.

The wolves were closer, tongues lolling as their huge paws slammed the crossties.

Bertha continued its sluggish acceleration into the yellow lights of the Thirty-fourth Street station. The columned landing was empty. From one story up, where the Sixth Avenue line ran, I could hear the dull echoes of a PA system and the din of commuters.

Shouts rang out: "There he is!" "Stop right there, Croft!"

NYPD officers were pounding down a stairwell and leaping busted turnstiles. I ducked low as I passed them. Shots popped off, flashing from the hood of the truck. I was almost clear of the station when a hard explosion rocked me. Bertha wobbled and canted left. A metallic keening sounded. In the side mirror I caught sparks spitting from her lower body.

Damn, they blew a tire.

The speedometer, which had been creeping up to forty miles per hour thudded back to the low thirties. Behind me, the wolves began to gain. Up ahead, NYPD officers would no doubt be scrambling to head me off. There was no going up an emergency staircase now, no making my way to the piers jutting into the Hudson. The New Jersey plan was scrapped.

That leaves the vampires, I thought grimly.

Fleeing to them would make me look guiltier than sin, yeah, but when the alternative was death...

Problem was, I was three miles from the Wall Street station. Not only that, I didn't know what I would find when I got there.

Given the vampires' vast security apparatus, I had to assume they'd barricaded the station to prevent infiltration from below. But I had a more immediate problem.

In the upcoming station, an assortment of abandoned maintenance vehicles were clogging the tracks. I was on a collision course.

I stood and aimed a hand at them. *"Vigore!"*

Hot energy erupted from my palm. The vehicles capsized in a wave, derailed, but now littering the track. Seizing Bertha's steering wheel in both hands, I ducked low as her large front fender plowed into the pile-up. Metal banged and whined. I braced for derailment, but Bertha held on like a champ, her mass heaving us through to the other side of the mess. The blown wheel in back clunked as I depressed the accelerator and urged us back up to speed.

In the rearview mirror, the wolves had arrived at the downed vehicles and begun leaping them. Something on one of the upturned trucks caught my eye: a cylindrical gas tank.

There she blows, I thought.

Bertha decelerated as I climbed onto the crash bars. Over the top of the equipment that rocked and jostled on the flatbed, I lined up my right palm with the tank and yelled, *"Forza dura!"*

The force of the invocation threw me back into the cab. Reclaiming the steering wheel, I peered into the side mirror. The vehicles had been blown skyward in a wave and were now crashing down. From inside the cacophony, a wolf yelped.

Should slow them, but I missed the damn tank.

The thought had barely formed when a white flash appeared amid the wreckage followed by a deafening detonation. An orange fireball swallowed the thrown vehicles and stormed down the tunnel. I crouched as it roared past, flames searing my arms and hunched-over back. I held my breath to the strangling heat while slapping out a small fire atop my hat.

After a moment, the flames receded along with the piteous cries of the wolves. With a choked gasp, I inhaled the stench of burning diesel and focused on the tracks ahead. They switched here and there, throwing us from local to express tracks and back. I had no control over the switches, just the steering to ensure Bertha's rubber tires remained aligned with the rails.

It was a matter now of staying the course.

The next station was empty as well as the one after that. I had no way of knowing what was happening above ground, but my guess was that the NYPD, having sent the bulk of its force to Midtown, was now struggling to get officers into the Broadway line south of me, where many of the entrances remained sealed. If that held, and with the wolves no longer in pursuit, my chances of reaching Arnaud's district were starting to look decent.

I checked the speedometer and then my watch. At our current speed, we'd be at the Wall Street station in under five.

As the seconds ticked by, my body felt like an exposed nerve. I marked off each station. *Prince Street … Canal Street*. The upcoming station was City Hall, which, two weeks before, had been the ghoul crematorium. The station had yet to be cleaned out. Bertha bumped over heaps of charred bones and through drifts of ash, the particles billowing up into the headlight beams.

I coughed as we thudded onward.

Only two stations from Wall Street. As Bertha rumbled through the Fulton Street stop, I rose from my seat to get a better look at the tunnel ahead. It ran around a bend, straightened, and then...

"Oh, shit."

I slammed the brakes hard. Too hard. The load in the flatbed trailer pushed against Bertha's rear, displacing the tires and metal wheels from the rails. I fought with the steering, but there was no correcting it. The truck and trailer jackknifed. I used the crash bars to brace myself as we capsized.

Bertha crashed and came to a sudden rest on her side. I'd managed to stay inside the cab, shocked but not hurt. I craned my neck to peer down the tracks. One of Bertha's headlights illuminated what I'd seen a moment before: an imposing steel wall and a line of government security guards standing in front of it. Their eyes glowed above their aimed pistols.

Distant commands sounded behind me—NYPD officers entering from the Fulton Street Station. Crackling power rushed to my prism, but I held back. The second I cast, I'd be shot dead.

"Yeah, yeah," I said tiredly, showing my hands. "I surrender."

"Music to my ears," a familiar voice said from the wolves. It was Flint, one of the wolves who had decked me in the West Village. On the outer edge of Bertha's light, his lupine teeth flashed. If his brother was among the dozen-odd wolves stalking toward me I couldn't see him.

"Where's Tweedledum?" I asked.

"I'd be worrying about yourself right now," Flint said with a snort. "I don't get you, Croft. You had official protection. Why'd your dumb ass throw it away? What'd the vamps promise you?"

"Nothing," I growled. "It's a goddamned lie."

"But at the first sign of heat, look where you ran." He glanced around. We must have been at Liberty Street. Aboveground—and below ground too, evidently—stood the forbidding Wall.

"Like I had a choice," I said. "The mayor's office planted that story about me. But you probably already know that."

"All I know are my orders."

"To bring me in?"

His delayed response told me everything. "Yeah, to bring you in."

I was being thrown to the wolves. Literally. Flint stepped forward, reached down, and seized my arm. His grip was crushing. I hooked an elbow around one of the crash bars and grabbed my wrist with the other hand.

"Let go," he ordered.

"No."

He would pry me away eventually, but my powers needed time to recharge. Then I'd figure out how in the hell to use them. I braced for a shoulder-dislocating jerk, but Flint's grip relaxed. He raised his face and sniffed. I noticed some of the other wolves doing the same.

Flint was opening his mouth when automatic gunfire broke from the tunnel behind me. Wolves shouted and went down, smoke blowing from their wounds. Silver rounds.

A spray of blood hit me across the face. Flint released me, seizing his throat as he fell.

Within seconds, it was over. Pounding boots replaced gunfire. Men in body armor appeared, wrestled me from the toppled maintenance vehicle, and began running me toward the steel barrier. They weren't NYPD, which the wolves had realized too late. I recognized them as members of the vampires' private security force, the ones who guarded the Wall.

Behind me, single shots cracked as the mercenaries finished off the survivors.

Hydraulics sounded, and the steel barrier shuddered and rose. The guards hustled me into a corridor, the tracks replaced by cement flooring. After a couple of turns, we stopped in front of an elevator door. I stared at my dazed and blood-spattered reflection in the metal, dimly aware I'd lost my fishing hat.

The doors slid open, and my mirror image was replaced by a familiar figure. Immaculate, pale-faced, and featuring short, straight bangs, the blood slave flashed a wicked grin.

"Welcome to the Financial District, Mr. Croft," Zarko said. "Mr. Thorne has been expecting you."

25

Still stunned from the chase, I rode the elevator with Arnaud's head blood slave in a buzzing silence. It was only when the doors opened on the top floor, and Arnaud's musky scent whisked in on the icy, climate-controlled air, that I realized we were in the vampire's building.

Zarko led me down the hallway toward Arnaud's office. Well before we arrived at the forbidding double doors, however, the blood slave stopped and turned toward another office. Producing a key, he unlocked and pushed open the door to an executive-level suite.

"There's a washroom in back, where you'll find a change of clothes," he said.

"What do I need to change for?"

I followed his gaze down my front. My sweat-sodden shirt was half unbuttoned, the sleeves and stomach stained with soot from the tunnels. Grease smeared the thighs of my pants.

"A high-level meeting," Zarko answered.

"With Arnaud?"

He leaned forward just enough to give a single sniff. "You should avail yourself of the shower as well," he said before stepping back, bowing, and closing the door behind him.

Vampires and their decorum.

But Zarko was right; I smelled like a bag of garbage left out in the sun.

Inside the bathroom, I found a dark suit hanging from the door beside a huge walk-in shower. I stripped off everything except my amulet and turned the controls to hot. Steaming water washed over me. I soaped and rinsed while I chanted Words of healing, blood and the filth of the tunnels sliding into the drain.

The shower was restorative, but I kept a keen vigil on the locked bathroom door. I had escaped the NYPD and wolves, yeah, but I wasn't exactly safe. I was in the stronghold of a killer—and naked in more ways than one. I bore no ring, no silver, nothing to keep the vampires off me. If Arnaud decided he wanted me dead, I was dead. Simple as that.

That I was here at his invitation offered little comfort. He would protect me only as long as he could use me. I didn't know what he had in mind, but I had a feeling I was about to find out.

I cut the water and grabbed the towel hanging on the shower's back wall.

I also have a feeling I'm not going to like it.

"Mr. Croft," Arnaud said with exaggerated pleasantness.

He stood from the head of a long, coffin-shaped conference table. He wasn't alone. Eight other faces turned toward me. I recognized them from the news and covers of business magazines. They were the heads of New York's giant financial institutions. Unlike Arnaud, they wore dour suits, ties cinched to their throats. Like Arnaud, they were all vampires.

I stiffened as their hungry eyes fixed on me.

Arnaud opened a hand toward the empty chair at the other end of the table, directly opposite him. "Please," he said, "come in and join us." He nodded at Zarko to close the door.

I willed myself forward, hoping my tailored vicuña suit radiated the control and confidence I presently lacked. The vampires' predatory gazes followed me as I fumbled to pull the chair out and sit. I scooted forward with just as much clumsiness, then cleared my throat.

"Thank you," I said in a hard voice, which came out false-sounding.

"Several of you remember the wizard Asmus Croft, with whom we joined forces in Europe some centuries ago," Arnaud said, adjusting his earpiece as he sat again. "Everson Croft is his grandson. I've had the pleasure of his—how shall we say—*collaboration* in recent months. And here he is again."

To my right, a graying vampire with a lean undertaker's face made a noise of interest. He looked like a creature who lured children into alleyways with promises of candy, then stared, smiling, into their dimming eyes as he strangled the life from them. His cheeks began to dimple.

I quickly averted my gaze.

"Did I not anticipate this day, Mr. Croft?" Arnaud asked over his steepled fingers. Before I could answer, he directed himself to the others. "You see, when the poor boy and I last spoke, I told him that should we ever meet again, it would be because *he* had come to *me*." His eyes cut back to mine. "Mr. Croft was dubious."

The vampires sniggered in a way that said they knew well the stupidity of mortals.

"Fortunately for him, we were monitoring the encrypted police frequencies to know he had arrived at our doorstep. I also anticipated the developments taking place in the city, but we'll get to that in a moment. First, I want to make one thing clear. As long as Mr. Croft is here, he is under my protection."

He spoke the words as though staking a claim. I understood then that the suit I wore was more than a clean change of clothing. In vampire society, it was a mark of ownership.

I shifted, the silky fabric suddenly stifling.

Arnaud stared around the table. Each vampire nodded his understanding of the claim, some more reluctantly than others, it seemed—especially the undertaker vampire beside me. Harsh energies moved throughout the room. A reinforcement of hierarchy? I shifted again, my neck damp with sweat.

When at last the energy settled, Arnaud's gaze returned to me. I read the glint in his stare: *Do not test me, Mr. Croft, for I am the only thing keeping them from your wizard's blood.*

I nodded, hardly aware I was doing it.

"Now to the business at hand," he said, breaking his eyes from mine. "The day has come, gentlemen. With one hand, City Hall is prying away the financial ties that have kept the city in our debt, and with the other, it seeks to drive the proverbial stake through our chests."

"The blasted werewolves are behind it," the youngest-looking vampire seethed.

"Now, now, Damien," Arnaud said. "Let's not fall victim to reductionist thinking. The werewolves have a role, yes, but there are *many* forces at work. The election, the upcoming bailout, the war against supernaturals—indeed, we're facing a perfect storm. One that will wipe us out if we do not keep our heads."

"You don't think Penny has awakened?" Damien persisted.

When Arnaud replied, vehemence scored his voice. "Penelope Lowder is not our concern."

I considered the vampire's question. Had Penny recovered? Had *she* been the one to link me to the vampires? The idea had flickered through my mind back in my classroom. There was certainly motive, namely that I had almost killed her. And then there was the age-old enmity between werewolves and vampires, as well as a more recent enmity between Arnaud and Penny. He had rejected her as his mate, and hell hath no fury...

But something didn't jibe.

Maybe it was the thought of Penny recovering from a prolonged coma and going directly on the offensive. A campaign of this scale would take time to plan and prepare and with no assurance of success.

Unless she's been awake this whole time, I thought.

I looked around the table. Could the eradication program have been a pretext to a larger war between werewolves and vampires?

"And no, Penelope has not awakened," Arnaud said to Damien, killing my idea. "Do you think I am so foolish as to not be monitoring the situation? Regardless, the wolves see opportunity in our predicament. As do the fae. We are beset on all sides."

Though he'd brought the fae up, Arnaud didn't seem to suspect them of outing the vampires.

"Something to share, Mr. Croft?" he asked.

I couldn't think about the fae without thinking about Caroline. The idea that she may have played a role in my betrayal savaged my heart. Still, a competing instinct to protect her persisted. Sensing the emotions clashing inside me, Arnaud arched a slender eyebrow.

"No," I said quietly.

"Very well."

Arnaud dropped his gaze. I didn't realize a control pad was inset in the table above his lap until he tapped something. The paneled wall behind him rotated to become a large flat screen. The screen showed a satellite image of skyscraper-packed lower Manhattan, its northern boundary demarcated by the Wall. I noticed that the streets beyond the Wall had been cleared for several blocks, and...

I squinted forward. Was that a line of tanks?

"We are under siege," Arnaud confirmed. "Tanks rumble from the north. Attack helicopters circle the skies. Gunboats have yet to appear, but they're coming. Fortunately, we keep an impressive military stock of our own. Defensively, we have land, air, and sea covered."

Along the top of the zoomed-in Wall, members of the vampires' security force manned what appeared to be anti-tank missiles. On the roofs of skyscrapers, anti-aircraft guns swiveled, tracking the helicopters' movements. The waterfront was manned as well, it appeared.

"Feeling safer, Mr. Croft?" Arnaud asked.

"For right now, yeah," I admitted. "But we're cut off. Nothing comes in or goes out."

"If you're worried about sustenance, you needn't. My fellow executives and I have our associates." Arnaud was referring to the blood slaves, from whom they could feed indefinitely. "As for you, we have independent sources of energy and clean water, as well as a large store of nonperishable goods. While you're inside our district, you'll want for nothing."

But what do you *want?* I wondered.

Instead, I asked, "What about the supernaturals? The wolves and the fae?"

"We'll worry about them when the time comes," he said. "Though I do wish you would have brought your fellows. To take nothing away from you, Mr. Croft, but a dozen wizards are better than one."

Especially when that one wizard is essentially unarmed, I thought. Absent my staff, sword, and spell items, what power I wielded was wild and would deplete quickly. But I stuffed such worries away, not wanting Arnaud to pick up on them and decide I wasn't worth protecting.

"What's the end game?" I asked.

Before Arnaud could answer, the door to the conference room opened. I turned to find Zarko holding a phone.

"It's Mayor Lowder, sir," he said to Arnaud. "He would like to speak with you."

Arnaud nodded as though he'd been expecting the call. Zarko set the phone on the table in front of him and activated the handless feature. Arnaud rested an arm over the back of his chair and laced his fingers.

"I'm disappointed in you, Mayor," he said. "I took you at your word."

I realized he was talking about the deal he had struck with Budge in which the vampire had protected the mayor's stepdaughter in exchange for amnesty. A hedge, he'd called it.

"*You're* disappointed?" Budge shot back. "How do you think I feel when I find out the star of my program is in your pay, trying to sabotage everything?"

"Bunch of B.S.," I muttered, anger toward the fae coiling my insides.

Arnaud showed a hand. "If you're referring to young Mr. Croft, he was not working at my behest, I assure you. He was entirely in your service, his intentions quite golden, actually."

"Was that him I just heard in the background?" Budge asked.

"I won't deny his presence among us, but where else was he to have gone? It's not as though you left him a choice, sending the wolves after him. Do you think they would have listened patiently, chins on their paws, while he pled his innocence? Even you're not that obtuse, Mayor."

"Well, we've got a problem."

"It would appear so," Arnaud replied, picking at a talon as though his fortress wasn't under siege.

"I've got thirty-six men in the morgue, and a city convinced that, not only did Everson put them there, but that he's working for you. Oh yeah, and that you're all vampires."

"And why should that concern me?" Arnaud asked.

"Have you looked out your window lately?" Budge said, incredulous.

"I have, Mayor. But you and I both know that the charges are mostly falsehoods."

The phone's speaker hummed for several seconds, and I imagined the mayor consulting with someone off to the side. Caroline? At last, he cleared his throat and said, "We'll pull back if you give us Everson. While we deal with him, I'll, ah, work on putting out the vampire rumors."

Give us Everson, Budge was saying, *and war will be averted.*

I pinched the corners of my eyes with a finger and thumb, trying to piece together what was happening on the mayor's end. If Caroline was there advising him, was she trying to help me? Or would I be grabbed and thrown into a trial for public consumption? A trial seemed the logical next step in the fae's campaign. They had already aroused the city's sympathies and fears; now they could stoke a communal lust for justice—all to Budge's and the fae's benefit. The fae would get their preferred candidate and, using the vampire rumor as leverage against Arnaud, access to the lower portal. That may have been their plan all along.

One in which I'd served as unwitting pawn.

When I lowered my hand, Arnaud's fellow executives were watching me. Loathing hardened their unblinking eyes. I was a threat to their security. They wanted me gone. Could I blame them? If I was in their position, I'd no doubt want the same. And if turning myself in meant preventing a war in which innocents could be killed, maybe I didn't have a choice.

I cleared my dry throat, but Arnaud showed me his palm.

"I'm afraid I can't accede to your request, Mayor," he said.

I blinked in surprise. Several of the vampires hissed their protests.

"Why not?" the mayor demanded.

"Because I know a bluff when I hear one."

Budge let out an aggrieved sigh. "You're not leaving me much choice, then."

"I'll trust you to make the right call," Arnaud said. "Your city is depending on you."

Budge raised his voice. "Everson, if you're there—"

"Good day, Mayor," Arnaud said and disconnected the call. He signaled for Zarko to remove the phone from the conference room.

Around me, the vampires' protests grew into bat-like shrieks. Without warning, something slammed into me. I toppled backwards in my chair and landed hard against the floor. The young-looking vampire was on top of me, pupils shrinking inside bright yellow irises, spiny teeth sprouting from his gums.

"You'll get us killed!" he screamed, and lunged for my throat.

A fist knocked Damien off me. By the time I straightened, Arnaud had the vampire pinned high against the wall. "Did I not say the wizard was under my protection?" he seethed, an inch from Damien's twisting face. "Subvert my authority again, and you *will* be killed."

Arnaud tossed the vampire aside and returned to the head of the table.

Damien shuffled back to his own seat, grumbling but chastised. The remaining vampires stopped screeching, their eyes shifting between me and Arnaud.

"My apologies," Arnaud said as I stood and righted my chair. "My fellow executives are on edge, and perhaps understandably. There is much at stake. *However...*" He peered around the table. "...I know what I'm doing. The eradication program would eventually have included us all. That day has only been moved up, an opportunity we should be embracing, not wringing our hands over like Nervous Nellies. The city has no intention of sparing us and never did. So now comes the question." Arnaud leveled his eyes at me as I sat again. "Will you renew the Pact between our kinds and defend our rightful place in this city? Or will you bow to the fears and prejudices of humanity?"

His musky scent grew inside the room, making my heart slam harder. I raised my eyes to the satellite image. The gunboats Arnaud had mentioned earlier were rushing in to surround lower Manhattan.

"I need to know your endgame," I said.

"There's a fitting quote, Mr. Croft: 'War is the continuation of politics by other means.'" He gave an almost paternal smile. "Don't be fooled by the show of force. What's happening is nothing more than politics writ large. All we need do is force a stalemate. Make it so further engagement will be too costly for the mayor's reelection chances."

"So your strategy is purely defensive?" I asked to be sure.

"We've nothing to gain by attacking the city," he replied. "With a successful stand, we win by default. The mayor will have no choice but to seek a negotiated settlement. We may have to make a concession or two, yes, but we'll find the ground on which we presently stand more solid. And that would include you, Mr. Croft, for whom the ground underfoot must feel like quicksand."

"*Assuming* we're successful," I said.

"Trust me." Arnaud's eyes gleamed. "I've anticipated this day."

A sick shiver passed through me. *Trust me.* As if I could ever trust someone so vile. But something in his words carried me back to my final meeting with Lady Bastet. There had been a moment when the mystic had stared into me, her third eye probing some future horizon. And what was it she'd said when she'd returned? Trust in the one you trust least?

I lowered my gaze back to Arnaud.

The one I trusted least was right in front of me.

"I'll repeat my offer from the bar," Arnaud said.

He reached into his shirt pocket and held out a silver band. His yellowing talons scraped as he turned the signet around to face me. I stared at a rearing dragon. Grandpa's ring. He was offering to return it to me. All I had to do was renew the strategic alliance between our kinds.

Trust in the one you trust least.

I clenched my jaw. How in the hell could I trust a monster?

"What say you?" Arnaud pressed.

26

I eyed the ring Arnaud's blood slave had broken my finger to remove. Containing the power of the Brasov Pact, the ring was a deterrent against vampire aggression. If I renewed the Pact, that power would only be enhanced. Arnaud and his ilk wouldn't be able to touch me.

"The offer will not stand forever," Arnaud said.

My legs tensed, as though to stand and claim the ring, but the rational part of my mind resisted. Aligning with Arnaud might mean protection, but at what cost? I would be committing to a war against City Hall as well as the werewolves, maybe even the fae. And something told me it wouldn't play out as neatly as Arnaud was forecasting.

Trust in the one you trust least. Lady Bastet's remembered words again.

Around me, Arnaud's musk was strengthening, stoking my adrenaline. I was having trouble breathing. As the ring glinted out in front of me, I felt pressed in from all sides.

"I need to make a phone call," I blurted out.

"To whom?" Arnaud asked, watching me for a lie.

"Detective Vega."

"For what purpose?"

My gaze moved around the table. I couldn't reason in here. My thoughts were slamming together. I needed to know what was happening outside, and Vega would give it to me straight.

"Information," I answered.

"Look at the screen, Mr. Croft. There is all the information you need."

"It will only take a minute."

Arnaud closed his fist around the ring. "Very well," he said. "Through that door, you will find a small office with a phone. You have exactly one minute."

I stared at him, making sure I'd heard him right.

"Run along," he said. "The second hand is ticking."

I hurried through the door he'd indicated and closed it behind me. A conference phone sat on one end of a desk. For a moment I considered calling Caroline, but I doubted her offer to help me still stood. Besides, there was too much she hadn't told me, and I wasn't going to waste my one minute on more vagueness. I pulled Detective Vega's business card from my wallet and dialed her cell.

"Vega," she answered.

"Before you say anything, let me explain—"

"Croft," she whispered. "What in the hell are you doing?"

"I ended up at Arnaud's, yeah. But listen, listen, listen," I said over the expected outburst. "I didn't have a choice. The wolves caught my scent. I got trapped in the subway tunnels and had nowhere to go but downtown. His men grabbed me at the Wall." All true on the surface.

She was quiet for a moment. "You're okay?"

"For right now," I said. "How about you?"

"Yeah. Told the officers you kicked my gun away and jumped out the window. But what in the hell are you gonna do now?"

"How bad is it out there?" I asked.

"On a scale of one to ten? Twenty. We've got just about every piece of military equipment aimed at the Financial District. There are some in the chain who want to start blasting."

"Where are you?"

"Police Plaza … inactive duty because of my knee."

The acidic churning in my stomach abated slightly. Vega wouldn't be involved in any fighting. "The mayor made Arnaud an offer," I said. "Turn me over and he'll pull back, quash the vampire rumors."

Vega snorted. "Budge would have a better chance putting out a volcano with a bucket of water."

That was what I'd been afraid of.

"The story's already caught fire, huh?" I asked.

"Put it this way. If you're looking for a crucifix or bulb of garlic, every store in the five boroughs sold out this morning." She lowered her voice further. "And the government security guards, Croft. They're working with the NYPD in ways I've never seen."

"The werewolves," I muttered. "Who's in charge?"

"Hard to say. Cole is down at command-and-control, but this feels higher up the chain. I could try to—"

"No, no," I said, seeing where she was going. "You've already helped me enough."

She'd also given me the straight answers I needed. Arnaud was right, dammit. The city meant war.

"I don't know how to tell you this, Croft. But you're trapped."

"Yeah," I said, sighing. "I'm starting to see it that way too."

There was another pause on her end. "Listen," she said, "you make some really aggravating decisions sometimes, but you try to do right. I know what they're saying about you is bullshit."

I thought about how that aggravation ran both ways but was too touched by her words to say it.

"Thanks, Vega. That means a lot. Especially coming from you."

"Just—" she started, but the room shook and the line went dead.

"Vega?"

A growing rumble sounded outside, like thunder. I hung up and made my way back to the conference room. On the flat-screen television, a white cloud had appeared among the skyscrapers. An answering explosion sounded, and one of the helicopters burst into flames. It went down in Battery Park, creating another small plume. More shots thudded and boomed.

"The war has begun," Arnaud said. "It is now or never, Mr. Croft."

The vampires along both sides of the table were watching the screen in rapt attention. But opposite me, Arnaud was holding out the ring again.

"Hey, uh, shouldn't we get out of the top of the tower?" I said.

Arnaud didn't answer. His eyes sharpened and pressed into mine.

Trust in the one I least trusted? It wasn't like I had a goddamned choice anymore.

"All right," I said, my stomach in a nauseating fist. "I agree to renew the Pact."

Across Arnaud's lips, a smile clicked on and off. He set the ring flat on the table and slid it toward me. The ring bisected the eight vampires and came to a rest in front of me. I pushed it on. The ring fit as I'd remembered, squeezing the base of my middle finger. A chill energy coursed down my body, and I imagined it circling the room, binding us all in the agreement.

The conference room shook again.

"The mayor has made the opening move," Arnaud announced. "Phase one of the war has begun. Go now. Assemble your slaves. Be ready to mobilize them. This is for our very existence, gentlemen."

Arnaud spoke with the authority of a general. The vampires stood and filed from the room, the Undertaker's eyes lingering on me. My attention remained fixed on the screen. Several of the tanks were in flames, and two sections of the Wall appeared to be smoldering.

"Come, Mr. Croft," Arnaud said. "Let's go to my office for a live view."

Zarko appeared and opened the conference room door for us. I pulled my gaze from the screen and fell in behind Arnaud. We followed Zarko to the end of the hallway, where he opened the office door. As I stepped past him and onto the plush carpet, I thought about my two prior visits. The first time, Arnaud had nearly sunk his teeth into my throat before banning me from the

Financial District. The second time, he had coerced me into a deal that had led to Vega's son being imperiled.

Third time's a charm? I thought cynically.

I joined Arnaud beside the window that took up the far wall. Through the brown-tinted glass, we looked over the battlefield. Smoke billowed here and there, probably from artillery fire and downed helicopters. Along the Wall, automatic weapons popped. Gas jetted out as an antitank missile took flight. Its target, an armored vehicle rolling down Broadway, exploded in flames.

"Sadly, it's a recurring scene in our history," Arnaud remarked, as though watching a television documentary. "A city come to storm the fortress walls, to drive our kind from their midst. But that is the advantage of immortality, no? One eventually knows what to expect."

Zarko appeared with two glasses of scotch. I shook my head, but Arnaud accepted his glass and took a thoughtful sip. I looked over at him, incredulous. How could he be indulging at a time like this?

A helicopter chopped past our view, gunfire bursting from a pair of muzzles. I shouted and reared back.

Arnaud swirled his glass. "At ease, Mr. Croft. The windows are made of reinforced laminate. The building is similarly blast resistant. It would take several direct hits for us to become imperiled, and the city's forces presently have their hands full."

The helicopter appeared again, this time spiraling beneath a trail of black smoke. Below us, it collided into a neighboring skyscraper, fire mushrooming from the impact site.

I peered up at the sky. "What's to stop them from dropping a giant bomb?"

"Resources, for one. I doubt they have anything like that in their arsenal. Money, for another. It's already going to cost the mayor a pretty piece of his budget to restore Central Park. Now imagine having to rebuild lower Manhattan from the ground up. Not even the federal government will spot the city that kind of capital." City Hall was hidden by a cluster of intervening skyscrapers, but a wedge of its park peered out. By the tenting, I guessed there was some construction going on. "No, the initial assault is meant to punch some holes in our defenses in preparation for the next wave," Arnaud went on. "Ah, and here it comes."

I squinted past the Wall. Though I didn't possess Arnaud's preternatural vision, I could see the tide of foot soldiers racing down the north-south corridors. More than a hundred of them. And too fast to be humans.

"Werewolves?" I asked.

"I knew Penny was amassing an army before her untimely bullet wound, but I must applaud her ambition. She apparently got her hands on some enchanted item or other. A half wolf couldn't have managed this kind of loyalty otherwise."

Automatic fire popped from the Wall. The advancing wolves were undeterred, converging toward several sections of the Wall that looked to have been damaged by tank fire.

"You, ah, planned for this, right?" I asked.

"The wolves, yes," Arnaud said, taking another sip of scotch. "But not necessarily the numbers. We're looking at the population of much of New England. It seems we're going to be getting our hands dirty, after all." Without looking, he handed his half-empty glass over his shoulder, where Zarko was standing. "Come," he said to me. "You too, Zarko."

"Hey, uh, I'm sort of weaponless."

With Grandpa's ring secure on my finger, I was no longer so concerned about the vampires. Werewolves were another story. Arnaud stopped and looked me up and down.

"I may have something for you in the armory," he said.

"Armory?"

Without a word, he and Zarko sped from the office. I pursued them down the corridor and into the elevator. We descended and stepped into a bunker-like basement. I had to run to keep up as they traversed a long corridor. Another elevator carried us up a short distance.

We stepped out into a warehouse-sized space. Colonies of blood slaves moved among rows of storage shelves. They no longer wore business attire, but suits of glittering chainmail. Several carried medieval weapons. As though summoned, one of the blood slaves darted over and stopped in front of us, chainmail hugging his body like a second skin.

"Isn't it beautiful? Titanium-silver alloy." Arnaud ran his fingers across the blood slave's chest, which, along with the shoulders and neck of his suit, featured extra plating. I noted he was wearing a blue armband with the corporate logo for Chillington Capital. In his hands, the slave clasped a pair of punching daggers—also silver. "Neither of our kinds react well to the element," Arnaud went on, "but it is especially toxic to wolves. Imagine their shock when they seize this man by the throat. Zarko, be a dear and find a suit for our friend."

Zarko bowed in consent. "This way, Mr. Croft."

I followed him to an open dressing room with racks and racks of armor. Locker room-type benches crossed the space in rows. Zarko left and reappeared a moment later with a chain mail suit.

"I believe this is your size," he said.

I accepted the suit and stripped down to my shirt and boxers. The suit was cold going over my skin, but much lighter than I'd expected. Zarko turned me around several times, tugging the chainmail here and there, before securing the waist with a thick leather belt. I sat to don the chainmail shoes. When I stood again, I jogged in place and circled my arms a few times.

"Not bad," I said. "What about offense?"

Zarko led me to the other end of the room, past racks of conventional weapons, to a display case that stood apart from the others. "These belonged to wizards once," he said.

"Donations, I assume?"

I could feel Zarko's grin behind me as I peered down on the items. There were wands of various woods and sizes, which I immediately eliminated from consideration—they took too long to train. No amulets for me, either. God only knew what kinds of enchantments hid inside them. I moved down to the weapons. There were no sword canes, but my gaze lingered on a pair of maces. I opened the case's glass lid and picked one up. It was light in my grasp, easy to wield. I looked over the flanged metal head. Its ambient energy suggested silver in the alloy. Between the sharp edges were cloudy blue stones.

I held the mace away from me and said, *"Illuminare."*

The weapon stiffened in my grip as a new energy coursed through it. The stones glowed, dimmed, and then burst with blue light. With another Word, I willed the light into a shield. I moved the mace into various defensive positions, assessing the shield for strength.

After another moment, I nodded and dispersed it.

I reached into the case for the second mace, this one featuring a single blue stone at the weapon's apex. I looked from the stone to a blood slave trotting past in full armor.

"A test?" I asked Zarko.

"Very well," he replied.

I aimed the mace at the armored blood slave and shouted, *"Vigore!"*

Like with the other mace, this one took a moment to process the peculiarities of my energy. Following a brief sputter, the weapon kicked in my hand and channeled the force. The emerging blast nailed the blood slave in the side and sent him skittering across the floor.

"I can use these," I said, fitting the maces into my leather belt.

Though not my sword and staff, they were worthy replacements. I glanced over the rest of the weapons, but nothing grabbed me. Beyond the end of the display case, a large round door stood in a steel section of wall. It looked like the entrance to a bank vault.

"What's in there?" I asked.

"Our contingency plan, Mr. Croft."

I turned at Arnaud's voice to find the vampire CEO transformed. Gone were the playboy suit, silk scarf, and Italian leather shoes. He strode up in full armor, a burgundy cape flowing behind him. Banded mail gleamed over his forearms and chest. Beneath his chainmail suit, which flared into a long skirt, metal boots rang over the floor in a martial rhythm. He could have been Vlad the Impaler, on whom the original legend of Dracula was based.

"Contingency?" A horrible thought struck me.

"I know you believe me a monster," Arnaud said, picking up

on the emotion, "but even I have my limits. As a werewolf-vampire hybrid she would have made a powerful weapon, yes, but you will not find my daughter inside. She is far, far from here. And though I'd rather not say where that is or what she is doing, I assure you that the mayor would be proud."

I relaxed at the knowledge that Alexandra was safe, likely in school somewhere.

"As for the contingency, there *is* an element of kinship there, I suppose." Arnaud lowered a studded metal helmet over his mane of white hair. His pale, predatory eyes peered from a pair of slanted holes. "Though let's hope we never need it," he said. "Have you found what *you* needed?"

I nodded, touching my two maces. "This is just a defensive stand, right?"

"Asserting our rightful place in the city," Arnaud reaffirmed. "Men!"

The blood slaves fell into formation behind him. From a side room, two more slaves appeared, straining to lead an armored warhorse. I stepped back as the giant black animal snorted and reared its head. I could see by its sunken red eyes that it had joined the ranks of the undead.

Arnaud accepted the reins and climbed deftly onto the horse's gilded saddle. Another blood slave handed up a long sword, which Arnaud held at his side. He trotted the horse toward a barren wall opposite the elevators. The rest of us followed. The horse stopped in front of the wall and pawed the floor with a thick hoof, its coat covered in an oily lather. From deep inside the wall, a pair of clunks sounded. Without warning, the entire wall fell out before a set of heavy iron chains caught it.

Black smoke and battle sounds flooded in. Through a hazy light, I could make out several downtown buildings. One was on fire. The wall clanked out the rest of the way, like a drawbridge.

Arnaud canted his head toward me. "Try to stay close, Mr. Croft."

The wall banged down to become part of a broad ramp that descended to Wall Street. Arnaud raised his sword straight overhead and aimed it forward. "To battle!" he cried as the horse charged outside.

"To battle!" the blood slaves echoed and followed.

I joined them, and we poured down the ramp.

27

L ed by a vampire on an undead horse, our nightmare force emerged onto Wall Street. Around us, stone buildings rose steeply into smoke and coughing antiaircraft fire.

In the adrenaline-pumping confusion, it took me a moment to get my bearings. The Federal Hall building coming up on our right helped. It was the site of the fae's lower portal. The private security forces and blood slaves that ringed the building were facing inward, in case anything tried to come through.

We veered left, pulling my eyes from the building. *South?*

"I thought the fight was at the Wall!" I shouted up at Arnaud.

"The other executives are taking their battalions there," Arnaud said. "However, there's been a breach in the subway line.

A pack of wolves mean to attack from the rear. We'll head them off at Bowling Green Plaza."

Though Arnaud wore an earpiece, he used it to communicate with his human security forces—the vampires were psychically linked to one another as well as to their slaves. So when Arnaud shouted for his battalion to split up, I understood the verbal order to be for effect. He was enjoying playing general. The slaves coursed around us like quicksilver, disappearing into the canyons that ran every which way in the oldest section of the city.

"Your hand," Arnaud called, reaching toward me.

I seized his plated arm shield, and he hefted me up behind him. I seized him around the waist, the muscles of the horse's flanks surging like giant pistons. We emerged onto Broadway. Ahead, an attack helicopter pivoted around and came at us low. In a deafening burst, gunfire blew up chunks of asphalt.

"They're trying to strafe us!" I shouted.

Before the lines of blown asphalt could reach us, Arnaud pulled the steed left, onto a narrow side street. The helicopter roared past. An explosive bout of antiaircraft fire sounded behind us.

The horse snorted and sprinted on.

"It seems the wolves are emerging," Arnaud said over his shoulder.

He took a sharp right, and the small gated park near the Bowling Green station appeared ahead of us. Werewolves in their creature forms were bounding up from the subway entrance and emptying onto the brick plaza outside the green. Blood slaves swarmed in to meet them.

With the preternatural speed of both creatures, the action was hard to follow. Claws and teeth flashed, blades glinted, smoke and blood erupted from locked and rolling bodies.

The blood slaves were outsized but not outmuscled.

Before I was ready, Arnaud charged his warhorse into the park. I worked one of the maces free from my belt while holding tight to Arnaud. The werewolves were wearing what looked like Kevlar suits, but Arnaud found their vulnerabilities with swift, precise strokes of his sword. I watched one werewolf fall away, his decapitated head hanging on by a thread of sinew. The horse trampled the wolf's body. Other wolves retreated from the bite of Arnaud's sword to regenerate—only to be piled upon by blood slaves armed with punching daggers.

But for every wolf that fell dead, two more seemed to appear from the subway.

I twisted one way and the other, swinging the mace desperately. One blow caught a wolf across the jaw. Blood blew from his mouth like spindrift. Slaves pulled the wolf from the horse's right flank, where he'd embedded his claws. I nailed another wolf behind the ear.

This is insane, I thought, swinging at a third lunging wolf. *I need eyes on every side of my head.*

By sheer luck, I glanced up in time to catch something plummeting toward the park.

"Protezione!" I cried.

The mace stiffened in my grasp and a blue shield appeared around us an instant before the mortar impacted to our right. The blast kicked us to the side, burying us in a wave of stone dust. Wolves and blood slaves that had been thrown skyward thudded down around us.

The horse bellowed, hooves hammering the blood-slick bricks as it struggled to stay upright. I squeezed Arnaud tighter as he fought to bring the horse around. A second mortar landed, slamming into the park on our other side. The horse was blown from its feet, and I lost my hold. I rolled over several times, coming to a rest against a mangled blood slave.

I peeked above his body. Through the thinning haze, I could make out the old U.S. Custom House across the plaza. I drew the other mace from my belt. The stone steps to the entrance would give me higher ground and protection from the rear. I'd be in a better position to cast.

Shouting to reinforce my shield, I crossed the plaza at a run, ears still ringing from the twin blasts. I veered around blood slaves grappling with giant wolves and pounded up the steps. At a landing where a pair of columns climbed the building's tall edifice, I turned to take in the scene from my new vantage.

Not good.

Arnaud and the blood slaves had recovered from the mortar shells and were re-engaging the wolves, but there must have been a second breach. A new wolf horde was swarming in from the east.

"Arnaud!" I shouted.

From his mount, the vampire turned his blood-streaked face. The eyes that met mine burned red from his helmet. Sword poised above his billowing cape, he could have been an angel of death. Arnaud wheeled the mount toward where I was pointing and saw the new front. He said something. From windows in the surrounding buildings, gunfire erupted. The vampires' private security force!

Several wolves tumbled from the charge. Blood slaves not

entangled formed a wall to meet the rest, but the slaves were still outnumbered. And that wasn't the worst of it—a third werewolf horde was coming in on their blind side. Who in the hell was coordinating them? And how?

"Forza dura!" I bellowed.

Power stormed from my mace and hit the incoming wave. Wolves were lifted from their feet and slammed into buildings. Several of the gunmen above switched their aim, lighting up the fallen beasts. The rest of the wolves recovered quickly. They split up, one group scaling the buildings to reach the gunmen, a second group bounding toward the battle in the green. From that group, half a dozen wolves splintered away and veered toward me.

I checked my shield and set my legs. I'd spaced out my invocations enough to keep Thelonious at bay and to allow my power time to recharge. My magic still held plenty of steel. And whether it was the rush of battle or the sum of my frustrations, I was burning to let that steel rip.

"Who's first?" I shouted at the charging wolves.

I didn't get the chance to find out. From around both sides of the Custom House, a new force appeared. Clad in the same chainmail as the foot soldiers in Arnaud's battalion, the blood slaves wore green armbands that bore the insignia of their vampire's firm. Bristling with swords and daggers, the slaves collapsed into the wolves at the base of the stairs.

The Undertaker galloped past them on a blood-red steed, a barbed lance braced between arm and armored chest. He grinned over at me before diving into the main battle. Wolves screamed as he skewered them two and three at a time and flung them from his path.

Never thought I'd be happy to see that creep, I thought.

I was looking for where I could help out when a snarl sounded below me. The giant red wolf that had been leading the charge shook himself from the bloody melee and bounded up the steps. His baleful eyes fixed on mine as he slowed to a hunched stalk. I recognized those eyes.

I met Evan's stare. "You miss your dead brother, huh? Maybe I can fix that."

The challenge pierced his human and animal mind, and he sprang. I brought a mace around and slammed him with a shield invocation. He staggered back, then lunged again. I met him with a Word—*"Respingere!"*—and blew him aside, his back cracking against the base of a statue.

"Is that all you've got?" I asked.

Anger seethed in Evan's eyes as he circled out in front of me, looking for an opening.

I didn't wait. Thrusting one mace toward his legs, I hit him with a force blast. With the other mace, I brought the shield down on his head, pinning him against the landing. Evan snarled as he struggled to free himself. I walked toward him, shaping the shield into a stockade that wrapped his neck and wrists. Blood soaked his coat as he barked and thrashed, fury engorging his eyes. I honed the edges of the shield until they were razor sharp.

"Sorry, pal," I said. "Bad day for revenge."

I raised the other mace and, with a force invocation as a propellant, brought it crashing down on the back of his skull. The metal flanges sank into bone, and the wolf's head sheared off at his neck. I dispersed the stockade as the wolf's two parts thudded to the ground.

Blowing out my breath, I lifted my gaze to the battle. One less wolf, but still plenty more. Several had reached the gunmen in the windows and were hurling them to their deaths. The rest swarmed the plaza and park. Arnaud and the Undertaker fought with their mounts back to back, the Undertaker wielding a black broadsword now. But even with the reinforcements, we were outnumbered— and losing. I watched the way the wolves moved, ever shifting and reassembling, concentrating their attack where the vampires were weakest.

I looked around, trying to pick out whomever was coordinating them.

Did werewolves have the same psychic linkup as vampires? I didn't think so. Which meant...

My gaze dropped to the severed head at my feet. In the hair around the wolf's ear, I spotted what I was looking for. After ensuring no wolves were coming, I knelt and worked my fingers into the blood-matted hair. A crescent-shaped band had been affixed behind his ear. I worked the band free. With it came two slender filaments, one emerging from the wolf's ear canal.

The filament that had been in the wolf's ear ended at a small speaker. Very carefully, I brought it to my own ear.

"...*Alpha Three, move now. Flank them north. Alpha One ... south ... bef...*"

The tinny voice crackled as my wizard's aura killed the communication device. But I had already recognized the voice's cadence. I examined the other filament, which ended at a dead lens.

"Well, hello there, Captain," I muttered and tossed the smoking device aside.

That explained the coordination between the NYPD and wolves. But Captain Cole would have to be lupine himself to command them, and I'd never sensed an aura around him. I thought about the powerful enchantment Arnaud had mentioned and remembered the ring with the dark gem Cole wore on his pinky finger. Besides controlling the wolves, it must have concealed his own wolf nature.

Across the plaza, the ferocious battle raged on. Arnaud and the Undertaker continued to hack and slash, but their slave battalions were dwindling. The wolves were too well coordinated. I looked high and low.

Where are you, Cole?

I knew from our work on the eradication campaign that he liked to be near the action for communication purposes. And what Vega had said on the phone about him being "down" at command-and-control seemed to confirm he was close. But how close?

I thought back to the view from Arnaud's office window earlier. That tenting I'd glimpsed at the southern end of City Hall Park ... I had assumed it was part of a construction project, but it was the same military-drab color as the tenting used in the other campaigns.

That's where he was, I decided. Close to the campaign but shielded by the intervening skyscrapers.

I cupped my hands to the sides of my mouth. "Arnaud!"

The vampire discerned my voice amid the chaos and looked up. His mount reared as he swung it toward me, hacking and trampling a swath from the battle. I met him at the bottom of the steps. He was covered in gore, his mane of hair soaked in blood.

Aiming a mace, I blasted back a pair of wolves that had broken from the battle to pursue him.

"You've found something?" Arnaud asked.

"There's a tent at the southern end of City Hall Park," I panted. "Captain Cole is inside, coordinating the assault. He's the one controlling the wolves."

Arnaud's eyes sharpened in understanding. But as he activated his earpiece, I thought about the police officers and technicians who would also be in the tent. And if Vega had ended up there for any reason...

"Wait!" I said. "No mass casualties. Have a sniper take him out."

Arnaud nodded and gave the order. His blood-bathed horse snorted, eager to rejoin the battle. I looked past Arnaud in time to see the Undertaker and his mount falling. The aging vampire's wailing cries pierced the snarls and barks of the wolves diving down to tear into him.

With the Undertaker's final moan, his blood slaves regained their mortality and stopped fighting. The ones he'd turned centuries before shriveled and broke apart. The younger ones aged, some crooking into the shapes of old men, others staring around in shock, wondering what kind of nightmare they had awakened to. The wolves showed no mercy.

Arnaud's remaining slaves continued to battle fiercely, but the force had been halved. A mass of wolves, more than a hundred strong, turned toward us. Arnaud's mount grunted and stamped the bricks at its feet. I squeezed the leather-bound grips of my maces.

"Stay behind me," Arnaud said, raising his sword.

The wolves' grizzly snouts peeled from their fanged teeth.

I threw up a shield invocation, knowing it would only buy us a few minutes. There were too damned many. They charged en masse—then stuttered to a stop. Muzzles lifted to the scents of death and carnage, then began to sniff one another, growls rippling in their chests.

"It seems you were right," Arnaud said. "I just received word the captain was taken out. An inter-pack alliance on this scale is unnatural. I suspect we're about to see it unravel."

A savage bark sounded, and a wolf seized another by the throat. More barks erupted as wolves from rival packs clashed, claws and teeth ripping into one another.

"Encircle them!" Arnaud called to the surviving blood slaves.

The slaves complied, several limping into position on mangled legs. The battle among the wolves was as brutal as it was quick. As maimed wolves attempted to escape their attackers, the blood slaves drove silver weapons into them. This went on until the final wolf was slain.

I relaxed my tensed arms as my gaze ranged over the slaughter. At the edge of the park, the Undertaker's mount had been dismembered, the Undertaker no doubt somewhere among the remains.

"Poor Luther," Arnaud said without a trace of sympathy. "It seems the rest of us will have to divide his assets." He looked down at me. "Well done, Mr. Croft. The assault on the Wall has disintegrated as well, I'm told."

"So ... what now?" I asked.

"We return to my offices and await the mayor's call."

"It's over?"

"Listen. Do you hear that?"

I stopped breathing and immediately understood what he meant. No shooting. No explosions. No shouts, snarls, or death cries. A deep, snowy silence had descended over lower Manhattan.

"It's the sound of success," he said, grinning. "Come, let us negotiate the terms of our future. Swiftly now."

Arnaud extended an arm toward me.

Ready for the alliance to end, I clasped his blood-caked hand and straddled the mount.

"Let's go," I said.

28

Trailed by the remaining blood slaves in Arnaud's battalion, we rode back to Wall Street. Fires burned here and there. Chunks of building littered several of the streets. But except for the crackling of the horse's hooves over glass, the downtown remained eerily silent.

We turned a corner and came up on Federal Hall, with its pillared façade and bronze statue of George Washington. Blood slaves and private security forces still ringed the building. A handful of carcasses lay across the street—bullet-riddled wolves reverted to their human forms—telling me the bulk of their attack had not penetrated the core of the Financial District.

"Anything?" Arnaud called up.

Several members of the security force stared back with shield sunglasses and shook their heads.

It looked as though the fae had stayed out of this one, which was not overly surprising. When it came to human affairs, their M.O. was to operate just out of sight, advising here, injecting money there. And they tended not to use magic unless threatened. The anxiety that Caroline and I might become actual adversaries let out a little. I exhaled a shaky breath as two more depleted slave battalions appeared, both led by vampires on horseback.

Arnaud trotted up to the closer group. "I understand we lost two defending the Wall."

The mounted vampire, who was too battle spattered for me to recognize, nodded. "Francis went down near the West Side Highway," he said. "Gordon was impaled on Maiden Lane."

"Victory always comes at a cost." Arnaud said.

The vampire farther back galloped forward. "Why stop here?" he demanded, eyes blazing inside his helmet. I recognized the young vampire, Damien, by his voice. "There remains a city to conquer!"

Arnaud looked as though he was going to respond, no doubt to talk him down, but he canted his head suddenly. I followed the vampire's gaze toward Federal Hall, where the security forces had fallen into crouches, automatic weapons aimed at the building. And then I heard it too—a dull, concussive sound, like something trying to pound its way out of a giant tomb.

The horses grunted and drew back.

"What's going on?" I asked, peering around.

The blood slaves looked jittery, eyes fixed on the building. A deep snap sounded, and then another. A member of the private security team emerged from beyond the pillars. "The slabs are fracturing," he barked. "Whatever's coming up is moving ten tons of reinforced concrete."

Coming up? The fae were sending something through the portal?

"Hold your positions!" Arnaud said severely, but I caught an odd strain in his voice. When his horse shuffled back another foot, Arnaud cracked its head with the pommel of his sword. "You too, cursed beast."

Arnaud must have had the portal sealed, but all manner of powerful beings dwelt in the faerie realm. Another pair of snaps sounded, followed by the unmistakable sound of heavy stone grating against heavy stone. From inside Federal Hall gunfire exploded. Other automatic weapons joined in. A man's scream rose above the noise and was just as suddenly strangled.

Anxiety sawed on my insides as I flipped through a mental reference of fae creatures.

Arnaud's men backed out between the pillars, guns cracking. A giant shadow pursued them. It wasn't until the shadow ducked beneath the pediment and rose to its full height that I recognized the iron-haired monstrosity.

"Oh, shit," I muttered.

"Does this present a problem, Mr. Croft?" Arnaud asked, holding his slaves back.

"A mountain troll?" I let out a harsh laugh. "Only if you expect to kill it."

I glimpsed the troll's volcanic gray face before he hefted an arm to keep the gunfire from his recessed eyes. With a grunt, he seized George Washington's upper body. Stone erupted from the foundation as the ten-foot-tall statue broke free. The troll wielded it overhead like a club, then swung it in a fierce arc, taking out two of the gunmen.

"Attack!" Arnaud called to his slaves.

Regenerated from their fight against the werewolves, the slaves surrounded the troll, blades glinting. Half a dozen of them slipped behind the creature, darted in—and exploded into flames.

For the first time, I noticed the way the air warped around the troll.

"It gets better," I shouted. "The troll's wrapped in some kind of enchantment, probably put there by the fae." An enchantment that torched the undead, apparently.

Leaving the blood slaves to burn, the troll bounded down the steps with surprising speed, swinging the statue again. More gunmen went airborne, their bodies broken. The rest retreated around the corners of buildings. The troll puffed his cheeks. When he blew out, the fae aura bent with the force of the gust, igniting a swath of blood slaves ahead of him.

For the first time, Arnaud walked his horse back. I followed the angle of his head to where two more mountain trolls were emerging from Federal Hall, their stony bodies glimmering inside the fae enchantment.

"Wonderful," I muttered.

The trolls assessed the scene and split up, running after the blood slaves like they were chasing mice.

Damien, the young vampire, had seen enough. With a cry, he dug the metal spikes on his boots into his mount and charged. The statue-wielding troll turned toward the piercing sound and roared, revealing a set of tombstone teeth. Damien evaded his downward swing, the statue busting into the street behind him. He charged past the troll and sliced his sword at the tendinous pocket behind the monster's knee. The blade fractured into pieces. When Damien brought the horse around, I could see flames licking out from beneath his right gauntlet.

Damien's eyes burned red as he let out a furious scream. The troll lunged toward him.

"Vigore!" I shouted, aiming one of my maces. But the force that rippled through the air dissipated upon reaching the troll's enchanted protection. I thrust forth the other mace. *"Protezione!"*

The shield that manifested over Damien burst apart beneath the troll's descending fist. Damien's scream was severed as the blow crushed his head and battered him and his mount against the blacktop. Both broke into flames. The horse's legs kicked for several beats, like a dead insect's, before falling still.

"My magic's no good!" I said. "And unless you have cold iron..." But Arnaud was already moving us away.

"Retreat!" he called, charging toward his building.

The wall we had emerged from earlier remained down. Our footfalls stampeded up the ramp and into the armory, a handful of gunmen at our backs blowing cover fire. I doubted it would do much against mountain troll hide. The bulk of us inside, the wall jerked from the ramp and embarked on a clanking rise as the chains retracted, pulling the wall back into place. Outside, the trolls ran toward us, their horny nails gouging up chunks of asphalt.

"Quickly!" Arnaud called.

One of the trolls seized a gunman who'd been left behind. I looked away, but not before he'd pushed the gunman into his chomping mouth. The statue-wielding troll brought George Washington down on a crippled blood slave, crushing him. He then swung the statue around, caving in the corner of a building across the street. The third troll broke into the lead and charged. The wall slammed closed ahead of his outstretched fingers.

A moment later, the armory shuddered around us. Weapons fell from shelves. The trolls were attacking the outside of the building. Blast-resistant stonework or not, the mountain trolls would eventually get inside or bring the entire building down on our heads.

Arnaud dismounted and helped me down. A pair of blood slaves led the torn and bloodied beast away. The other slaves traded their silver blades for those forged from iron. Arnaud stared around for a moment. When his eyes locked on the other vampire's, I caught something I'd never observed in their kind before. Uncertainty. That uncertainty was also manifesting in their blood slaves, who, though freshly armed, backed from the shaking walls.

"Come, Mr. Croft," Arnaud snapped.

I followed him to the vault-like door I'd observed earlier. His contingency plan. Trepidation shook through me as he seized the hand wheel. The round door released from the wall with a dull bang and swung outward. It took a moment for my eyes to adjust to the tomb-like chamber.

What the...?

I had been expecting a creature of some kind. Instead, I was looking at an ornate casting circle painted on the floor in what looked like blood and bone dust. Dark candles stood at the points of the circle's star-shaped pattern. I raised my gaze to an altar above the circle. It featured an old iron chest about the size of a cinderblock, thick candles bracketing it. When I leaned my head toward the claustrophobic space, I picked up the stink of rancid blood.

Arnaud placed a chilly hand on my back. "I believe you'll find everything you need."

"Everything I need for what?"

The armory shook again, this time toppling several of the racks of weapons. Arnaud removed his helmet and shook out his hair. He looked as if he was wearing a grotesque mask, the dried blood thick over his jaw and around his eyes but absent from the rest of his pale face.

"I don't need to spell out our situation," he said when the noise settled. "I underestimated our opponents, or at least the lengths they were prepared to go. They have already decimated half our ranks. They mean to finish the job. Our only recourse now is the Scaig Box."

I studied the trunk on the altar. "Scaig Box?"

A cold force seemed to emanate from the word, like fingernails dragging across stone.

Outside, the pounding continued. A giant crack appeared in the drawbridge-like wall.

"Listen to me, Mr. Croft," Arnaud said quickly. "The box holds an ancient being, a precursor to vampirekind. We will use the being to destroy the trolls, then order it back into its hold."

I jerked away, understanding what he wanted. "Are you fucking insane? No, I'm not calling forth any *ancient being*. I'm forbidden for one, and for another ... That thing's related to you? Yeah, no."

"You're bound by the Pact." Arnaud's eyes burned into mine.

"To aid you in battle, not unleash some ancient evil on the world."

"I know how summonings work," he pressed. "The circle I've prepared is extraordinarily powerful. The being will remain under *your* control. You can test the circle for yourself."

The armory shuddered again, rubble falling from a fresh proliferation of cracks. The image of the troll shoving the gunman into his mouth flashed through my mind.

I eyed the casting circle. Though it had elements that looked vaguely Sumerian, the pattern wasn't one I'd seen before. With a flick of my mace, I cast an ounce of energy toward it. The circle gobbled it up. A moment later, the pattern began to pulse like a heart, amplifying the energy several fold. Alright, so it passed the power test. But what in the hell would I be calling forth?

I raised my eyes to the iron trunk. It sat on its dark altar perch as though biding its time.

This had disaster written all over it.

"I hear more of them out there," Arnaud said above the thundering blows.

My heart slammed in my chest. It was only a matter of time, I got it. But summonings never worked out for me, from my first experience with Thelonious to nearly succumbing to a gatekeeper a few weeks ago. And then there was Chicory's warning—not only about the penalty for summoning, but why the Order forbade the practice. I could be opening a fissure...

To the Whisperer, I thought, *the being who nearly destroyed the Elders.*

"I can't do it," I said.

"Can't or won't?" Arnaud asked.

"It doesn't matter. It's not happening."

"What about your *mother?*" he asked, his narrow tongue spearing the word.

I stiffened. "What about her?"

"Well, if I understood your grandfather correctly, she was slaughtered like a little lamb. If you fall today, who's left to avenge her death?" Though he spoke softly, almost teasingly, I could smell his musk, could feel my already-racing pulse kicking into a higher gear. He was inciting my anger.

"They've won," I said.

Arnaud stared at me. "I don't believe I heard you."

"There are creatures out there we can't kill," I said, "and a being in that box that might be even worse. Our best option is to contact City Hall, have the fae call off the trolls, and then see if we have any chips left to bargain with. If nothing else, it buys us time."

My mind made up, I turned toward the elevator.

"Oh, Mr. Croft," Arnaud said. "I did hope it wouldn't come to this."

I was still processing his words when he swooped in behind me and seized my wrists. The talons of his thumbs pierced the network of tendons below my palms, and my hands jerked open, dropping the maces.

Fear and anger spiked hot inside me. He was attacking me in violation of the Pact!

I twisted my right fist around until the ring was aimed at him. *"Balaur!"* I shouted.

The cold metal remained inert.

"You poor fool," he hissed in my ear. "Do you think I would hand you a loaded weapon? The design is identical, yes, and there are magnetic elements that might feel like power, but the ring is a worthless copy. Now," he said, steering me back toward the vault, "I believe we have a summoning to perform."

The son of a bitch had tricked me.

Furious, I snapped my head back to smash his face, but he was too quick. Far, far too quick. Cold breath brushed my exposed throat an instant before his spiny teeth plunged in.

29

My eyes shot wide.

He's doing it. He's actually biting me.

In an instant, the piercing pain was replaced by a warmth that flooded my system, relaxing everything. It was like slipping into the warmest, most lavish bath. Though my mind struggled, my body relaxed into Arnaud's embrace, his high-pitched suckling. I couldn't stop him. Couldn't dam the endorphins dumping into my bloodstream. And that was the worst part. Despite the horror of what he was doing, my brain was flashing pleasure signals.

My eyelids fluttered, even as I strained to keep them open.

No, dammit! No, no, no!

I felt Arnaud slipping into my mind, growing inside it like

a fluid-filled sac. He was turning me into one of his minions. I groped for my mental prism, found it, but couldn't summon the will to cast through it. Arnaud controlled that will now. And with it, he controlled me.

Arnaud broke away with a wet gasp.

He turned me until I was facing him, my blood glistening across his mouth like a lurid lip gloss. His swollen pupils narrowed to pin points. Wizard's energy pulsed around him.

I stared back dumbly.

"Be grateful, Mr. Croft," he said, releasing my wrist. "I could have taken far more."

I saw one of the maces on the floor at my feet. I felt myself stooping for it, seizing the leather-bound grip, swinging the silver-edged flanges into Arnaud's head. But, in fact, I hadn't moved, couldn't move.

Arnaud tsked. "What a cruel thing to want to do to your master."

He's inside my damn head, my thoughts.

"Indeed, I am," he said. "Behold."

Arnaud turned and walked toward the vault. I followed, my legs kicking into a series of jerky steps. I couldn't stop them. The vault swallowed us into its frigid hold. Arnaud stepped aside, and I fell to my knees inside the casting circle, as though thrust down. Arnaud moved in beside me.

"Cerrare," a foreign voice spoke.

No, *my* voice. The word had been spoken through my mouth.

Could Arnaud direct my magic? Certainly not. But energy was already pouring through my mental prism and down my body. The casting circle glowed with protective power. Flames sprouted from the candles.

That's why he held back, I thought. *Not out of charity, but to preserve my prism.*

"*Den-lil lugal kur-kur-ra ab-ba.*"

Arnaud moved my lips and tongue around the Sumerian words.

"*Re-ne-ke inim gi-na-ni-ta.*"

Ropey strands of dark energy sprang into being, linking Arnaud to the Scaig Box on the altar. The summoning was starting, and God only knew how it was going to end.

"*Gir-su dsara-bi ki e-ne-sur.*"

The trunk stirred. Something inside strained against the hinges, but they were bound by a powerful magic. Hope found a fingerhold inside me. Maybe the binding magic would be too strong for me to dispel. But the magic was familiar. Like the long-forgotten scent of a childhood home, I felt the magic resonating on a limbic level. I'd sensed it before.

"Yes," Arnaud whispered. "Your grandfather sealed this box, centuries ago. Only someone of his bloodline can unseal it. How fortunate that I found you—or more accurately, that you found me."

What in the world's in there?

"A forebear, Mr. Croft."

"*Ensi ummaki-ke nam inim-ma.*"

The magical binding released in a pair of audible pops.

"Soon, the city will look on me as a god."

"*Diri-diri-se e-ak!*"

The lid cannoned open and a horrible shadow rose. It took form above the trunk, unfurling a pair of ragged black wings. A black bat's face squinted down at us, fangs jutting up from its lower jaw. I'd been right to be wary. Arnaud had just summoned a shadow fiend.

"Arnaud Thorne," the fiend said in a voice that sounded like a rusty nail being drawn from wood. "You dare call me forth after hundreds of years of neglect. Hundreds of years in which I've foundered in the blackest shadows. Why should I not destroy you here and now?"

I expected Arnaud to cower from the towering creature. Instead, he stepped forward.

"I am protected, for one," he replied from inside the circle. "And two, I have bound you to me."

The fiend's eyes burned as it raised a taloned hand.

"Gal bi-su!" Arnaud had me shout.

The ropey umbilicus connecting him to the fiend looped around the creature's neck, becoming a barbed collar. The fiend's hands flew to its throat as Arnaud tugged the cord. Arnaud yanked again, and the massive fiend fell to the floor, as though it were bowing before the vampire.

"Any attempt to harm me will redound on you a hundredfold," Arnaud said. "Are we clear?"

The fiend's face twisted in evident pain. "I will obey."

I looked on, horrified. Combining the ancient ritual with my power, Arnaud had taken complete control over the entity. And something told me Arnaud had larger ambitions beyond troll killing.

"Get up," he commanded.

The being flapped to its feet. "What is your bidding?"

Arnaud's eyes cut toward me, and I could see the calculation in them. He had what he wanted: the Scaig Box opened, the shadow fiend in his command. He was no longer dependent on my magic. And that wasn't all. Arnaud's access to my thoughts ran both ways. Before he could cover the keyhole on his end, I saw the full extent to which he had manipulated me.

Everson, I thought, *you ever-loving idiot.*

Late last night, Arnaud learned the mayor's wife had succumbed to the bullet I'd lodged in her aorta. Penelope Lowder was dead. With the head of the werewolves gone, he saw an opportunity. The false story about me working for the vampires hadn't been planted by the fae and City Hall. The timing of the story—on the heels of the Central Park disaster—had only made it seem that way.

The story had been planted by Arnaud.

It was brilliant, really. Drive me to him, force the city into a confrontation, and then use my powers to unleash his fiend. The coordinated werewolf attack *had* surprised him. He hadn't known Cole was the second wolf in command. The captain had fooled us both, apparently. But with that battle won, Arnaud's plan was back on track. And the fae's response helped—or so he thought. He had believed the trolls would convince me to summon the shadow fiend.

They hadn't, and so here we were.

"The mayor was already threatening to end my empire," Arnaud said, having followed my thoughts. "I merely forced his hand. And now that he has sown the wind, his city shall reap the whirlwind. Remember what I told you, Mr. Croft. 'War is the continuation of politics by other means.' So too is terror. Rise, please." When he gestured, my body jerked like a marionette, and I was on my feet. "And step outside the circle."

I fought with everything I had—the circle was my only defense against the shadow fiend—but it was no use. My right leg broke through the circle's humming border, breaking it. My left leg followed.

Arnaud had his control over the creature to protect him, but I was exposed now. Nightmare images ripped through my mind as the fiend crawled toward me, its dreadful eyes boring into mine. It reeked of sulfur and carrion. I tried to squint away but couldn't even do that.

Beyond the vault's entrance, gunfire erupted in fresh bursts. A large stone shot past.

Arnaud sighed. "It seems the trolls have made their way inside. Come," he said, jerking the fiend by the collar toward the vault door. "I have work for you."

I could only stare as the immense being rose and drifted past me.

"We shouldn't be long, Mr. Croft," Arnaud said. "Call if you need anything."

His fangs grinned through my drying blood as he slammed the door closed, extinguishing the candles and sealing me in blackness.

30

I'd read that an attack from a shadow fiend was like being disemboweled while having your brains sucked out through the back of your skull—the victim conscious the entire time. I almost pitied the trolls. Beyond the thick wall of the vault, I heard the first one being set upon, his grunts and roars followed by an unearthly scream and then a foundation-shaking collapse.

In the darkness, I felt over the metal door. Arnaud was no longer in direct control of me, but I couldn't cast, dammit. It was as though my prism was stranded in the middle of a huge chasm. I doubted I'd be able to raise a hand against Arnaud, either. I was his slave now. Maybe not to the degree of the others, but still doomed to serve him. Until his fiend killed me.

The inside of the door was smooth metal, nothing to grasp or turn. I put my shoulder to it and shoved, but I'd heard the giant magnets engage after the door had swung closed. It wasn't going anywhere.

Another troll screamed. The vault shook with his collapse.

Okay, calm down, I told myself. *Relax. Remember your training.*

I heard Lazlo's voice from years before. *A wizard who cannot cast is a dead wizard.*

Leaning my arms against the door, I inhaled through my nose and exhaled through pursed lips. I recited my centering mantra.

After several cycles, I saw it wasn't going to work. Arnaud had siphoned out too much of me. The distance between where I stood and where I needed to be remained too vast.

Arnaud was the bridge, and unless he commanded it, I couldn't cast.

I straightened and pulled my coin pendant from beneath the collar of my shirt. I ran my thumb over the symbol. It was the first magical item of his Grandpa had given me, the only one he'd given me while living. I'd acquired the sword and ring after his death—*and managed to lose both,* I thought bitterly. Right now, the ring's loss was the more damning.

The coin's metal pulsed warmly in my hand.

As I considered its round shape, I thought about Grandpa's penchant for acquiring things in pairs: tools, slippers, straight razors. *To have an immediate replacement,* my grandmother had said. What about the Brasov Pact? Grandpa hadn't owned a second ring, but he would have wanted a backup. My thumb made another pass over the symbol. The coin could cast light and protect against lesser beings. Might Grandpa have also instilled it with the power of the Pact? It was the only other wearable ornament he'd possessed.

As though in answer, the coin let out another pulse.

Hope kicked inside me. Yes, the enchantment was buried, but it was in there! I could feel it! It was just a matter of manifesting enough magic to access the enchantment, to release its power.

"*Illuminare,*" I said, concentrating into the coin. I waited for several moments before repeating the word. But no energy stirred. No light shone forth. The vault remained as dark as my situation.

I twisted off the fake ring Arnaud had given me and threw it with all of my strength. "Goddammit!" I shouted, the echoes seeming to chase the clattering ring around the vault before both fell silent. With my back to the door, I slid to the vault floor, landing with a rustle of chainmail.

Another troll's scream pierced the vault.

I closed my eyes. Backup or no backup, I was powerless to cast. The vampire had won.

Checkmate.

I could search the vault in the hopes of finding something to use as a weapon. Perhaps the iron trunk the shadow fiend had emerged from. I could stand to one side of the door and await Arnaud's return. I could bring the trunk down on his head, or attempt to. And it would all be for nothing. At every turn, Arnaud had been a dozen steps ahead of me. He'd enticed me, repelled me, vexed me, possessed me—all moves in a complex dance that he'd been leading the entire time. He hadn't come this far to be foiled by a box on his head.

Exhaling, I muttered, "Trust in the one you trust least."

I cast back to that final moment with Lady Bastet. I remembered the feel of the stone table beneath my forearms, the tendrils of incense in the air, the strand of my mother's hair. I remembered Lady Bastet staring into me, losing herself so completely that she didn't remember the experience. Could she have erred? Gotten her signals crossed? *Trust in the one you trust least.* From the mouth of an oracle. And the one I trusted least was Arnaud. Zero doubt.

But that's not what Lady Bastet had said, I realized. Not exactly.

In my memory, I watched her violet lips shape the message. *Trust in the one your* heart *trusts least.*

Yes, that's what she'd said. *Heart.* And that one word changed everything. The divination no longer fit Arnaud Thorne, but it conformed perfectly to my feelings for Caroline Reid. *Caroline* was the one I was supposed to have trusted—the one who had been offering to help me the whole time.

I kicked the floor in disgust.

Tabitha had been right. I'd let my wounded heart play foil. I was so hell bent on punishing Caroline for choosing Angelus and the fae over me, that I slammed the door on her offer, on her.

"I'm sorry," I said.

The words weren't just meant for Caroline, who had *always* helped me—how could I have forgotten that? The apology was also for my mother, who had sacrificed her life for my future. It was for my grandfather, who had protected me in ways I still couldn't quite understand. My self-disgust took on the ponderous weight of disappointment.

I had failed them. And in doing so, I'd unleashed a frigging shadow fiend.

I'd also lost any chance at retribution against my mother's killer, the head of a group that could still be plotting against the Order.

"I'm sorry," I repeated, the darkness swallowing my voice.

I sighed and touched the coin dangling from my neck. Whatever warmth I'd imagined emanating from the metal earlier was gone. I began to tuck it back inside my shirt—and froze.

Ed.

A strangled laugh escaped my throat.

Ed! My golem! The one I'd animated to follow Hoffman. He could still be out there, the amulet that powered him dangling from his clay neck. When did Hoffman say he'd seen him? A week ago?

I stood and paced in a circle, not wanting to get too excited, but not wanting to release the slender hope, either. As my golem, Ed would be accessible to me. That didn't require magic, just focus.

A kaleidoscope of colors danced before my eyes as I sat in my centering pose. It was a long shot—I hadn't expected Ed to hold out for more than a few days. But hadn't a rover or two tooled over the Mars surface years beyond their life expectancies? I was mixing robotics and magic in my thinking, sure, but still ... I needed Ed to have that same plucky resilience.

I took a calming breath, closed my eyes, and focused on my creation.

A moment later, the world lurched into motion.

"...matter of finding the right *enterprise*, you see what I'm sayin'?"

Like coming to the end of a merry-go-round ride, the up-down, round-and-round motion slowed, then stopped. From what felt like the inside of a full-body cast, I peered out at a room of muddy shapes.

I—I'm out of the vault. It worked!

"And man, don't listen to what they're sayin' on the streets," the sleepy voice beside me continued. "Shit. There's money to be made if you got the right enterprise. Then all you need is *capital*."

My, or rather Ed's, legs were stretched out in front of me. I recognized the pants I'd given him, though they were caked with filth now. His shoes had either come off or been stolen. Two sets of gray, blocky toes stared back at me. Beyond his feet, the rest of the room came into dull focus. I was in a bedroom layered with mattresses and languid bodies. The bodies sprawled across one another, smoke drifting from their sallow fingers and lips.

Somehow Ed had landed in a flophouse.

Newspapers slid off me as I tested my right arm, then my left. The movements were stiff and clunky. I pawed my chest for the amulet. Still under the shirt, though the power that sustained Ed's life was ebbing.

When I tried to stand, an arm around my neck restrained me.

"Hold on a sec, man," the sleepy voice said. "You need *capital*, which means you got to look for *investors*. But it's better to secure a loan, see? Then you don't got to share ownership. Problem is, my credit's shot to shit. Rap sheet don't help none, either. That's where I could use you."

The man leaning into me was gaunt, his eyebrows and mustache threadbare scratches on the skeletal contours of his face. With his free hand, he combed back a pile of brittle-looking hair.

He blinked a few times, his hooded eyes like muscadine grapes in the deep pits of his sockets.

I tried to tell him to let go, that I needed to take off, but all that emerged were lumpy mumbles.

The man's mouth stretched into a grin. "Yeah, man, you see where I'm goin' with this. Fifty-fifty split. Even Steven. You secure the loans, I manage the enterprise." He cinched me closer, until the bill of my Mets cap was indenting his brow. "Look man, I don't say this to just anyone, but you got that look about you. I trust you. And I'll tell you right now, I'm an honest Joe. I don't lie, cheat, steal. None of that. Not anymore. That shit's all behind me, sure as I'm sitting here."

I could have pointed out that he was sitting on a filthy mattress in a drug den, but the clock was ticking. I peeled his clammy arm from around my neck and struggled to my feet.

Have to figure out where I am.

"Hey, man, where you going?"

Unaccustomed to piloting Ed's body, I stumbled over an array of junkies in front of a window and parted the blinds' plastic slats. The view was of a fenced back lot and a crumbling field of buildings. I wasn't one hundred percent, but it looked like the Lower East Side.

The man behind me tried to stand. "I haven't told you my idea for our enterprise."

I emerged into a living room that featured a pair of old couches and another sprawl of bodies.

"Soft pretzels, man," he called from the back room.

I searched the living room for a phone, but if there were any around, they were buried.

Staggering through a stench of urine and sweat, I made my way to the front door and into a hallway. From there, I found a stairwell. I fell several times on my journey to the lobby. Ed had no sensation in his extremities and zero peripheral vision. It was a wonder he had managed these last days.

By the time I reached the street, I was moving more like a man buzzed than blottoed. The street sign on the corner told me I was in the Bowery.

Need to find a working phone.

I lumbered south to Canal Street, aware that the fiend could return to the vault at any moment. I was on borrowed time, and little more. A payphone leaned at the corner. When I rounded it, though, I discovered that the receiver had been torn out. Wires sprayed from the bottom of the dented box.

"Shit," I managed to grunt.

"Hey, there you are!"

I turned to find the man with the soft pretzel plan hustling to catch up, his peeling loafers slapping the sidewalk as he lurched this way and that. He came to a wheezing stop in front of me, a filthy floral shirt hanging from the thin rack of his shoulders. "Why'd you bail, man?"

Because I need to make a goddamned phone call, I tried to say. But with the amulet's power ebbing, the only intelligible words that emerged from Ed's mouth were "need" and "phone."

"The hell didn't you say so?" Pretzel reached into his shirt pocket, pulled out a flip phone, and pried it open. "Got it from my sister." He squinted over the display as he coughed into his fist. "One bar of battery left, man."

I nodded and gave his shoulder an enthusiastic pat that almost knocked him to the ground. *God bless this man.* He handed over the phone, but my fingers were too fat to punch in the numbers. On my second try, I nearly dropped the phone. My clay face creased with stress.

I don't have time for this.

"Here, man, give me the digits." Pretzel took his sister's phone back.

With monumental concentration, I articulated each number. Pretzel entered them, then held the phone up to my ear. I felt the blood I'd used in creating Ed pumping through me. The call hadn't gone straight to voicemail. For the first time in months, Caroline's line was ringing.

"Hello?" she answered.

"Carllln," I said, feeling like I was speaking through a mouthful of M&Ms.

"Who is this?"

"Eh-eh-sn."

"I can't understand you."

In the background I heard heated conversation. The mayor's distinct voice rose above the others—the sound of it, anyway. I couldn't make out any words, but it told me Caroline was at City Hall. I tried to repeat my name, but the more I forced it, the more jumbled it came out.

"I'm sorry," she said. "I'm ending the call."

"Whu-ait!" My mind scrambled for some way I could get her to understand me.

"Look, sir. I don't recognize your number, and I'm in the middle of something."

"Sub!" I blurted out. The old joke between us for all the times she used to cover my classes.

A silence followed. "Everson?"

"Y-ysh!" If Ed had tear ducts, I'm pretty sure they would have been gushing with joy.

The voices around her diminished as though she were walking into another room. "Thank God," she breathed. "What's wrong? Where are you?"

Okay, she knew it was me, but how was I going to get her to understand a single thing I said. The situation was too complex to grunt out in monosyllables over a phone. If I was going to warn her, I needed a face-to-face.

"M-meet," I managed.

"You want to meet? Where?" No hesitation.

I thought for a moment. The streets around City Hall were probably closed. The checkpoints would be a nightmare. I came up with a place about halfway between us and within walking distance.

"Clum-ba Pa," I said.

"I didn't get that, Everson."

I balled up my fists and tried again. "Clum-ba-ba Pa."

Pretzel pulled the phone from my ear. "I think he's trying to say Columbus Park, lady."

I nodded fervently.

"He's saying yes," Pretzel said. He stuck the phone back against my ear and bounced his eyebrows. "She sounds fiiine."

"Columbus Park," Caroline repeated. "All right. I'm heading there now. I'll meet you at the pavilion." She ended the call before I could attempt to thank her. Probably just as well.

Wavering on his feet, Pretzel slid me a wasted grin. "Need a wingman?" he asked.

31

Our staggering journey took us down Chinatown's narrow streets. The amulet's energy flagged and surged like a dying electrical appliance, and I had to lean on Pretzel for support several times. Thankfully, the sidewalks were empty, the shops closed. The thundering concussions from the battle that afternoon had likely driven everyone inside.

Almost everyone.

At the next intersection, a gang of young men in white suits appeared. I recognized them as White Hand enforcers, employees of Bashi. They patrolled the street in a V formation.

Crap.

I searched around for a place to hide. The gang spotted us and veered our way.

Double crap.

I didn't have time to be interrogated. The amulet fueling me was already in the red, and if the White Hand decided to remove it, Ed would collapse into a mound of clay, and I'd land back in the vault. I lowered my head, hoping the gang would allow a pair of common vagrants to shuffle past. But Pretzel chose that moment to pick up his business pitch.

"The thing with soft pretzels, man, is they don't discriminate. They're for everyone, you know? Race, age, creed—none of that shit matters. Come one, come all. The only thing might change is what's put on 'em. Some like mustard, others like that horseradish."

The members of the White Hand surrounded us.

"Oh, hey," my partner said. "What do you guys like on your pretzels? Sweet and sour sauce?"

Oh, Christ.

The man in the lead position stared down at him. "What are you doing here?"

"We're goin' on a date," Pretzel answered proudly.

"With each other?"

The other gang members laughed. Not realizing we were the butt of the joke, Pretzel laughed along with them. The leader's mouth didn't budge. He had the deadened eyes of a killer. They cut over to me. "What's the matter with your boyfriend?" he asked Pretzel. "Someone shoot off his tongue?"

"Aw, he don't say much," Pretzel explained. "But when he does, pure genius, man."

"Is that right?" The leader drew a black Beretta from his waist band. "Let's hear some of that genius, *tùzi*."

I looked past him. The park was only a block and a half away.

"Hey," he snapped. "I'm talking to you." He flipped my bill and the Mets cap tumbled off my head.

When the leader drew back, I raised an arm in anticipation of being pistol whipped, but his eyes were large and startled. Amid muttered swears, the others in the gang eased back too. The leader recomposed himself, his eyes going dead again. "Get out of our neighborhood," he said to Pretzel. "I never want to see that deformed piece of shit around here again."

Pretzel gave his lazy smile. "Yeah, man, he's cool."

I retrieved my hat as the gang moved on, their members peering back with unsettled looks. I leaned toward my reflection in a car window and understood. Out in the summer heat, and with the amulet flagging, Ed's face had started to melt. One eye was a good two inches below the other, and what remained of his nose had skewed to the left of his lips. It was a disturbing sight. With a stab of self-consciousness, I replaced the hat and pulled the bill as low as it would go.

Caroline was already at the pavilion when Pretzel and I shambled up. She must have sensed my presence in the pile of clay, because she hurried toward us. "Everson?" she asked.

I nodded and gestured to my body. *Just a loaner,* I tried to say, but it came out a clumpy moan. Speech gone. Power spent. The park around us was beginning to feel insubstantial too, like a fading dream. For a moment, I felt the cold floor of the vault beneath me.

No...

Pretzel stumbled in front of Caroline. "I spoke to you on the phone, lady. I'm his business partner."

His voice brought me snapping back. As Caroline accepted Pretzel's dirty hand, I pawed at my chest. Her head tilted in momentary question before nodding. She could see the energy that emanated from the amulet to power my form, could sense its weakening field.

Pulling her hand from Pretzel's, she stepped in close and pressed her palm to the amulet. Maybe it was seeing Caroline through Ed's eyes, but she looked even less human now, more fae. From the amulet, a scent of honeydew rose and a soft, prickling wave swept over my skin. My body began to straighten and tighten, facial features migrating back into place. As the recharge finished, I decided that, yes, Caroline was definitely more fae.

She stepped back, eyes dark with concern.

"Thank you," I said, the words wooden but much easier to form.

"What's going on?" she asked.

I looked over at Pretzel, who was staring up at Caroline with a dreamy expression. "Hey, mind giving us a minute?" I said.

"Oh, yeah, sure." Pretzel staggered off several paces before turning. "Ask if she's got a friend," he called back in a loud whisper. He found a park bench and collapsed onto his back.

I looked at Caroline again. "I'm at Arnaud's."

"I know. We've been trying to get you out of there."

"The situation's become more complicated," I said with a wince. "Arnaud ... bit me."

Caroline's face paled. "Bit you?"

"He took over my mind and forced me to call up a shadow fiend. I couldn't stop him. I'm pretty sure he intends to turn the fiend loose on the city after it takes care of the trolls. And me."

Caroline searched my eyes, appearing to weigh the information.

"I'm not asking you to help me," I said. "I've blown my chances, and it's too dangerous anyway. But I can tell you something Arnaud never intended for anyone to find out. He bound the shadow fiend to himself in a way that makes it dependent on his life force. This guarantees the fiend will remain loyal to Arnaud, but it's also an Achilles heel."

"Kill Arnaud, and the fiend perishes," Caroline said.

"Exactly. Meaning there can't be any more negotiations with the vampires. They'll only stall for advantage. Arnaud has to be destroyed."

Caroline nodded. "We'll take your heed."

"Good," I said, noting how she was even starting to talk like a fae. "And, look, whatever happens ... I want you to know I'm sorry. I should have listened to you."

"It's not your fault. I gave you ample reason to distrust me." Caroline smiled tightly. "The fae and their secrecy ... I wasn't to discuss my involvement in the mayor's programs with anyone else. Nor was I to intervene directly in the outcomes of those programs."

"You saw the potential for complications, though," I said.

She nodded. "Including the vampires trying to twist the eradication program to their own ends. That story about you ... I knew it came from Arnaud. But Captain Cole reacted first, preempting the mayor. He organized the hunt for you and lay siege to the Financial District. City Hall had to play catch up."

The war has begun, I remembered Arnaud telling me as his building shook.

"Arnaud fired the first shot, didn't he?" I said, coming to yet another realization of how thoroughly I'd been duped. She nodded. "So Budge's offer to end the siege in exchange for my extradition...?"

"Was to get you to safety," Caroline affirmed. "We were in the process of clearing your name."

"And the trolls?"

"Sent to help you."

I shook my head in anguish. Who knew how many would die before the shadow fiend—and Arnaud—could be stopped. *If* they could be stopped. And all because I'd wanted to prove Caroline wrong.

She cupped my chin and raised it until our eyes aligned. "When we spoke in your classroom a few weeks ago, I told you I had worked out an exception in your case. I was granted three chances to intervene on your behalf. The first was convincing Budge to negotiate for your release, the second was deploying the trolls. Everson, I still have one more chance to help you. If you'll let me."

"At what cost to you?"

The skin between her brows dimpled.

"Oh, c'mon," I said, "I know the fae well enough to know there are no freebies. I mean, you gave up your mortality to help your father. What did you have to give up to help me?"

She hesitated. "My feelings for you."

That was why she'd kept her distance. She had known this moment was coming.

"And with this third chance, the deal's sealed?" I asked. "The feelings go away?"

The moisture in her eyes answered the question for her. I looked over her face, trying to frame it in my memory: every perfect line, every sensual color, from the blush of her lips to the blue-green spires of her irises.

Over on the bench, Pretzel began to croon about faded love.

No kidding, I thought. *Caroline will never look at me this way again.*

I drew a deep breath and, nodding, took her hand.

"Let's make it a good one, then," I said.

32

I stood slowly, feeling my way up the vault door.

The merry-go-round motion had stopped moments before, and I'd opened my eyes. Gone was the hazy light of the park, Pretzel's singing, Caroline's tender touch, the clean scent of fae magic. There was only a soulless darkness that smelled of sulfur and rancid blood.

But I was still alive.

I pressed my ear to the door's cold metal. I couldn't hear anything. Had the troll massacre ended? Where had Arnaud and the shadow fiend gone? Not out into the city, I hoped.

Okay, need to focus. Need to—

"You're up, I see," Arnaud said.

Blood roared in my ears as I spun toward his voice. No, it was too soon!

From the far end of the vault, footsteps clicked toward me. "You were lying so still, I feared you'd succumbed to the transformation. Not everyone has the constitution for it, I'm afraid. I would wager that for every young man I enslave, three to four die. A horrible inefficiency—a nuisance, really. Especially when one is trying his best to play down his true nature."

I pressed myself flat against the vault door and edged away from his voice, from the soul-raking presence of the shadow fiend.

"But at last the days of hiding are behind us, Mr. Croft. The trick was making the cost of persecution too high. Today, the city received a taste. Tonight, we will give them so much more." Arnaud's eyes shone red in the darkness. Several feet above him, a larger pair of eyes peered hungrily down.

"You promised the battle would be defensive," I stammered.

Arnaud chuckled. "Well, you know what they say. The best defense is a good offense."

"You lied to me."

"Yes, about that..." He and the shadow fiend continued to stalk me in the dark. "I take my pledges very seriously. I have a reputation for my word being as reliable as gold. It's what elevated me to the heights of lower Manhattan while lesser of my kind ended up in the filth of Forty-second Street. The late Sonny Shoat, for example. But in your case, Mr. Croft, I made an exception to my own rule. And you have your grandfather to blame."

"My grandfather? What in the hell does he have to do with this?"

I could feel the talons of Arnaud's mind probing my thoughts. What he found was terror and uncertainty.

"You know about the original Pact, of course," Arnaud said. "The union between wizards and vampires to resist the enforcers of the Inquisition. Why, you used the Pact's binding power against me in our first meeting. That never should have happened. Your dear grandfather violated the Pact when he double-crossed not only me, but his fellow wizards."

Anger flared hot in my cheeks. "Bullshit."

"Oh, I don't blame you for not knowing, Mr. Croft. He hid the deception very well. Indeed, even I wasn't aware of what he'd done until after his death. But I received a visit one day from someone in your *Order*. A representative, I suppose. The fellow asked some interesting questions, and though he disguised his mission well, I soon understood what he was after. You see, during the campaign in Eastern Europe, some powerful artifacts were stolen, including the Scaig Box over there. I, along with others, had always assumed the Church to have taken and destroyed them. But by the nature of the fellow's questions, it became clear he suspected a vampire of the thefts—me, in particular, given my movements during the war. I must have said enough to convince him otherwise, because he left, and I never saw or heard from him again. It got me thinking back, though. Your grandfather, the Grand Mage himself, had been with me or close by during much of the war. He was at the same places the fellow from the Order had mentioned during our interview."

I continued to ease along the wall of the vault as he talked, chanting quietly.

"Fortunately, I kept close tabs on your grandfather since his arrival in Manhattan. He was behaving quite curiously, performing work far beneath his station. A stage magician and insurance man? I was convinced the war had addled his mind. Some form of shell shock. But after the fellow's visit, I began to wonder whether your grandfather had been hiding something."

Though I kept up the chant, I couldn't help but think about Grandpa's strange habits, his odd hours.

"Every so often he would take a trip out to Port Gurney. If you haven't been, it's a waterfront town, very working class. Old dockyards, warehouses, a few bars as well. Your grandfather would go directly to one bar in particular—a place called the Rhein House—and sit on the same stool, sometimes for hours. He would then emerge, perfectly sober, and drive home, scarcely having spoken. Maybe the man just liked to spend time in a place suggestive of his German past. Or maybe, I thought, there was more going on than met the eye. Late one night, following the fellow's visit, I dispatched a pair of slaves to that waterfront bar to have a look around. And do you know what they discovered?"

"What?"

"A vault in the bar's basement. Despite considerable coercion, the owner seemed not to know how to open it, claiming the vault was closed and locked when he bought the establishment. After a bit of research, I discovered a strange clause in the property deed. The vault could not be considered a part of any subsequent sale. Very curious, wouldn't you agree?"

"What's your point?"

"When we finally managed to open the vault, we found the Scaig Box alongside a host of artifacts. Ones belonging to both vampires and wizards. It appears your grandfather used the Pact to steal them. I don't care about the wizards' grievances— that is for them to sort out. But he stole from *me*. Did you know the earliest vampires were shadow fiends? Only a precious handful remain, and your grandfather took one for himself, the thief."

From the darkness above, the shadow fiend smacked its lips.

"So yes, Mr. Croft," Arnaud said, swooping in close, "my *point* is that your grandfather violated the Pact first, effectively dissolving it."

I kept moving, trying not to allow Arnaud's words to challenge my concentration. But the things he was saying … The vampire had no reason to deceive me now, unless it was to incite confusion and dismay, to fill the vault with more of my stress hormones. But I had *felt* Grandpa's magic on the Scaig Box. And if Grandpa was as powerful as he seemed, he could easily have cast a projection spell to make it seem as though he were at the bar, drinking for hours, while, in fact, he was down inside the vault, checking on the artifacts.

But why?

"I'm not my grandfather," I said defiantly.

"Of course not, Mr. Croft," Arnaud agreed. "If you were even a tenth of the man, you would not be in this precarious position. But that's neither here nor there. The penalty for violating the Pact is death, and since your grandfather is no longer among us, that penalty defaults to his descendants. Or descend*ant* in this case. Be grateful you didn't sire children."

I was at the back of the vault now, moving past the altar.

Almost ready…

"One final thing," Arnaud said, his voice tightening. "You called me a liar, but remember this. Every mistruth, every furtive act, was in accordance with seeing justice through."

"How noble," I scoffed. "You just left out the part about using me to take over the city."

"I merely saw an opportunity. And opportunities are my livelihood."

I nodded to myself. Everything was in place.

"Cerrare," I called.

Across the vault, the door rang with the power of the Word. The glow it cast outlined Arnaud and the fiend in a wavering blue light. Arnaud snapped his head toward the door and back to me. His blood-masked face remained placid, but I sensed surprise beyond his eyes.

"Perhaps you're more resourceful than I've given you credit for." His voice, though cutting, was slightly off. "You've tapped into some reserve, I see. But why seal yourself inside?"

I felt his talons plunge deeper into my thoughts. Or rather, what he believed to be my thoughts. In addition to restoring my magic, Caroline had cast a mental glamour: a *mirage* of my thoughts—in this case random jags of confusion and terror where none existed.

"The locking spell?" I replied evenly. "Oh, that's to keep anyone from coming to help you."

He stopped digging, eyes narrowing in on mine.

I grinned and shouted, *"Balaur!"*

Blue light crackled around the coin pendant over my chest and shot a bright beam at Arnaud. The power of the Pact was not only present in the pendant, but just as potent. With an ear-splitting scream, the fiend sliced in front of Arnaud, absorbing the beam into the shadow of its body. The fiend staggered to the floor, smoke rising from its twisting wings.

"That bit about not giving you enough credit..." Arnaud said from behind me.

I wheeled, but he had already pulled the necklace over my head.

"...I take it back."

I lunged for the coin pendant. Arnaud smashed me in the jaw with a backhand. The vault whorled and dove as the sting of copper filled my mouth.

"Were you *really* trying to bait me into that clumsy trap?" he asked. "I don't know whether to feel flattered or insulted."

Another fist smashed me in the right temple, dropping me to my knees.

I pawed toward Arnaud, but the recovered fiend grasped me from behind. Though a shadow, the fiend was far from immaterial. The talons of one hand gripped my gut while the other hand clamped my mouth so I couldn't cast. As its foul, bristling wings wrapped me around, I felt the jagged fangs of its underbite nestle into the shelf at the base of my skull.

"A moment," Arnaud said, pacing to the center of the vault where he could face me.

I stared back at him, eyes pleading.

"I was prepared to make your death quick, Mr. Croft. A reward for your service, naively given, though it was." He twirled the necklace around a finger. "But since you insist on being a petulant little bastard, I am going to allow the fiend to savor you while I watch. Perhaps it will help resolve some of the anger I've accrued toward your grandfather these past years."

He wasn't a thief, I thought so Arnaud could hear.

"No?" he answered. "The evidence suggests otherwise."

The fiend ran its sharp tongue against the back of my head, leaving a burning trail of saliva. I grunted in pain but held still for fear the slightest stimulus would send the fangs into my skull.

You don't know what my grandfather's intentions were, I thought. *No one does.*

"And never will, Mr. Croft. This closes the case as far as I'm concerned." Arnaud raised his eyes to the fiend.

He helped you, goddammit!

"And deceived me. I do not suffer betrayal lightly."

He gave the necklace another twirl and caught the coin pendant in his hand. As he stroked the symbol with a finger, I remembered the night Grandpa had appeared the necklace from his sleeve.

The necklace is an heirloom, he'd said. *It is meant to protect.*

Thank you, I'd replied. *But protect against what?*

Instead of answering, Grandpa had taken the necklace by the chain and placed it around my neck, the heavy coin settling over my sternum, where I could feel its deep, tidal energy.

Wear it in the city, he'd said, *under your shirt.*

"Oh, does this have sentimental value for you, Mr. Croft?" Arnaud asked in a teasing voice.

I raised my eyes to his. *You don't deserve to be in the same room with it, much less touching it.*

The vampire cocked an eyebrow and placed the necklace around his armored neck. "I don't know, Mr. Croft. I think it rather suits me." He turned from side to side, the coin sliding over metal plating. "Perhaps it will become *my* sentimental piece, something to remember the end of the Croft line."

He watched my eyes for my reaction.

I'd been keeping a silent countdown in my head. Things had moved more quickly than I'd planned, but through a series of challenges and subtle suggestions, I'd gotten Arnaud to don the necklace. Underneath the shadow fiend's hand, my mashed lips twisted into a smile.

Checkmate, you arrogant son of a bitch.

Arnaud's mouth straightened. "How dare you—"

...one.

The shield I'd built around the coin fractured. Amassed energy detonated in a nova of blinding white light, swallowing Arnaud. The explosion cannoned the fiend and me backwards. As we smashed through the wooden altar, I felt the fiend's fangs clench, only to break into smoke. Where Arnaud had been stood an afterimage, a formidable vampire one moment, a decimation of atoms the next. Blown apart by the power of the Pact.

The vampire's scream rang around the vault for several seconds, a shrill, lingering echo. Beneath the pain, I heard raw rage. The wrath of a creature who had won centuries' worth of battles only to lose the final war—and in the time it took to understand he'd been outwitted by a mortal.

Pushing myself to my feet, I coughed out a weak laugh. "Not bad for a petulant little bastard."

In the center of the vault, Grandpa's coin pendant rattled to a rest.

33

"So let's see if we can break this down for everyone," Courtney said. "You were acting as a double *double* agent?"

"Well, it's sort of complicated," I stammered.

I had sworn off press conferences, but Mayor Lowder argued this wouldn't be a press conference, but a relaxed interview. "You want your life back, don't you?" he asked. He had me there. After the NYPD had extracted me from the ruins of downtown, I had spent the next two weeks in hiding until City Hall could leak the "actual" account of my involvement. "Anyway," Budge said, "I gave Courtney over at TV 20 first rights to your story." I wondered if that had anything to do with Budge being a bachelor again and Courtney being gorgeous.

"'Complicated' is an understatement," the blond anchor said with a small laugh. "You had *everyone* fooled."

A tide of assenting murmurs went up. I glanced around. While the interview was relaxed in the sense I was wearing jeans, Budge failed to mention it would be held in front of a packed auditorium at City Hall.

I swallowed. "Yeah, I guess so."

"The simple answer is this," Budge cut in. "I knew the vampires were planning something, but I didn't know what. So I had Everson here infiltrate their ranks. And when the vampires attacked, guess who was on the inside?" Budge slapped my knee. "My good old secret weapon."

"Five vampires destroyed, including Arnaud Thorne," Courtney cited. "Two captured..."

Leaderless, and their blood slaves decimated, two of the remaining vampires had fled while two others surrendered to the NYPD. At my suggestion, the vampires were bolted inside steel coffins and their slaves imprisoned in a reinforced shipping container until the city could figure out what to do with them. A short ethics debate followed. In the end, the vampires were executed by cremation in order to restore their blood slaves to mortality. Those young enough to survive the transformation went into immediate therapy.

"All thanks to Everson's fine job," Budge said.

"So, the Central Park campaign...?" Courtney asked.

"Mistakes were made," Budge cut in, "but the buck stops with me and no one else. Especially not Everson here, who risked his life trying to get the other officers out of the park that night."

Courtney smiled and tilted her head in approval.

"And we learned from that experience," Budge went on. "The fight was better waged from the air, which is what we did. The city's had to deal with a lot of smoke these past several days—and I do apologize for that—but Central Park is officially clear now. The monsters that once terrorized the woods and meadows are now the ashes from which a new, improved park will rise."

"And to that end, I understand you'll be announcing a jobs program soon?"

Budge's embarrassed laugh sounded like part of a script he and Courtney had worked out beforehand. "You're preempting me a little here, but yeah. With Central Park and the downtown in need of rebuilding, we're allotting a portion of the federal package to put New Yorkers back to work. There are going to be a ton of new jobs." He turned toward the crowd. "That is, if you would do me the honor this fall of allowing me to serve a second term."

"That seems in little doubt now," Courtney said above the whoops and applause.

Budge waved his hand modestly, but Courtney was right. The death of Budge's wife coupled with his victory over the vampires had vaulted him to a twelve-point lead in the latest poll. The jobs program would only build on that. I had to hand it to him and Caroline. They had conducted a near-flawless campaign, he for the mayorship, she for the fae portal.

Courtney returned to me. "And will you have a role in the second administration?"

"I'm planning a little time off, actually," I said. "There are some things I need to take care of."

"I hear you'll have a new title at Midtown College when you return."

"That's true." I couldn't help but smile. "Tenured professor. I received the news this week."

"Well, congratulations," Courtney said as more applause rose up.

I nodded and gave the same modest wave as the mayor. I wasn't there when Chairman Cowper announced my tenure to the rest of the faculty, but I was told Professor Snodgrass went into a convulsion that locked his entire body. He was carried out on a stretcher, one of his heeled shoes protruding from his mouth to prevent him from biting through his tongue.

I had his secretary retrieve my cane from his office.

"And the honorariums don't end there," Courtney said with a sly smile. "Mayor?"

I turned toward Budge with more than a stab of dread. *Okay, what's going on?*

"As mayor of New York," he proclaimed reaching inside his jacket and withdrawing an oblong black case, "I hereby present Everson Croft with our city's highest honor." When he opened the case, a ceremonial key to the city glittered for everyone to see. "May you remain a trusted friend."

A fresh storm of applause rolled in as cameras flashed and audience members stood from their seats. Budge signaled for me to stand as well. He seized my right hand and held the open case between us.

"You're one lucky bastard," he said through his enormous smile. "City was ready to rip you to shreds. Press had practically written your obituary."

"No shit," I replied through my own fixed smile. "Thanks for bringing me back to life."

"Thank Caroline. Hell of a body count you left down there."

"Wasn't all me," I said. "But I am sorry about the wolves."

"Ehh, I never much cared for them. Wife excluded, of course."

"About that…" I started to say, but he gave my hand a harder squeeze.

Following the photo op, the interview turned into a campaign platform for Budge, which was fine by me. Among other things, he announced a wave of hirings in government security—the werewolves' former domain—trimming New York's unemployment rate by a half point. I sat back and studied the key, wondering how long the good will would last. New York had a short attention span and an even shorter memory.

When the interview concluded, Courtney, Budge, and I stood and shook hands. While the audience filed out and the camera crew packed it in, Budge pulled me aside.

"Listen," he said in a lowered voice, "you don't need to apologize about my wife. I was there last spring. I saw what happened. Heat of battle, and all that." He snuffed out a laugh. "She was a helluva fighter, though, huh? I wanted her to pull through, I did, but … The damned thing of it is, if she'd lived to know you finished off Arnaud, she'd have forgiven you everything."

"Really?"

"Hey, I know my Penny." He smiled sadly before changing the subject. "Do you know how long you're gonna be away on your sabbatical?"

"I don't," I said, thinking about the Order, blood magic, my mother…

"Well, be sure to check in when you get back. I could use you around here for my second term."

As he gave my hand a final solid shake, it struck me that from our meeting in the warehouse until now, a few attempts at coercion aside, Budge had shot pretty straight with me.

"Will do," I said.

I watched him walk to the wing of the stage, where Angelus and Caroline were waiting for him. Caroline glanced past his shoulder. When our gazes met, her face showed recognition but nothing deeper. Per her arrangement, her feelings for me had vanished. Poof.

I raised a hand anyway. She responded with a nod before turning and disappearing with her husband and the mayor.

I stared after her for several seconds.

You didn't have a choice, I reminded myself. *Neither of you did.*

And the truth was she was becoming more and more fae by the day. Her sacrifice to help me had only sped her departure from my world. I thought about our final moments in Columbus Park, her awesome power riffling through the conduit that connected Ed back to me, restoring my mind, my magic. I would have had to let her go eventually. The knowledge didn't make it hurt any less, though. I blinked and rubbed the heels of my palms across my eyes.

"There he is."

I gave myself another moment before turning. I spotted Vega limping up the steps to the auditorium, her son clinging to her trailing hand. She flashed a smile when she saw me walking over.

"Somebody's been dying to meet you," she said to me.

When my brow wrinkled in question she cocked her head down at her son.

"Oh, yeah?" I lowered myself to a knee and extended a hand. "Tony, right?"

The one time I'd seen him had been after Arnaud's slaves had returned him to Vega. He'd probably been too shocked to remember me then, and I was frankly surprised Vega was introducing him to me now. I guess blowing up the vampire responsible for his kidnapping had boosted my stock in Vega's portfolio. I smiled when the six-year-old boy edged further behind her braced leg.

"Go on," Vega said to him. "Shake the man's hand."

Eyes fixed on Grandpa's ring, which I'd recovered from a vault in Arnaud's office, Tony stretched an arm forward and clasped my fingers.

"He's been talking about you ever since the story broke," Vega said. "Thinks you're a superhero."

I shook his warm hand and stood again. "What, and you don't?"

"Well, you've got more lives than anyone I've ever met. I'll give you that."

"You're partly to blame this time," I pointed out.

"And you managed to make me not regret it."

We both smiled and looked over at Tony, who had picked up my cane from the chair I'd been sitting in for the interview.

"It's all right," I said before she could tell her son to leave it alone. "It's safe. He won't be able to open it." For several seconds, we watched him cane-fight an imaginary foe.

"So what's this about you taking time off?" she asked.

I reflected on the past several weeks. In one form or another, I'd been involved with clearing the ghouls from the subway lines, the goblins from Central Park, not to mention decimating the city's werewolf and vampire populations. And that was on top of learning about the dark mage. "I haven't earned it?" I teased Vega. "Nah, it's just some personal time."

Her eyes narrowed. "Anything to do with Lady Bastet's murder?"

Crap. We'd never buried that hatchet. "A lot, actually," I admitted. "I think the person who killed her also killed my mother."

"You never told me your mother was murdered."

"I didn't know until that night you caught me at LB's. I saw something in her scrying globe."

"Do you have a name for me?"

"Not yet." I checked my watch. "And I've gotta run."

"We're not gonna play this game again, are we?" she asked.

She was right. I owed her more. "I'll tell you anything I find out. *If,*" I added, "you let me call the shots." *And if,* I thought, *I'm not in terminal trouble with the Order.* "This is a whole different level of menace."

Vega's lips torqued as she considered my terms.

A small hand tugged at my pant leg. I looked down to find Tony holding my cane up for me.

"Here, Mr. Croft," he said, his brown eyes as intense as his mother's. "To fight the monsters."

"Thanks, big man." I smiled at Vega. "He'd make a great sidekick."

She ruffled his feathery curls. "Yeah, when he's not too busy making trouble."

"Hey, listen," I said. "I'm glad we're talking again."

When she replied, it was with an edge of warning. "Let's try to keep it that way."

"I'll be in touch," I assured her.

"I'm counting on it."

I kissed her cheek in farewell—why not?—and gave Tony a high five. Vega seemed not to mind either gesture. As I pattered down the auditorium steps, her son's voice rang out behind me.

"Bye-bye, Mr. Croft!"

34

"You're late," Chicory said when I entered my apartment.

"Yeah, sorry about that." I hung my cane on the coat rack and hustled to the sitting area in front of the stone fireplace. "The interview went longer than expected. Can I get you anything?" I ran through a mental inventory of what I had on hand. "Water? Um ... cheese?"

"No," he said. "Have a seat."

From the reading chair, my mentor nodded to the couch opposite him. He was buried under Tabitha whose purrs sounded like a small tractor. His eyes glowered at me over her orange mass.

"The Order received your communication."

I'd thought his scheduled visit might have something to do with that. I sat carefully.

"Let me hear it from you," he said.

"Okay." I cleared my throat and started into a verbal account of what I'd sent the week before. Bringing my mother's hair to Lady Bastet, the mystic's murder, the residue found on the slaughtered cats, my attempt to cast through said residue and the resulting encounter with the dark mage, the vision in the scrying globe of my mother's murder ... I told him everything. Even the part about the mage stealing my blood. Blood I had given to Lady Bastet willingly.

My only omission was Arnaud's claim that Grandpa had stolen the wizard artifacts.

When I finished, Chicory watched me for several long seconds, fingers digging into the hair on Tabitha's crown. Sweat dewed over my brow. For a moment I was back in Romania awaiting Lazlo's verdict: train me or destroy me. I flinched as the repaired AC huffed on.

"You violated a cardinal tenant of the Order," Chicory said at last. "Several, in fact."

"Several?"

He arched a bushy eyebrow. "Summoning a shadow fiend?"

"Oh, c'mon. You're going to stick *that* on me? I was under a vampire's control. I didn't have a choice. And in case you didn't notice, I took care of the vampire in question. The shadow fiend, too."

"Yet another example of giving your blood willingly," Chicory said.

"What, you think I offered Arnaud my neck? 'Here, turn me into one of your mindless undead. Enslave me for all eternity. I'm begging you.'" I sighed at the ridiculousness of it.

"The point, Everson, is that you contravened the rules. Something you've done time and again. Your potential for magic is enormous, but so too is your potential for causing great harm. You dabble in things you shouldn't, despite any and all warnings to the contrary. You're a danger to yourself, your city, and to the Order of Magi and Magical Beings."

I could tell by his tone he was building up to a verdict. I made a circular motion with my shaking hand. "Just cut to the chase, please."

"Everson, this is the part of my job I least enjoy..."

"You're giving me more preamble," I said.

Chicory let out a heavy sigh. "The Order is through issuing warnings. The penalty this time is ... severe."

"Death?" The word scratched from my throat.

I remembered the sensation of falling into the In Between, that realm of luminescent darkness and haunting gatekeepers. I hadn't been ready to pass then, and I wasn't ready now.

"Possibly," Chicory answered.

"Possibly?" I stared at him. "What's that supposed to mean?"

Tabitha stirred on his lap and murmured, "Less talking, more scratching."

"The dark mage's name is Marlow," Chicory said. "He was once a member of the Order. A lot like you, in fact. Curious. Headstrong. *Impetuous.* And it was this last quality that got him into trouble. He discovered an old book by Lich, the member of the First Order who aspired to the power of his siblings and opened the seam to the Whisperer. The book contained Lich's original notes. Notes on his spell experiments as well as pages of invective against the First Order: their iniquities, their disproportionate power. The charges inflamed Marlow's mind. He formed a splinter group known as the Front to ascend to the power of Lich."

"Why didn't the Order stop him?" I asked.

"Marlow kept his activities well cloaked. When the Order began to suspect him, they sent an agent to infiltrate the Front to learn more."

"My mother," I said.

Chicory nodded. "It's why the Order kept no records on her. Rest assured, Everson, I'm told she performed her job very capably. But all it took was one intercepted message, apparently."

"And they killed her."

"Marlow sent the Order her ashes in a trash bag."

My face burned. "So why in the hell wasn't he punished?"

"Marlow and the Front went into deeper hiding. By that time, they had acquired sufficient power to stay hidden."

"Even against the Elders?" I asked, incredulous.

"I'm afraid so."

"I thought you said there had only been one rebellion against the Order."

"Yes, but a second is coming," Chicory said. "Of that the Order has little doubt. It just hasn't started yet."

"So what does this have to do with my sentence of *possible* death?"

"The Order believes there was a reason Marlow didn't want you to learn about your mother's murder."

"And what was that?"

"He knew you would want to come after him."

I barked out a laugh. "Why should that bother him? The *Elders* can't even touch him."

"This is different, Everson. As a descendant, you would be able to penetrate his veiling and defensive spells in ways others can't. Perhaps even get close to him unnoticed."

"Descendant? What in the hell are you talking about?"

"Based on the information you shared," Chicory said, "the Order believes Marlow is your father."

For a vertiginous moment, my soul seemed to leave my body. Far away, I felt the ice-cold brush of the AC, heard Tabitha's chopping purrs. And then I was back, my heart resuming its hard, flip-flopping rhythm.

"How sure are they?" I asked.

"That's what they want to find out. And that's where your sentencing comes in. As of now, the Order is suspending your other activities. Your new mandate is to find Marlow and destroy Lich's book. It's where he derives his power. If Marlow *is* your father, you should succeed in the first."

I didn't like the qualifying *should.* "What about the second?"

Beneath the wiry shelf of his brows, Chicory's eyes turned dark. "Marlow is also known as the Death Mage. There's a reason for that."

I nodded, fully present now. I didn't care what his name implied. This was bigger than my mother's murder, bigger than vengeance. I would be picking up where my mother had left off, countering a threat to the Order, to humankind. This was about legacy.

I met Chicory's waiting gaze.

"When do I begin?"

THE SERIES CONTINUES...

DEATH MAGE (PROF CROFT, BOOK 4)

On sale now!

About the Author

Brad Magnarella is an author of good-guy urban fantasy. His books include the popular Prof Croft novels and his newest series, Blue Wolf. Raised in Gainesville, Florida, he now calls various cities home. He currently lives and writes abroad.

www.bradmagnarella.com

BOOKS IN THE CROFTVERSE

THE PROF CROFT SERIES
Book of Souls

Demon Moon

Blood Deal

Purge City

Death Mage

Black Luck

Power Game

Druid Bond

THE BLUE WOLF SERIES
Blue Curse

Blue Shadow

Blue Howl

Blue Venom

MORE COMING!